QUANDARY FARM

QUANDARY FARM
A Novel

Jack F. Reynolds

iUniverse, Inc.
New York   Bloomington

QUANDARY FARM
A Novel

First edition and this Second edition, both copyrights owned by J & G Reynolds

Copyright © 2008, 2009 by J&G Reynolds.

All rights reserved. No part of this book may be used or reproduced by any means, graphic, electronic, or mechanical, including photocopying, recording, taping or by any information storage retrieval system without the written permission of the publisher except in the case of brief quotations embodied in critical articles and reviews.

This is a work of fiction. All of the characters, names, incidents, organizations, and dialogue in this novel are either the products of the author's imagination or are used fictitiously.

iUniverse books may be ordered through booksellers or by contacting:

iUniverse
1663 Liberty Drive
Bloomington, IN 47403
www.iuniverse.com
1-800-Authors (1-800-288-4677)

Because of the dynamic nature of the Internet, any Web addresses or links contained in this book may have changed since publication and may no longer be valid. The views expressed in this work are solely those of the author and do not necessarily reflect the views of the publisher, and the publisher hereby disclaims any responsibility for them.

Second Edition edited by Neal Marlow

ISBN: 978-0-595-46098-4 (pbk)
ISBN: 978-0-595-90398-6 (ebk)

Printed in the United States of America

iUniverse rev. date: 3/06/2009

Also available by Jack F Reynolds

A Curse on the Cruise
Selected Poems 1947-1998

I

"David W. Dimble," the door said.

Your ordinary polished oak door says things like "David W. Dimble" in genteel, graven brass, or perhaps with pink paint on grey slate. David W. Dimble's door spoke audibly. It said "David W. Dimble" in mellifluous, rounded tones, as pear-shaped as the personage named.

Plug Shavaughn, his outsized boots hiding most of David W. Dimble's monogrammed doormat, shuffled half-a-pound of Connecticut agriculture mud into the two "D"s, missing the "W" by virtue of his agrarian stance, and said, "Hi! How are ya? I'm Plug Shavaughn. I have this letter. You wanted...."

He was about to report the essence of the letter he had received on the impressive, embossed letterhead of David W. Dimble, the essence being Mr. Dimble's undersigned assurance that, if Mr. William Thackeray Shavaughn would visit the offices of David W. Dimble at 10 a.m. on Monday, May 6th, he—Mr. William Thackeray Shavaughn—would be told something very much to his advantage.

Plug was interrupted in his attempted rehearsal of the essence. The door spoke again. It repeated the "David W. Dimble". This time it added, "Please come in".

Feeling that, while it was undoubtedly true that one should not allow oneself to be drawn into conversations with doors, it was equally true that doors should not initiate these little chats. Plug turned the vast brass knob and went in. His hand swallowed the vast brass knob.

Inside, in turn, he was swallowed to ankle depth by what he took to be a growing carpet. Also, he was dramatically confronted by a pair of immensely wide eyes shaded by up to eight millimeters of applied eyelash. The lashes gently brushed him through another highly polished door into the presence of what could only be David W. Dimble.

Standing with his fingertips on his desk, that gentleman smiled the smile he had learned from Dale Carnegie in the lesson called "Truly Sincere Sincerity." David W. Dimble had evidently been placed in his pear-shaped suit that morning by an especially meticulous brain surgeon. He managed to suggest that he had already shaken hands with the less scrupulously dressed Plug without exposing himself to the indignity of doing so.

"You are Mr. Shavaughn? Mr. William Thackeray Shavaughn?"

Plug assented with a nod, adding orally that he responded better to the simpler, colloquial form, Plug. David W. Dimble refused to accept this information.

"Mr. Shavaughn, you are a very fortunate man. A very *rich* man! I am in a position to give you one hundred thousand dollars. One hundred thousand good American dollars I will give you, for that tiny, infertile little farm of yours. One hundred ... Mr. Shavaughn? Mr. Shavaughn, I'm talking to you!"

But David W. Dimble was not, in fact, talking to Plug at all. Plug was not in the room. He was already out among the eyelashes, and David W. Dimble was talking to the high polish on his own side of the inner sanctum door. Where Plug was, a voice rose from beneath the lashes, evidently speaking in organ chords.

"We were expecting you *yesterday*, Mr. Shavaughn; Monday."

Plug kept right on high stepping through the field of carpet.

"Yeah," he said. "I tried to make it but the right wing came off 'Theplane.' Took all damn day to screw the wing back on." And he was gone. The vexed eyelashes spent two hours dragging mud from the tentacled carpet.

All this took place in those long gone good old days, the late 1950's. It was a rich, Eisenhovian era before homebuilding had been overtaken by evangelism as America's leading source of hasty bucks. Everywhere, the purpose-built slums were gushing coin, and the only difficulty faced by the practitioners of the art was the acquisition of more land upon which to build more purpose-built slums.

Plug refused weekly offers from persons of the David W. Dimble ilk, most of them less sartorially sublime than D.W.D. (as he was known to his friend), but all of them deeply involved in what they chose to call 'home construction' in the Nutmeg State. Most of them lied with smaller numbers than David W. Dimble, but they all wanted Plug's farm so badly that they bulged at the eyeball when he spilled little pieces of it into their visiting automobiles, over their office Persians, around the brass rails of sumptuous bars, or even back onto the acreage from when it came. By now, Plug knew most of the developers by name. But he had previously missed David W. Dimble because David W. Dimble usually specialized in the major depredation of office space.

Now, it should be known that David W. Dimble lied, cheated, bribed, and swindled as if these activities were going out of style, although they certainly were not. But he rarely cried. At this moment, however, his eyes were moist. The ducts were ducting, in part, because he could see through the appropriately one-way glass of his office window, the car—the automotive thing—in which Plug drove away. D.W.D. chose always to think of America as a rich nation without want, so it hurt him that anyone should be reduced to driving in—that!

But even more inductive to the tears was his realization that he would have to raise his offer for Plug Shavaughn's farm. And for him, raising an offer always created serious emotional problems.

Plug took one of his several devious routes out of town. His vehicle did, indeed, suffer a severe degree of cosmetic disability. He took a winsome pleasure in wheeling it past the Department of Motor Vehicles, although only once had an Inspector of the Department, looking out the window while awake, actually seen the car pass. The man had put his coffee cup down very carefully and turned his back resolutely on the window, gasping.

As he drove toward the farm, Plug thought about David W. Dimble. The letterhead summoning him to Hartford had implied 'lawyer' rather than 'developer', though it had specified neither, and Plug had responded in the distant hope that someone might have died and left him a few dollars. He could think of nobody qualified for that high order of achievement, but it had seemed worth the trip at the time. People do die and leave things. His Uncle Selkirk had died and left him a major part of what was now Quandary Farm. Selkirk-like, of course, his will had also left an open question about a band of land running right down the middle of the farm. Midge worried about that. She tended to worry about trivialities, like who owned the middle of their farm. She was of the theory that everyone should invest a few minutes every day worrying. "On account," as she said, "one never knew when there might be something that needed worrying about, and it was only prudent to be in credit."

Plug was currently of the opinion that she should worry only about the whereabouts of the small tractor when she was taking off in the family aircraft.

QUANDARY FARM

It was she who had been responsible for removing the lower right wing the prior morning.

At nine a.m. she had towed the plane to the top of the south rise with the tractor—standard operational procedure in getting airborne from the farm. The land was decidedly "rolling" and when Plug had first come home with the many pieces of the ancient biplane they had decided that it would be futile to try to flatten a landing strip. And it would obviate the whole point of owning the thing if they were to keep it at an airport, the nearest being twelve miles away and expensive. They had, as they so often did, devised a way.

With the aircraft at the top of the south rise, Midge had carefully removed the towbar from the left undercarriage, neglected the towbar on the right undercarriage, and wheeled the small tractor around to the side of the plane. With the engine at full throttle, she released the brakes. She confidently expected to roll vigorously down the rise and become airborne in time to evade the various impedimenta behind the milking barn.

Instead, releasing the brake slewed her around. The lower right wing hung up neatly on the small tractor, and then slowly peeled away from the fuselage. Midge, ordinarily a pretty sound case, cranially, was crestfallen, and Plug spent all day working out an interesting new technology to attach wing to fuselage.

Now, a bit better than a day later, he judged that Midge should be just about arriving at Catton Farm, a few miles from Providence. She had gone for the periodic duty visit to Uncle Selkirk Catton's widow, Aunt Gladys. If the wing stayed on!

While Midge flew, Plug sped along toward the farm. In deference to a car once owned by an old college chum, Plug had plagiarized the name 'Catastrophobia' for the vehicle. It looked the part.

The airplane had not received formal nomenclature—it was known around the farm as only 'Theplane.' It had some numbers painted on the yellow underside of the wings, simply because most planes had. Plug was fully aware that those others had acquired their numbers along with their licenses and certificates of airworthiness, but the economic circumstances at the farm suggested that there was no real sense in arousing sleeping officialdom by taking 'Theplane' around for certification which would undoubtedly cost money. Surely, the chosen numbers—Midge's birthdate—were perfectly satisfactory.

The plane had been flown only six or seven times, but unknown to Plug each flight had accounted for upwards of half-a-dozen cardiac arrests, swallowed cigarettes, and raw, terse understatements like "there's one going down in sector Alpha Omega."

These reactions occurred among the baffled air traffic control people who occasionally found this vagrant blip on their radar screens, only to lose it again. There were also varied reactions among the public bodies called out to locate the wreckage. More than one State Police car had rolled in haste over the top of Plug's hill. There the trooper stopped to gaze at the beauty of the land, incidentally seeking a minced airplane or a telltale pillar of smoke. Always, by the time the seekers arrived, 'Theplane' was quietly closeted in the wing hangar Plug had dug under the old piggery. Only 'Theplane's' tail was in the open, and that was made unobtrusive by the large tarpaulin thrown over it.

Nobody, of course, ever considered the idea that a plane could be brought to earth intentionally anywhere within the voluptuous topography of the farm. So, after a while, Police, Fire, and Civilian Defense functionaries lost interest in the downed aircraft that was now and again reported in the area.

Wheeling Catastrophobia into the muddy farmyard, Plug parked it and stomped toward the house. He was a good solid block of man, just turned thirty and just showing the first superficial signs, the first residual scars, of his chosen way of life. Overturned tractors, minor and major pitchfork wounds, falls into silos—these trivia accumulate and leave their little telltale marks; mildly arthritic knees, a reluctance to sleep on this rib or that hip, little things.

The wounded body had, perhaps, begun to complain slightly, but there was no effect whatever on the ever-welling zest and spirit with which Plug Shavaughn worked his vital earth. Sometimes, twenty hours a day.

In the kitchen as expected, he found Able Mabel, the factotum who referred to herself as "the family slave," and more or less was. Some people take to slavery. Able Mabel had never been caught not working. She had been known to knit through dinner, which calls for a lot of dexterity, especially when one is dining and serving too. It was a degree of dexterity belied by her brief, broad fingers. She was essentially spherical and probably the world cheese soufflé champion. Anyone can make a soufflé, even a good one. But, the magnificent cheese soufflé created consistently but to constantly changing quantity-demands, and baked in an oven periodically rocked by seismic shock (Plug, tossing a bale of hay onto the porch!)—that is a cheese soufflé of worth in a wicked world.

Sitting at the big kitchen table, patting Able Mabel's round rump each time she passed—which she did with such frequency as was beginning to tire him— was Zeke Smithooski, the hired hand.

No one, naturally, is really named Zeke Smithooski. It's just that there is thought to be such an excess of John Smiths in Connecticut that "John" became "Zeke" the first time, and quite possibly the last time, he was seen chewing on a straw. The appendage was put on the "Smith" out of sheer deviltry. In the land of the melting pot, a fellow should not have to go about without a little snap to his name. Plain "Smith" lacks pizzazz!

So, at Hartford Hospital, where he was born, he was rightly listed as John Smith—not even, as he observed in plaint, a middle moniker. But elsewhere, especially on the side of his fire-orange racing stock cars, he was identified as Zeke Smithooski. Most of the people who saw him barreling a car around dirt tracks of New England and New York State believed that they were really watching a maniacal type preposterously name Zeke Smithooski.

Zeke had listened to Plug drive in. He said, "There must be something wrong under the hood. It sounded almost like an internal combustion engine."

Zeke was prone to the diagnosis and treatment of automotive deficiencies and felt cheated when none presented itself to his acute ear. Catastrophobia was, if Plug's property, Zeke's toy. He felt that looks were unimportant in a car—except of course, his track cars—and he cared not that the looks of Catastrophobia pained others. But, the engines were crucial, and her engine was out of a Cadillac hearse some twenty years younger than the chassis-and-baubles that made up her visible parts. The car purred, which confused people who saw it but could not hear it, and he had had it up to 130 mph.

On that May day, a sunny Tuesday, Plug packed away a meal that was somewhere between brunch, lunch, and high tea and then wandered out to the vehicle barn. All afternoon he tractored up and down the picturesque ribs and ridges of Quandary Farm, breaking earth for the corn crop. The fragile, watery green of spring was everywhere around him. Above, a bright blue sky smiled on the brown rows piling up behind the tractor. Plug could feel the latent life beneath his wheels, and he knew that nobody was going to build quickie houses on that ground while he lived.

Toward five, he noticed Zeke on the far side of the valley, waving violently and pointing toward the top of the hill. The racket of the tractor had completely screened the sound of 'Theplane,' but as he looked up Midge slipped the aged flying machine over the crest, shooting through the narrow break where Plug had cut out half-a-dozen trees—his sole concession to the logic of manned flight. Sliding through the gap, Midge barely stalled the craft, then gunned the ancient engine to keep it from falling completely dead.

Those many years ago, Midge was a petite bewitcher who had never even ridden in an airplane until Plug started carting the pieces of one into the yard. But all 98 pounds of her can gentle a one-ton horse to do her bidding, or weld I-beams for a new hay barn, or win crewel work prizes at the Berlin Fair—or analyze the interior line blunders of the New York Giants. It follows that before the re-construction of the historic aircraft was complete, she could fly it, and indeed was licensed to fly anything short of multi-engined craft. She accepted flight much as a hummingbird—or condor—accepts flight, giving it the same intuitive care and attention they give it.

As Plug watched, she bounced down the topography on three points, a bit raggedly. But, she had landed safely in a space something under three hundred yards, including the steep uphill—or braking portion of a dubious landing strip. Suddenly she was taxiing toward the subterranean hangar. Plug turned his tractor smartly and raced for the crest, planting the machine firmly across the dirt road that any curious policeman, fireman, or thrill seeker would have to use. None appeared. Pragmatists all, they preferred to believe that a plane they never found was never there. Plug gave himself about two minutes on roadblock duty, then retired for the day.

Half-an-hour later Midge looked at the place on her wrist where her watch would have been if she had not left it at sinkside in the Rhode Island farmhouse, and declared it was the cocktail hour.

This gave an element of legitimacy to Plug, who was pouring big gin and trivial vermouth over too much ice. Midge declared further, "You know what that stupid Aunt Gladys of yours has done?" The query was clearly aimed at Plug, and he didn't.

"She's sent your Uncle Selkirk's will to some lawyer in Hartford named Whiffletree."

Plug stirred, paused, and considered. Finally he said, "There must be something wrong with that, but I can't just put my pinkie on it. The will's long ago probated. Why send it to some shyster in Hartford? Even one named Whiffletree? He can't help his name. His parents foisted it on him, along with his china blue eyes and thin blond mustache, or whatever else is wrong with the poor devil."

"This stupid will," Midge explained, "that your stupid aunt sent to this lawyer Gooseplod or whatever his name is—it's not the main will. It's the famous long-lost codicil to the main will. The thoughtless afterthought! It covers the middle strip of *this* farm, the strip that Uncle Selkirk acquired separately—and left separately—from the rest of the farm. *This* farm, I repeat.

"Anyway, this afterthought of his, this codicil, it wills the whole damned center strip of this farm to a *blank space*! He signed the bloody thing, but he never filled in a name. Evidently couldn't make up his alleged mind who he was going to leave the middle of *our* farm to. And your simple-minded aunt didn't even have the wit to fill in a name like William Thackeray Shavaughn or Amenhotep III—*anything* but a blank space."

Plug, of course, knew all about the codicil—a minor technicality to him. By now he had poured, sipped, re-poured, and was just bending his head to the re-drinking position. "You mean," he asked, "this lawyer, this Thisletop or

O'Sheopstien or whatever—he is now in possession of the paper, in effect a deed to the middle of Quandary Farm, signed by Uncle Selkirk but with no legatee named? Attorney Mulchstomper can fill in his own choice of names?"

"How's that for an aunt-and-a-half's worth of applied idiocy", Midge asked. "I was going to strangle her, but I had an egg salad sandwich in my hands. But, really, Plug, she is the outside, everlasting *limit*!"

"Where does this Wafflebot or Stoutfellow or whatever—where's his office? I can go along to see him without an egg salad sandwich. I'll just take a pen that can spell Shavaughn!"

"My program, exactly," Midge told him. "Pearl Street—right in the heart of the high-shyster district." She took a card from her bag and handed it to him.

"Giuliano's Nursery?" Plug read. With his crisp martini a pencil, he drew a question mark in the atmosphere. Midge reached up, took the card from his hand, turned it over, and handed it back to him. There, in her hand and in pencil was written,

Thos. S. Whiffletree Suite 23
Commercial and Guardian Building
Pearl Street Hartford, Connecticut
203-568-5554

By the time Plug got to reading the telephone number, he had arrived at the telephone. Nobody answered at Suite 23. Plug's watch said 5:45. Plug said severe things. Then he sat down to kill the can of martinis.

About 6:00 he relinquished his glass and went out into the darkness to cold-finger a few cows. Zeke and a kid from down the road had the milking pretty well in hand, the electrical sockets doing the old pocketa-pocketa and the cows standing about setting new records for phlegmatic vacuity. Plug was uncivil enough to think how like the average cow was to Aunt Gladys.

Jack F. Reynolds

This is the ancient biplane which Plug assembled from parts

II

At 10:29 the next morning Plug was standing at the threshold of Attorney Whiffletree's Suite 23, his second sequential day in the metropolis. At 10:45 he was standing back out in Pearl Street, convinced that Whiffletree was at a hearing and wouldn't be on tap until mid-afternoon. The firm, polite, formal, built, blond-haired dish who served as secretary to Whiffletree hadn't said anything very substantive. Plug had the feeling that she could probably find Richelieu swinging in her family tree. She seemed particularly skilled at divulging zero information about mail received within the week from places like Catton Farm in Rhode Island.

Standing in Pearl Street, Plug was unexpectedly lapel-clutched by David W. Dimble, who seemed to favor black shoes with a shine like the onyx bar in a brothel, extremely dark blue suits assembled on his person, neckties of Coolidgean conservatism, and black hats of the Homburg persuasion. Plug, of course, was less formally attired, the motif being basic sweatshirt.

"One hundred thousand dollars is an awful lot of money, Mr. Shavaughn!" David W. Dimble evidently had no faith in preliminaries like, "Hello." He sped on, "But listen to this Mr. Shavaughn. I am prepared to increase even that stupendously generous offer for that wretched little rock pile of yours. Mind, it won't be easy to get my money back, but I'm pretty good at bargaining—when I'm *selling*, of course! How about one hundred and *five* thousand dollars, Mr. Shavaughn? How about that? You can retire in luxury. No more feeding the cows. No more egging the chickens. No more getting up at—at—at some ridiculous hour of the night. And my suburban shop can even show you some magnificent retirement homes. Best addresses in Bloomfield, or even Avon—and for as little as fifty-thou!"

It had never occurred to Plug to sell Quandary Farm. It had also never occurred to him that people sold houses for as much as fifty thousand dollars; some of the hustlers had been offering that little for the farm. We are, one must remember, discussing 1958.

He looked David W. Dimble straight in his left, pale grey eye and said, "One million dollars! And your suburban office throws in two houses, free. My hired man'll need a place." Zeke, in fact, had a comfortable apartment in Rocky Hill and a spacious cottage on Cape Cod; he was in the habit of winning his stock car races.

Suddenly, David W. Dimble's entire face matched the color of his left eye. He much resembled the television pictures of the time, black and white and grey and grainy. He regularly dealt with figures like one million dollars, but he suffered from a congenital condition that made him go all black and white and grey and grainy when other people tried to put the bite on him for that amount. And, because people do not jest about sacred things like a million dollars, it did not occur to him that Plug might be pulling his pedal extremity.

Plug left D.W.D. standing in Pearl Street, the paradigm of sartorial splendor—but sad.

He strolled around a couple of corners and into Paddy's restaurant. At this hour, even Paddy wasn't in the place. One of the waitresses opened the dispensary; Plug still enjoyed a certain amount of residual popularity from his pre-Midge days. He sat in a far corner reading the waitress' Daily News and sipping his earliest Jack Daniels in some time.

Occasionally his busy mind would be distracted by a headline. "27 Die at Sex Party." Or, on the next page, "32 Die at Sex Party." But mostly he was wondering about getting the right name filled in on that ridiculous coda to Uncle Selkirk's will.

The solution, he convinced himself, was simple. Steal the paper from the lawyer's office. And fill in the appropriate name, which, conveniently, he had learned to spell in the first grade. Return the paper to the lawyer's office. And send Aunt Gladys a basket of flowers with a puff adder stuffed up the begonia!

He decided he'd better get Midge and Zeke into the act. Lawyers were known to be sneaky, and it is always unwise to underestimate a sneaky. Especially one with a blonde Bismarck in the front office. Six light-fingered hands would be better than two.

QUANDARY FARM

He got on the phone to Midge and an hour later, that lady could be seen at Quandary Farm slipping into the right hand seat of Zeke's street vehicle—having waited in ladylike fashion for Zeke to bring the car around.

Simultaneously, in a ground floor corridor of Hartford's Federal building, Attorney Thos. S. Whiffletree was doing a bit of nervous sidling. His sidle-ee—if so trivial a term can designate so momentous a Somebody—was none other than State Senator Hadley Ware. *The Hadley Ware.*

Even among the rich, who are generally perceived to be "different", Hadley ware is different. Hardly a month had passed in his fifty-five years without some distant, often unknown and invariably stinking rich relative dying—and adding, forever adding, always and again adding to the mountain of gold ingots, guaranteed trusts, oil wells, stock certificates, diamond mines, and antique cameos which are the sole cause of Hadley Ware's distinction. And he doesn't give a warm damn about antique cameos!

As commanded in the King James Bible, the by-laws of the Bullion Brook Country Club, and his marriage vows, Hadley Ware is a Republican. He is a living, breathing, tall and slightly paunchy Republican, trapped in the Connecticut State Senate, a body of no legislative significance, which in normal times hardly tolerates and certainly does not encourage Republicans.

Measured objectively, his Senate seat is no more than a mild eccentricity—a whim akin to that of a Five Star Admiral patronizing a one star whorehouse. It didn't cost him much, and it is, after all, simply an easy, inexpensive way to provide himself with free stationery and an extra title. And titles, as the British aristocracy has long understood, are commercially valuable.

Having completed his sidle, Thos. S. Whiffletree stretched a comradely—no, rather let us say an all-American sycophantic—hand onto Hadley Ware's shoulder. Ware stands six feet—so the hand placing exercise was awkward for Thos. S., who doesn't. Measured scientifically, Whiffletree is tall in excess of five feet, but not in excess of five feet, one inch.

His left hand stretch, coupled with the weight of a fearsome briefcase in his right hand, left him looking like an off-balance discuss thrower about to do the gut-bust. He looked remarkably foolish, but he felt just grand. It isn't everyday that a mere eighty-five thousand dollar a year lawyer is seen walking and talking with a man as rich as Hadley Ware!

The sensitivity of the Senator is such that the hand on his shoulder went unnoticed. True, it is a small hand. But he would have been equally perceptive had it been the Hand of Fate! It is a peculiarity of Ware's that his head waggles when he walks. The motion is similar to that of those spring-loaded plastic dogs that certain motorists choose to place in the rear windows of their automobiles, and of essentially the same intellectual content.

Waggling to its right, the head happened to notice Whiffletree at five-o'clock low. To the joy—ecstasy, really—of the little lawyer Hadley Ware came to a full stop, turned slightly, and thrust out a digital ham for shaking purposes. There were people in the corridor to witness this act of seigniorial recognition. Whiffletree's cup was awash!

"Hullo, Whif. How's the wife and kids and girlfriend?"

The Senator always asked that friendly question, no matter what crumb he had to speak to. There were advantages. Now, for instance, vocalizing the questions gave him time to remember what it was he wanted from *this* crumb. That Whiffletree was unmarried, non-paternal and almost congenitally un-girlfriended, Ware knew not, nor cared. He was merely conscious that this greeting constituted some kind of drollery, though he never understood why.

Attorney Whiffletree habitually avoids contradicting his betters, so now he stated flatly that his wife, children and girlfriend were all fine, just fine, thanks. "Fine, Mr. Ware—er, Hadley, ah—Senator. Just fine, thanks." He went on to delve into the condition of the Ware family, expecting and getting no response whatever.

Instead, Ware instructed him that he wanted to see him. Then, perceiving that fulfillment had overtaken anticipation on that score, he emended. "Want to come into your office with one of my—associates. This afternoon. About five. Meant to phone you. Forgot about you! Got a little—conveyancing job. Right up your alley. See you around five." In fifty-five years, other people's convenience had never even been mentioned to a man as wealthy as Hadley Ware. With a nod, he was gone.

He left Whiffletree euphoric. In his thirty-eight years, no one's convenience had ever been considered when men as wealthy as Hadley Ware were concerned. He would simply have to postpone his brother and his brother's committee. They, too, had a date for five o'clock in his office. He'd just call Gregory and tell him he'd have to wait. Ware wouldn't.

Glowing like a man who'd just shaken hands with eight pounds of radioactive isotopes, Thos. S. Whiffletree scurried jauntily out into the street, displaying that hypnotic wheels-within-wheels motion of the legs, observable in short men scurrying jauntily out into the street.

He arrived back at his Pearl Street suite at about the same time Zeke and Midge were parking Zeke's missile on the third floor of the Allyn Street municipal garage. This left the farmers and the lawyer only a couple blocks apart physically though the spiritual separation could best be described in light years.

In Suite 23, Attorney Whiffletree pondered an appropriate gesture of celebration. Even without deluding himself that he actually liked Hadley

Ware, he judged that one should always celebrate the advent of new clients who were, well, practically billionaires. Blithely, even airily, he instructed Miss Giordano to bring him not only his usual roast beef on rye—well done, no butter—but a celebrative raspberry yogurt as well!

"Whoops," thought La Giordano as she swiveled a wild figure into the elevator. "Joy Boy must have found a loophole wrapped in an escape clause secreted in an ambiguity. Gone all depraved. If I'm not careful, he'll be staring at my shins instead of my ankles."

Thus preoccupied, Gemma Giordano strolled into the basement sandwich shop. Intentionally, she ordered the sandwich, and the stockbroker that ultimately, wholly unknown to Gemma, broke up a home in South Windsor. Simultaneously, and equally unintentionally, she caused a sixty-four year old gynecologist to drop his hot dog. Gemma Giordano doesn't go about trying to cause these little contretemps. It's just that where she happens, they happen. And it's all due to the shape of her body and the fact that she is most extremely pretty. At 32, she's blonde and 38-23-36. Other women hate her for this.

In her innocence, Gemma rode back up to the second floor, completed her delivery of dead steer and live cream, abandoned her employer to his saturnalia and strolled off to get her own lunch.

As was customary three days a week, she met a girlfriend who was also on the defensive. Without ever spelling out the position, the two girls understood that they provided one another with safe social mobility. Both had been divorced for some time. Each realized that she was playing in the toughest possible arena— trying to get fitted under the right man while staying out from under all the wrong ones.

The girls decided on Paddy's for lunch. Within a few minutes of that expensive but correct decision, they were cooling their fingers and warming their souls on a brace of Paddy's crisp, splintery Gibsons.

Plug Shavaughn, his broad back now separated from Gemma Giordano's shapely back only by the upholstered back of one of Paddy's booths, went right on explaining his plot against her employer. Midge and Zeke sat listening to him in some awe, wondering how he could have been so careless as to lose his mind between breakfast and lunch.

"His secretary," Plug continued, "is one of these real cool cookies. Let's on about nothing. Dishy as hell, but all business. Really built, and she's got that kind of hair that looks as if it's gone white—whaddaya call it?"

Midge rightly perceived that this question was her responsibility and said, "You mean like the girl behind you? That's platinum. Scientifically assisted platinum!"

Without a thought for decorum, Plug twisted around far enough to get a sidelong glance at Gemma. His eyebrows rose and he snapped back into his seat.

His eyes bulged and he became suddenly—and most uncharacteristically—stealthy, insofar as that is possibly while seated and motionless.

"That's her," he wheezed.

Midge had known him off and on for nearly a dozen years, but she had never before heard his voice crack. In a more dulcet tone of her own she said, "Careful—*care*ful. You go jerking around like that, you could do yourself an injury. For a chilly bon-bon, she seems to grab you where it counts. And I hereby retract my earlier remarks. You don't have to pursue this idiot program of yours alone. Where *you* go, if *she's* there, *I* go!"

Plug had given up extraneous girls on the day of his marriage—several months before it, in fact. Despite the delicious condition of Gemma Giordano, he hadn't really appreciated her during his brief morning visit to Suite 23, so now he had no real reason to understand that he was witnessing Midge in the role of inflamed defender of the hearth, claws unsheathed and fangs honed. Rather he was simply happy that she had come around to his way of thinking.

"That's better," he whispered, the better to conceal his plans from the white haired girls behind him. "We'll go up there around three and just sort of slop around and see if we can spot this document of Uncle Selkirk's. If one of us sees it, he just puts on the pilfer. Slip the paper into a warm spot next to your heart. If it works, great! 'It doesn't, you keep the broad busy ...'"—this secretive instruction was aimed at Midge—"and Zeke and I will have a little chat with Whistlestop. Persuade him!"

At this innocently sinister moment, there was a strident interruption. Leaning suddenly into the booth, ignoring Midge and Zeke, David W. Dimble spoke earnestly to Plug.

"A hundred and *fifty* thousand dollars, Mr. Shavaughn. How about a hundred and *fifty* thousand dollars. You couldn't be serious about that—a, figure—you mentioned this morning. Just your way of bargaining, eh, Mr. Shavaughn? But we can make a very profitable deal for a hundred and fifty thousand. Profitable for *you*, profitable for *you*!"

As D.W.D. continued to press his offer, Plug stood up. The slow manner in which he rose could have been viewed as purposeful. Actually, he thought that Plug was going to strike him. The Dimble commercial tenacity took hold. The Dimble instinctive greed obtained. He sought, and he thought he had found, a bargaining advantage. If punched, he reasoned, he would have a much stronger bargaining posture; possibly legally, certainly psychologically. Fearlessly he presented his chin for punching, slamming his eyes shut.

Bravely he awaited the expected blow—wondering if from the prone position, he could possibly get the offer down to a hundred and *forty* thousand. Maybe even one-thirty-five?

Instead of the expected blow, Plug poured a small dollop of water over the upturned face. Ice water, from his tumbler. Perhaps a tablespoonful. Then another!

David W. Dimble stood there, teeth clenched, chin thrust courageously forward, while Plug intermittently dribbled ice water on the face. Water glass in hand, wrist turning delicately, Plug worked diligently.

Conversation at the surrounding tables and booths ceased. That part of the lunchtime crowd seated in the taproom gave full attention to D.W.D.'s moist mush. It was, even for Paddy's, unusual. Plug stood there, drippity, drip-drip, dripping.

The Dimble voice quavered. Then it gargled. "One hundred and *sixty* thousand?" ice water gurgled joyfully over his chin, babbled about his starched collar, ran on and dampened his inflexible suit. By now, Midge had passed the tolerant giggling stage and had been reduced to the kind of head-shaking disbelief reserved for those who watch David W. Dimble engaging in high-level financial negotiations with Plug Shavaughn.

Also hanging in there was Zeke Smithooski. He, however, had just abandoned that inadequately classy name. Leaning forward across the spot where Plug had lately been seated, John Smith was suddenly eyeball to eyeball with Gemma Giordano. She, like everybody else in the place, had turned to see what was going on. She saw, she smiled, she was puzzled—and then she saw Zeke. Nee John. In that instant, she and Zeke went all stupid in concert. They froze where their eyes had met—he leaning forward about three-quarters of his considerable length, she swiveled in a manner that even her remarkable structure didn't really allow. They stared at one another.

Finally, Zeke said, "My name's John Smith."

Gemma moaned a little—she didn't believe him. "That's okay," she said, "it doesn't matter. Call me Mary Jones. Will you join us …?" She didn't need to complete her invitation. Zeke—he felt needed because he thought he had heard the faintest suggestion of a moan in her glorious voice—was already stepping around the eroding Dimble to sit beside the only girl who had ever existed.

Meanwhile, back at the bourse, David W. was wiping his face on a large white napkin handed to him by the proprietor. Paddy had come to see what was interfering with the turnover. Now he stood with his back to the damp Dimble and shook a questioning grin at Plug. Paddy was no advocate of water, but neither was he a major fan of David W. Dimble, who drank very little else. His smiling admonition finished, Paddy plucked his napery from a moist hand and led the Great Negotiator to the furthest end of the bar. Oblivious to the crowd, David

W. Dimble made a last, straight-faced sally at Plug. "Think about a hundred and sixty-*five* thousand, Mr. Shavaughn. *Very* generous offer!"

Plug, normally a man of some diffidence, made a modest bow to the staring lunchers—acknowledgement of the scattered applause. Then he resumed his seat and reached for his drink. Only after a comforting draft did he realize that the personnel count had changed.

"Where's Zeke?"

Again, Midge indicated the platinum blond girl behind him—now deep in conversation with the missing man. Again, Plug twisted far enough to get a sidelong glance at Gemma. "What," he queried, "is he doing over there? That's Wafflebat's secretary!"

"I haven't consulted him," Midge reported, "but any boy over twelve should be able to figure out what he's doing. And speaking as a girl over twelve, I'd say he would definitely get it done. I suppose I used to wear expressions like that when you came on the scene. That poor girl is totally helpless!"

Plug, his back still between himself and the next booth, felt that he must be missing something fascinating. He turned again. Gemma Giordano and Zeke were still staring at each other, their eyes about six inches apart, their drinks and Gemma's girlfriend ignored. The latter caught Plug's gaze. She slid out of her seat and approached the Shavaughn's. She spoke, mostly to Midge.

"Does your friend hypnotize all the girls like that?"

Midge slid further into her booth and nodded the girl into a seat. Plug made motions like standing and sitting while the girl accepted the invitation. Midge did the talking.

"I've only seen that look on his face once before. Somebody loaned him a 1935 Lagonda for a weekend. He looks like a little boy with eleven new puppies. You're sure she's not hypnotizing *him*! I'm Midge Shavaughn. Gunga Din, here, is my husband, called William or Plug depending on your taste or lack of it. I use

"Plug" because *he* affects *me* the way *she* affects *him*." She nodded at the couple alone in the next booth. "Alone in the world. In the macrocosm!"

"Lucky," the girl said. And then, less soulfully, she added, "My name's Nola Klim. Used to be Klimkowski, but I can't spell it. The girl half of that rehearsal for a blue movie over there, that's Gemma Giordano. She can spell it, but right now, I think she's working on changing it. Normally, she shows signs of sanity."

The conversation was friendly enough, but it sort of trailed off after awhile. Nola finally decided that she'd better go back to work—and allowed that the next time she came in she thought she'd have lunch. There were friendly goodbyes, and she was away. She paused long enough to pat Gemma on the arm and say, "so long." There was a kind of bemused nod from Gemma, suggesting that she was alive.

Plug is a romantic, but only after his own fashion. He decided that he could wait as long as Zeke was in captivity—because he really couldn't do his little search and collect mission without Zeke. After a quick phone call to the farm, alerting Able Mabel that she and the kid from up the road would be milking fifty cows that evening, he returned to the booth where Midge sat watching romance bloom. He slid in and settled down for a long siege.

It was, in fact, well over two hours before the pair in the next booth came around enough to move and complete the circle of introductions. By then, Midge was feeling gayer than she thought she should in the middle of the day, and the taproom was nearly empty. They sat some more, in a foursome, while Zeke and Gemma held hands.

III

As far back as 1785, a Scottish poet noticed that "... the best laid plans of mice and men gang aft a-gley."

Which was a pretty weird way of expressing it, of course, but it's hard to argue with his intent. What he was trying to express, however awkwardly, was that the best laid plans of mice and men frequently come apart at the seams.

The whole concept is Scottish to the core, truly Gaelic in its dour despondency. Barren. Desolate. Perfectly true, of course, but a touch emphatic on the sad side.

The poet—R. Burns, it was—would have been better advised to balance his cautionary lament with the equally true observation that many of the plans of man—we really can't speak authoritatively for mice—well or badly laid, often go straight down the pike to happy fruition. As in the present case.

Plug, as we know, had spent the best part of an hour trying to convince Midge and Zeke that they should practically rob a lawyer's office. Yet all three were honest folk, so the "let's-rob-the-lawyer's-office-a-little-bit" caper didn't really have much going for it. Beyond necessity! It didn't have what an ordinary *ad hoc* committee of decent citizens would be able to agree upon as the moral content and practical feasibility to recommend its adoption. It had nothing going for it at all, except the incomprehensible stupidity of Aunt Gladys. She of the jellied cerebellum!

But now, out of nowhere, the hastily laid plans of Midge and her man were suddenly going straight down the pike toward happy fruition. The active ingredient in this pleasant circumstance being, as we have seen, LOVE.

Gemma Giordano was precipitantly in love with a man whose name she couldn't believe was John Smith. John Smith was equally off his trolley over a girl whose name he was—pretty sure—was Mary Smith; she had, after all, said so. And their time together since meeting had been so—well, so *together*—as to preclude getting the details ironed out. And this girl was secretary to Thos S. Whiffletree, the very attorney whose office was so desperately in need of a little white robbery. That, surely, is going straight down the pike … etc.

Still, while we here on the printed page can comprehend these matters in seconds, it naturally took the listed personnel a little longer. In fact, it was mid-day the next day before the various arrangements were settled. But even that was pretty good going, considering how wholly preoccupied some of the leading players had been.

The arrangements that were settled were as follows. Gemma, or whatever her name was, was engaged to be married to—well, maybe his name actually was John Smith. She, at least, was suddenly aware that, despite all the clichés to the contrary, she had never actually known anyone named John Smith. And he, not really caring a damn *what* her name might be, was engaged to be married to her. And there was that other trivial detail. Some silly document that John's friends wanted to see, some silly piece of paper that was just cluttering up Attorney Whiffletree's office. Good heavens! Have paper, will filch! For John, she would have held up the Hartford National Bank and Trust Company's main office, barefoot, left-handed and blindfolded. Not right at this moment, of course. She was otherwise engaged!

The following lunchtime the entire assembly was back in Paddy's—lacking only Nola Klim and David W. Dimble. Gemma walked in smiling, nodded happily at Midge, handed Plug the silly document, curled an arm around Zeke's arm, and pressed herself quite indecently into the booth against him.

Plug felt that the several circumstances called for celebration. Champagne appeared forthwith, despite Gemma's arcane suggestion that raspberry yogurt might be in order. That remark confused Plug, but he had never really understood other guy's girls. Midge found it a perfectly sensible remark. Referring, obviously, to somebody who actually celebrated with raspberry yogurt. God knows … then Midge brightened. Maybe it was Gemma's boss, lawyer Eafflenob! Which would be just splendid—one couldn't feel guilty about putting the purloin on a man who did things like that!

While the bubbly bubbled, Plug took his newly liberated document and buttonholed Paddy at the bar. Moments later the two men were in Paddy's small office behind the kitchen. Moments after that Plug said a grateful "Thanks" to

Paddy and returned to the celebration with the magic words, "... my nephew, William Thackeray Shavaughn ..." neatly typed into what had lately been a blank space. He handed the paper to Gemma who put it in her bag, ready for replacement in the Whiffletree files.

Zeke nibbled at his drink and thought about the magnificent creature nestled against him. He now knew that she had an engine to match the chassis, but there was also some indefinable something extra, which juggled him all over the room. After much thought he decided that women must have some hidden something that makes them different from cars. He felt that he was onto an important discovery.

While Zeke philosophized, Midge and Gemma talked about marriage. Midge had several good words to say for it, while Gemma conceded that she was deep into the 'hope-over-experience' syndrome. Plug went right on not worrying about the things he had not been worrying about before, but admitting to himself that he was pleased with the day's doings. It was comforting to know who owned the middle of his farm, nice to know that business was finished. But, as R. Burns said, it wasn't.

And the reason it wasn't is that there is always some rotten SOB out there who just can't get through the day without living somebody else's life. Let us back up a bit and look in on a couple of these noodniks, one of whom we have already met. The other, be warned, is no improvement.

Some twenty-four hours prior to the small feast of celebration we have just attended—back in that innocent age when Plug had hardly started plotting and Zeke had yet to discover the secret of eternal bliss—some of those rotten SOB's were out there getting on with it, each doing his own thing. Several of which things, strictly observed, might seem to be crooked. Or, viewed socially, these things were engaged in by persons of the highest social and professional standing, and were therefore either shrewd or positively clever. So, in our pleasant little provincial capital, the status was quo and things were pretty alright!

Senator Hadley Ware, as we know, separated himself from Attorney Whiffletree in the lobby of Hartford's Federal Building. He then departed that scene by a rear exit, hoping that no one of significance had seen him talking with a nonentity like little whatsisname. And, while a euphoric Whiffletree strolled jauntily back to his Pearl Street office, legs hypnotically achurn, a grouchy Hadley Ware directed his driver to drive—to the Shaker Club.

On balance, Hartford is not prone to ostentation. It could be argued that practically all of the city's lavishness is carefully hidden away in the elegant rooms of the Shaker Club. Which, in the tradition of Hartford's good things, isn't in Hartford at all. The better not to disturb the peasantry.

It is a rule of modern money that rousing passion in the peasantry is as evil as dipping into the capital. Eviler! And the passion the arousal of which clongs the gong is ENVY. Nothing is more detrimental to domestic tranquility than envy in the hearts of nature's untouchables. And if the slobs don't see what you do with the money they earn for you, they won't envy you. Which must be good for them.

The Shaker Club, therefore, is located in a graciously retiring mansion in a diffident neighborhood of a reticent suburb, albeit only minutes from the Federal Building if traffic is flowing properly.

On the day in question, traffic so flowed that Senator Hadley Ware hardly had the lint of Thos. S. Whiffletree brushed from what compassion causes us to call his 'mind' before he was gazing at the shining skull of Gilbert deVille, smack in the center of the Shaker Club's Gold Room.

The room is, in fact, tastefully done in white with green accents. But in a niche above the bar, set securely in concrete, steel, and shockproof glass, is the single ingot of gold for which the room is named—four hundred ounces of applied ostentation and technical illegality. For, in the late fifties it was not within the law for private individuals, or even very private clubs, to hold gold. Perhaps not too strangely, nobody in the law enforcement business had ever thought it worthwhile to nudge that sleeping dog which, by whim or waspishness—envy, possibly?—the highly budgeted decorator had included as a kind of inspired token. Its position, both physical and spiritual, was equivalent in the Shaker Club's Gold Room to that of the Host in a Roman Catholic Cathedral— central, and handy to the bread and wine.

His back to the sacrament, deVille grunted a grunt and bestowed upon Had-ley Ware a rheumatic nod, indicating a heavy, embroidered chair. In nodding, deVille's head necessarily moved, nearly blinding Ware. Some men are bald. Some men are starkly bald. Gilbert deVille is starkly, buffed and polished dazzling bald. He is, at age sixty-three, still the victim of an affliction of his youth. His youth had happened to him during that thoughtless national experiment with moral coercion, which caused young men to drink alcoholic beverages from teacups. DeVille lost his hair through an unfortunate choice of whisky at a time when choice was, candidly, uniformly unfortunate. He hadn't had a hair up there for thirty years. And during those decades, had drunk only tea in bar rooms. Often, treacherously, from whisky glasses.

Surprisingly, this latter peculiarity is still unknown to a few of those naifs who tend to believe that deVille is drinking whisky simply because they seem to see him doing so. Over the years, this misconception has cost the business community a lot of money, almost all of which is still in the possession of the shiny-bald tea-tippler. It's a trivial, but telling, aspect of deVille's approach to business.

It is his oft expressed, if immodest, belief that, "It's no good fighting deVille." In general, his opinions are novel. Some have thought that they could find traits of Thuggee or early Shinto in his utterances. Less often, he will share a concept with the John Birch Society: "less often", because of his conviction that the membership of that organization is riddled with commies. Too, he takes very seriously his self-appointed role as the paradigm of Yankee virtue, perhaps because he is not a Yankee. His family was evidently Dutch, or perhaps Albanian. Like the Rejuvenation Insurance Society of which he is Chairman and Chief Executive Officer, the name was founded by Gilbert's great-grandfather while nobody was looking.

If the beacon atop the rival Travelers Insurance Companies Tower symbolizes the Insurance City to the world, the shine atop deVille's skull symbolizes it to all right thinking, *far* right thinking, locals. Starting at the top in Rejuvenation, deVille had hacked his way over the bodies of assorted uncles, cousins and other interlopers, each of whom thought he had some vague right to Chair the board. Subtly, Gilbert knew better. Now they know. And he has demonstrated his finer qualities by not actually demanding physical obeisance from the shards of these men.

"Have you got the Shavaughn parcel?" he asked Hadley Ware. Like David W. Dimble, Gilbert deVille seldom beat about the bush when he could get on with making money or emasculating somebody.

"I'm seeing Whiffletree this afternoon—and I'd like to have you come along. He's got the assignment document. It's a codicil to the prior owner's will. Believe it or not, there's no assignee. Put your name in, if you like. I had to go to Providence and see the old guy's widow. I told her there was legal requirement that she send the document to Whiffletree. People'll believe anything! Anyway, now it's in the State and we're ready to go. Is five o'clock in Pearl Street alright?"

Always methodical, though by no means as intellectually up-market as he believed himself to be, Gilbert deVille answered the questions in the order presented.

"You don't need me on display. I won't be there and keep my name totally and unconditionally out of it! Why'd you pick Whiffletree? He's not much brighter than that widow. Well, this gives us every necessary parcel in the township, doesn't it? Except the rest of the Shavaughn farm, of course. We'll have that clod-buster out of there in a few months at most, and cheap. Have a drink?"

Appropriately, the waiter awaited. Thirty feet away, behind the bar and busy polishing glassware, he divined deVille's summons: the faintest flick

QUANDARY FARM

of an arthritic hand, seen apparently by radar and for not more than a millisecond, and the man presented himself at deVille's side.

This is Catastrophobia, the car that looked beat up, but Zeke could get her going at 130 mph. She is parked by one of the barns on the farm

IV

While Gilbert deVille ignores his cold tea and Hadley Ware grimaces over his Chivas Regal, let us leave them to their hatreds and look into the matter of parcels, as referred to by deVille.

Christmas goodies and wet fish are not the only things that come in parcels. Land does, too. And at the time we are viewing, the relatively progressive State of Connecticut was getting under way with its commendable road-building program, inevitably involving LAND!

A few miles from Hartford, a minor connector road was to be laid, tying together two extant main arteries—and thereby catering for a proposed industrial park. The connector road would be anything from four to seven miles long, depending on a final choice of site. Its ultimate position at this time consisted of a half-a-dozen tentative pencil lines on some State Highway Department maps. Each line undulated sinuously over land!

At five or six million dollars a mile, the four-mile route had a certain charm and personality, from the viewpoint of the taxpayer that the seven-mile alternative lacked. But these things are never simple. The four-mile route would be, by far, the least convenient—the least economical—for the ultimate users of the road, the workers, shippers and suppliers of the industrial park. So it stood that the State might save ten or twenty million dollars by putting the road in one place. But, that sum and far more would be lost by the road users within a couple of years. Individual working men, for instance and ironically, would be putting an extra four or five miles a day on their cars because the shorter road would mean longer approaches for most of them.

How like the horns of the blue-tailed dilemma, you may think. Certainly, there were varied responses to the problem. The Fairfield County Republican spokesmen—thousands of them—represented working men none of whom would be apt, ever, to see the road in question. The Fairfield County Republican spokesmen—thousands of them—were very big taxpayers. They saw with crystal clarity the manifest *truth! That is, only a criminally psychopathic communist imbecile would even consider building the road at any point but the shortest. And instead of the projected four-lane divided highway demanded by safety engineers, why not a good honest Yankee dirt road, a one-laner like the kind that was good enough for George Washington and Calvin Coolidge? In fact, it was pretty damned questionable whether there was any need for any road at all! Just Hartford crooks, trying to rob the honest coupon clipper!*

The officers of Local 1432, Amalgamated Thrust Bearing Grinders and Cherry Pickers, AFL-CIO, meeting for dinner at the Yankee Silversmith, wondered why a small assessment might not be made against the wealthier, outlying counties—Fairfield, for instance—to get some of the tax burden off the back of the downtrodden working stiff. The motion was read by delegate Moriarty who, unlike the blackguard Ware, didn't grimace at all over his Chivas Regal, not even while reading.

There was even a local Chamber of Commerce that found itself in an uncomfortable—and unfamiliar—position, agreeing with those Luddite Union racketeers and disagreeing with the decent, upright Republicans down in Fairfield! The ramifications and permutations of ramifications were endless!

And how, and why, does all this impinge upon simple country folk like Plug and Midge Shavaughn? Or complex exurban folk like Gilbert deVille, whose swimming pool (never swum in the presence of Gilbert deVille) is larger than Plug's barns? Or statuesque girls like Gemma Giordano? Even Senators named Ware and Attorneys named Whiffletree and real estate hustlers named David W. Dimble?

With respect a suggestion; let us first wonder about the impingement upon Attorney Whiffletree. It will assist in carrying this narrative forward in an orderly fashion.

You will recall the progress of Thos. S. that day. While Hadley Ware was grouching his way to the Shaker Club, Whiffletree had done his jaunty churning bit in the streets, and by the time the subtleties of Gilbert deVille were drawing the waiter's attention in the Gold Room, Attorney Whiffletree had been handed his celebrative yogurt by Gemma Giordano—herself just returned from causing a sixty-four year old practitioner of gynecology to drop his Frankfurt. Gemma—we now know—had then gone on to better things, to indeed, the very best of things!

Whiffletree chewed his way through the roast beef sandwich. A small light of anticipation appeared in his eye as he periodically caught sight of the small carton of yogurt. He also fingered his way through his desk diary, wrote in "Senator Hadley Ware and colleagues" for five o'clock—and tried to phone his brother with the news that Ware was on and brother was off.

The last bit of roast beef disappeared. With a bright smile, he reached for the yogurt. As he leaned forward, his eye caught a note he had made on the calendar. It said, "Query R.I. testament."

He pushed the buzzer on his desk and waited for the unimpeachable Mrs. Giordano to appear. She didn't. He gleaned that she, too, was at lunch. He pushed the yogurt aside with a splendid feeling of heroic deprivation and went into the outer office to find the document in question. It had appeared in his mail the prior day and had meant nothing to him. But then, he received lots of mail that meant nothing to him. Some were ultimately explained. Some weren't. Every lawyer's office has a few floating around.

He found the document, of course, on Mrs. Giordano's desk—in a pile of papers to be filed. She never failed! He took it back to his office, sat down with deep satisfaction, and peeled the lid from the raspberry yogurt. Life was good.

He read through the brief document again. Strange. It transferred a small piece of land downstate to nobody in particular. The legatee wasn't named but the paper was clearly signed by someone named Selkirk I. Catton, and the signature was witnessed by a Providence notary and a second party. Probably the notary's secretary. Damned careless. The paper was as good as a title to the land, an odd, narrow parcel to be sure. But—no legatee. He made a note to give Mrs. Giordano a note of inquiry to the Providence notary. Then, his duties performed, he leaned back and abandoned himself to the sensuality of raspberry yogurt.

Time passed, in the time-honored way time has.

Years of experience should have taught Attorney Whiffletree that when things are going well, when life is filled with a myriad of joys, when its yogurt time in Pearl Street, when all seems bright in the world, it's time to call your insurance man. Or a cop. Maybe a priest. *Somebody. A lawyer, even.*

God and nature were about to lower the boom on Thos.

On this day of all days—his heart light with anticipation of the forthcoming visit of Senator Hadley Ware, his tum just pleasantly heavy—on this day the unimpeachable Mrs. Giordano suddenly proved impeachable. Worse, she proved invisible. For, as we know but Attorney Whiffletree could not know, Gemma was in Paddy's busy falling in love.

Her lunch hour was ordinarily flexible, at her employer's convenience, of course, not hers. But she never overstayed her allotted hour. And now, here it was four o'clock. Senator Ware would arrive at five.

Whiffletree's attorneyesque mind went to work. He phoned Hartford Hospital, where Gemma Giordano was unknown, although they did have a nice little boy named Jimmy Jordan, if that would help.

He tried to get a temporary secretary and was told that the bureau would have a top-notch girl there at nine sharp in the morning. Whiffletree's attorneyesque mind disengaged.

He had no idea where his secretary normally went for lunch, but he thought of making the rounds of drug stores and lunch counters. He abandoned that idea, horrified at the inherent threat—Senator Hadley Ware might arrive and find NOBODY present. His attorneyesque mind switched to 'Full Off.'

Basically, Thos. S. Whiffletree is a sound enough business lawyer. He understands things that boy scouts and serious churchgoers should never be told. If a man of such essentially conservative accomplishments can be faulted, or even peccadillo'd, the fault—or peccadillo—would be perturbability.

When others fret, Whiffletree worries. While they worry a bit, Whiffletree's nervous breakdown occurs in stereo and Technicolor. Those moments when a display of the popular old nerveless, steely-eyed stuff seems indicated; at just such moments does one find the quiet, staid Whiffletree standing on his chair, screaming.

His forebears were English and it would seem likely that they were not so much emigrants as deportees. They were presumably of that cut that would have stayed at Dunkirk, brushing up on their German, or turned their furious gallop furiously westward at Balaclava. They would have been among that tiny minority of Britons congenitally afflicted with squishy upper lips.

Their seventh generation Hartford heir was prone to panic under heavy pressure such as a stiff shove with a dove's wing. His reactions were well recorded. Up the wall! Aquiver, augmented by palpitations. Standing aghast and blenching. All these he was known to do well, and had at least once achieved tremble, shudder, flutter and quaver in complete harmony, all the while wincing and flinching. Fortunately, he is a small man and people often don't notice.

Indeed, as 4:30 p.m. passed into history (for, it must be admitted, the severalth time) there was still nobody around to do any noticing.

Jack F. Reynolds

This is a photo of some of the detail of the Connecticut State Capitol Building in Hartford. This is an archway over one of the doors.

V

Whiffletree wasn't actually prone, but he had a very pronounced slump when Gemma finally pushed through the door at 4:45, as rue-filled as a Paris map and profuse with apologies, which Thos. S. was quite relieved to accept. Ecstatic explanations followed. Thos. S. was wholly unable to comprehend these. His apperception stock in matters of love is severely circumscribed.

Despite her joyful guilt, Gemma was able to recognize two immediate duties. She had to introduce her employer to John Smith who was tagging along very close behind her. And she had to assist the frazzled Whiffletree to his own inner office and minister to him with the hot, black tea.

This was quite the worst attack of jangled employer she had yet witnessed, but her therapeutic techniques were sensational. Thos. was alive and well and very nearly living in Suite 23 by the time five o'clock happened. Zeke noticed the operation had several similarities with the demise and rise of Lazarus, so colorfully reported by the Gospeller John and his famous XI, 1–44.

As the awaited moment arrived, so did Senator Hadley Ware—and a fat, friendly man from the Southern New England Bell Telephone Company, the latter intent upon repairing a Southern New England Bell Telephone. Detached and disabused by Gemma, the man re-read his order, discovering that he had everything right but the street, the building, and the client name.

As the closing door finally shut off the departing man's non-stop apologies, the convalescent Thos. S. Whiffletree appeared at the door of his inner office, his face agleam with his very best effort at a smile of welcome for Hadley Ware. He strode forward, his hand outstretched, and went into a high parabola over a low table, arriving at the feet of his newfound patron headfirst. This caused him to become unconscious.

At precisely that ironically stimulating moment, Thos.'s brother Gregory arrived—with spear bearers—all unaware that he was unwanted. There was now much milling about in Suite 23, momentarily augmented by the repairman from Southern New England Bell Telephone, returned to ask if anyone knew the whereabouts of Gold Street. Senator Hadley Ware stood apart, displaying solemn indifference.

Slowly, things settled down. The only further difficulty was a minor one suffered—as one would expect—by the fallen Whiffletree. Even so, within the quarter-hour he was back at the semi-sedentary vertical, albeit by no means cleared for active duty.

Various diagnostic possibilities were suggested by various people, and when the words "fractured skull" were mentioned, Hadley Ware decided to get the hell out—immediately. No need to have his name publicly connected with any unpleasantness. He left the offices of Thos. S. Whiffletree, having first instructed the latter's secretary that she should find, segregate and preserve a document lately mailed from Rhode Island. It was she was told, an important codicil to a will and pertinent to a parcel of downstate land called Quandary Farm.

Zeke was supporting Whiffletree's head when this instruction was thrust at his beloved. It was an unfortunate thrust; Zeke dropped the head. But, as noted the setback was trivial and had no real effect upon the recovery of the patient.

The Whiffletree, once articulate, expressed the heartfelt wish that he might have died. Viewed objectively, he might have. Rarely has anyone of his age group achieved that particular shade of bleached moss and survived!

Gregory and his delegation were still hovering about in the wings. Flaked, as he was, Thos.—deprived of the apogee of his career by the departure of Senator Hadley Ware—felt duty bound to listen to the strange tale unfolded by these gentlemen. Perhaps not so much "unfolded" as dragged out of the hamper of mixed up minds and dumped on the floor.

It seemed that brother Gregory, Deputy Sub-Assistant Something in his small sector of the State Bureaucracy, kept losing airplanes. That was the claim of others, of course. Naturally, he, Gregory, had never lost an airplane in his life, nor would his natural conscientiousness allow such grossly uneconomic carelessness. But, his department had ultimate responsibility for the department that was finally responsible for the Air Traffic Control people in several of the State's airports. Under Federal surveillance, naturally. And it was the real, on-the-scene air traffic controllers who kept losing the airplanes, and Gregory wondered if his brother, as an attorney, couldn't do something to get the pressure off Gregory.

In the ordinary way, the kind of carelessness that Gregory was so unjustly accused of, would get a civil servant transferred. Or at least promoted out of harm's way. Gregory would welcome either if Thos. could manipulate in that direction. He shared his sibling's hereditary perturbability, and he realized that his was not the ideal make-up for any association, however remote, with air traffic control. Not that he had ever asked to be assigned to such a field of endeavor. He had clearly and specifically requested Debenture Adjustments.

Brother Thos. was not really absorbing all this, but Gregory pressed on; an opportunity for lamentation was not to be missed merely because of a pair of glazed eyes.

Not only did the airplanes keep disappearing, Gregory went on, there was never a corpus delecti. Seven or eight times this phenomenon had occurred, but nobody had ever found a bent airplane.

Several hundred local policemen, dozens of State policemen, and half a gross of volunteer firemen had, at one time or another, searched for the downed aircraft. None was ever found. Gregory wondered if there might be some diabolical plot against himself. There had even been insinuations around the department that Gregory might benefit from a few weeks off, resting in some establishment where he would receive tender loving care and lots of warm milk.

Thos. was suffering. That, of course, he did most days, but salvation by explosion is not, at least for him, an everyday event. So even his advanced fragility couldn't prevent him from following the stampede to the window—following slowly, to be sure.

The stampede was caused by the explosion which sounded like a major social event right outside the office window—an event of such decibelic magnitude as to grab command of all the *medullae oblongata in the neighborhood.*

One must suppose that, in a history that long predates the foundation of such Johnny-come-lately communities as Madras, Melbourne, Minneapolis, Montreal, and Murmansk, Hartford had experienced the odd moment of excitement. But not often. And surely not in Pearl Street!

Pearl Street, in fact, was never the scene for your casual thrill seeker, nor was it any place for comings-off or goings-on. Pearl Street was, then as now, home to the fiduciary mafia, to bankers, lawyers, brokers, usurers, and other of high birth and gentle intent, and hardly to be considered for public vulgarities like explosions.

So the rush hour blast in that decorous street raised a very large number of eyebrows, several dozens of the old-fashioned windows which in those days could be raised, and one carefully selected State Senator.

The law of gravity has an excellent record of incorruptibility. So, when Senator Hadley Ware, complete with limousine, chauffeur, briefcase, and a small green pamphlet lately pressed into his hand by the ardent advocate of some profound but esoteric movement, had risen smartly off the surface of Pearl Street in response to the explosion, it followed that, in response to that incorruptible law, the Senator with all his accouterments would return to the surface of Pearl Street with severe impact. And so it was.

Certain mutations were immediately visible. The car, askew in the crowded street, was straddling a ragged new hole and was a great deal less shiny than had been the case moments before. The chauffeur, lately alert, was now inert. Several by-standers had become by-sitters.

Senator Ware tried to stand up in the back of his limousine, a trick that he could not have performed under any circumstances. He found himself in an undignified position, trying to stride from the car on his knees, just as the first— fortuitous—cop got to the closed door. It became apparent that this was a very useful cop. It also became apparent that the car was on fire. The young policeman wrenched the door open, dragged Hadley Ware into the road at a steepish angle and assisted him to the sidewalk with a Herculean shove. The Senator flew to and across the walk, caromed off a bank and ended up down. This was not his style at all, but it was a vast improvement on being back in the limo.

While the Senator was still bouncing off the bank, the cop was carrying courage almost to excess amid the roaring gasoline. By brute force he got the chauffeur's door open and dragged that fortunate man—if you can view being blown up and knocked out as fortunate—awkwardly but effectively away from the now incandescent car. The chauffeur proved to be but slightly injured, although subsequently very outspoken!

Pearl Street, as its nature would suggest, enjoys a number of amenities, not the least of which at a moment like this is a big old cuddly, lovable fire station. From this suddenly debouched a platoon of very efficient Johnnies who did a lovely job of hasty mountain building. Working under decidedly hostile conditions, they had the blazing limousine completely hidden under a mountain of foam within a couple of minutes. The fire, grossly outnumbered by the bubbles, gave up.

The rush hour crowd had retreated as the pyre rose, some of them having to get up off the ground to do it. Now they pressed forward as the foam rose. They even had the decency to applaud as the firemen brought their entertainment to a conclusion. So devastatingly dull is the life of the office worker that any little respite is received in gratitude.

This is a 2005 photograph of the State Capitol where Senator Hadley Ware had his office. It is an extremely ornate building covered with statuary and scenes of Hartford history.

VI

"Now that love and stealing have put the world to rights," Midge said, "maybe we'd better write to Aunt Gladys the Gullible and let her know that virtue has triumphed over her vacuity."

It was that indeterminate era that qualifies as breakfast-time at Quandary Farm, that period between dawn and noon when the preparation and service of traditional fast-breaking comestibles like coffee, hotcakes, pan-fried potatoes, cold apple pie, orange juice, steaming codfish cakes, bubbling oatmeal, and last night's leftover Caponata Siciliana, keep Able Mabel's left hand more or less occupied while she paints the pantry and re-weaves the worn spot in the upstairs Persian rug.

Plug and Zeke had taken about 300 quarts of milk out of the bovine vacuities, set the animals loose to stoke up, and come themselves to the kitchen on a similar errand. As Plug piled butter on a muffin, he considered his wife's suggestion. And this brought to mind a question he had meant to ask before.

"Why?" "Why did the old darlin' suddenly come up with this ingenious trick of sending utterly incomplete legal documents to utterly unknown Whiffletrees? Did you query her about that little idiocy? Did you ask her what she thought she was doing, sitting over there in Rhode Island trying to give away the middle of our farm? She's got a farm of her own. She could give away the middle of *it* a lot easier. No postage. Nothing."

Midge unbit the slice of apple she was about to devour. She stated that, of course, she had asked. "And she gave me the kind of dumb answer you'd expect from the kind of dumb Aunt who would do a double-dumb thing like that. She said a man called at the farm, Catton Farm, and told her to do it. She said he was a nice tall man who looked very official. He told her the codicil had to go for 'endorsement,' whatever that's supposed to mean. He told her to send it to Whiffletree and that he'd take care of it. And she told him she didn't know where it was. So he told her to damn well find it. So she spent two days looking for it and she found it and sent it to Whiffletree."

Plug's big, chiseled face wore the kind of expression one associates with the Biblical loser, Job. "Jesus," he said as Midge finished, "one less brain cell and she'd be her own clone. Anyway, the stupid thing is found and fixed. Last time I asked her about it, three or four years ago, she had no idea where it was. Told me it was 'put away' with Uncle Selkirk's stuff. She should be put away."

As this forgivable unkindness passes his lips, Plug was nudged by Zeke. The latter had been ladling shredded wheat into his face and looking over the morning Courant. Now he mumbled, "This guy, Hadley Ware, *is* the one who was up in Whiffletree's office." Zeke pointed to the Bacharach portrait of Ware on the front page.

"Like I told you last night, he came in a little strong, and then he sort of melted away after Whiffletree fell on his head. Says here ..." Zeke read from the lead article.

"Senator Ware, thought to be one of the wealthiest men in the State, is believed to have had a business appointment in Pearl Street.

"His limousine had been parked in the area for some minutes and had apparently just picked him up and moved off when the blast occurred. The Senator was not available for comment after the incident, either at his home or at his office.

"An extensive check of hospitals and other medical facilities failed to show him receiving treatment, although his chauffeur, Giuseppe Diano, 40, of Newington, was admitted to Hartford Hospital for observation shortly after the explosion.

"Mr. Diano was reported to be suffering from shock, contusions, and, according to a resident physician who requested anonymity, outrage ..." "And so on," Zeke ended his reading. Then he picked up his own narrative of the prior evening and half the morning.

"Anyway, the cops say it was a bomb, no question. And I'm here to tell you it *sounded* like a bomb. Took out windows all over the area, mostly across the street. Our side, the blast must have come pretty much straight up."

Zeke went on. "Ware must have been the one Whiffletree was in such a sweat about. He kept telling Gemma that the most important client he'd ever had was coming in. You know, I feel a little guilty. If I hadn't moved that coffee table out of Gemma's way while she was playing Florence Nightingale, it wouldn't have been in his way when he came dancing out to meet this Ware.

"Altogether, we had a very exciting time. Nervous breakdowns, fractured dignities, concussed skulls, attempted assassinations, all in beautiful downtown Hartford, just as the inmates were escaping from the insurance companies."

"Gemma says Whiffletree is a real weirdo. Comes all apart and has fainting spells at twenty-minute intervals. Last week he got a paper cut from one of his legal documents and called his doctor!

"I think I better take her away from all that. You know, I bet that girl could produce complete babies in four-and-a-half months, forged, machined, burred, polished, and rustproofed. Did you see the way ..."

Midge came in loud and laughing. "Shaddup, already! We've heard nothing but the shape of her this-and-that's for two days. I like her, I like her. I think she's a great girl. But I'm not suffering the same gonadal twitch that's got you all ignited. *Enough* about Gemma's gems!"

"Anyway," she went on, "this Hadley Ware is a nooknik. Of him, I've had experience. He was on that legislative committee I was up against last year with the Farm Ladies League. He couldn't and wouldn't understand anything about anything. 'Course, he doesn't have to. God gave him all the money ever invented. I'll have to speak to God about that if the opportunity arises. Even *He* blows a few!" She turned to Plug.

"Whaddaya think? Should I let Aunt Gladys know that all is well? I *did* make some pretty pointed remarks when I was over there."

Plug put the question to rest. "I still vote for the bouquet. But," he added, "I'm not absolutely sure it should go to the beloved but senescent Aunt. Who the hell was it who went around to her with this bright idea about sending the codicil to Whiffenpoof? How does he get in the act? And why? And how the hell does he even know there *is* a codicil. Maybe I'm getting paranoid, but every time somebody says 'lawyer,' I go into a high adrenalin syndrome and start counting the silverware."

Sounds of munching prevailed, then Plug mused further.

"Every goddam contractor in Connecticut wants to build houses in my cornfield. And some of these guys are *not* paragons of virtue. So how does this grab you? Some house building mafooch finds out about the will somehow. And nips over to Rhode Island to liberate it. He goes around to Aunt Gladys and immediately notices that she has gelled between the ears—a four-second conversation would tell him that. And he gets the message that she really doesn't know where the hell the thing is. So he says to himself, 'Goodie, Goodie.' 'If she can't find it she can't dispose of it.' But to her, he says, 'find it! And send it to this lawyer.'"

"Anything's possible," Midge interjected. "But how does this guy know there is such a thing in the first place?"

"Like you say," Plug countered, "anything's possible. For instance, back when they were probating Uncle Selkirk's will, seven or eight years ago, any shyster who happened to walk through the court could have heard about it. I reckon some hood with a congenital lust for land could have filed away that little bit of information. Is this Hadley Ware a lawyer?"

"*Every*body's a lawyer," Zeke offered. "We ought to be able to find out easy enough."

Plug and Zeke went into a profound analysis of how to find out if Hadley Ware were a lawyer. Midge zephyred out of the kitchen. Three minutes later, she returned and broke up the ongoing analysis.

"Hadley Ware *is* a lawyer. He used to practice probate law, but no longer practices law at all because of his deep commitment to public service. Unquote.

"I called his office and asked. Why is everything so difficult for you two intellectual heavyweights?"

"Well, that suggests to me that our ointment is positively infested by the very fly Senator Hadley Ware. He even specialized in probate law. Not that he can give us any trouble now. Thanks to the Smithooski sex appeal, that little codicil now comes complete with the correct name. But I think we'd be wise to get the damned paper back from Waffleknit and tell him to butt out. Then we can get the deeds to the place fixed up to show the new, unexpurgated version. You gotta hand it to that Ware, though. If he is the one, he's got no competitors for sheer midtown chutzpah. What's the easiest way, do you think? Just ask Gemma to bring the thing out again—only this time, don't ask her to take it back?"

"Oh, no!" Zeke was on the defensive. "We don't put her in jeopardy anymore. I'll just get the key from her and slip into her office tonight and pick it up."

"Oh, that'd be *so* lovely," Midge interpolated. "Then we could have one of those wonderful, tender, headline romances: She sits at home for twenty years being loyal, while you sit in Danbury being buggered."

"Good trick," Plug added. Midge cut him off.

"Let's forget the illegals and get our own lawyer. There has to be one honest one hiding out somewhere."

"Okay," Plug said. "I'll pop out to the haystack and get the needle while you get the honest lawyer. Meantime, one more question. *If* this Ware is the culprit!

And presuming none of us put an infernal machine in his motor car! Who did it? And why? And is there connection?"

"You don't count well, there are no answers, and this Ware seems to be the kind of guy who naturally elicits bombs. Why not just get a lawyer and sleep on it?" This from Zeke.

"Alright," Plug said. "Lawyer, yes. Sleep, no. We've still got about a zillion acres to chop up in neat little rows. Fifty, anyway. And today is your turn in the barrel."

This is a 2005 photo of Quandary Farm touched up to look as it must have looked in the 1950's. Some of the farm buildings are visible on top of the hill in the background

VII

His luncheon companions were blinking badly, but Gilbert deVille was accustomed to that. Still, on this day his dome outshone itself, largely because of the flaming rage he thought he was containing so well.

"You goddam assholes told me that this codicil to Selkirk Catton's will was incomplete! No legatee designated, you told me. Can either of you read? Like here, on the legatee line, where it says 'William Thackeray Shavaughn' in plain American typewriter?"

He was waving the offending document before them, obscuring their views of, respectively, a superb Shaker Club finnan haddie—Ware—and an untouched roast beef on rye, well done, no butter—Whiffletree.

The latter was not enjoying, despite earlier intense anticipation, his first luncheon in the august Club. Even Ware, normally subject to minimal browbeating by anybody, was feeling the heat.

Seated side by side opposite deVille, six-feet of Ware and five-feet-nothing of Whiffletree stared at their tormentor from very different altitudes, causing him to wave his luminous head much as Hadley Ware habitually bobbed his, but with far flashier result.

DeVille's language was just that bit outside the accepted norms of the Shaker Club, but none of the other diners chose to tell him so. Rather, they were dancing about in search of the Club Manager. They wished to delegate the telling of Mr. deVille to him. But Mr. Zeldinian, the Manager, was hiding.

"So what the hell happened?" deVille demanded, very loudly. "When the will was probated, there was no legatee designated in the codicil, and the codicil was not accepted for probate. The farmer's lawyer moved to probate the main will and sent to Rhode Island for a search of the old man's effects, a search for a complete codicil. The judge went along. I know. I was there."

DeVille's scalp became shinier. "That was years ago, you moron."

Ware was beginning to twitch under deVille's abuse. He spoke with an edge on his voice. "It was also just last week, according to the Catton woman. She told me that no other codicil had turned up. I didn't look at this one myself, because she couldn't find it while I was there. But Whif says it was still blank when it got to him. And stop being so goddam snotty!"

Thos. S. Whiffletree wished that he had *not* mentioned that it was blank when it got to him. He also wished that it *had* never got to him and he wished he were Napoleon, in which case he would have been dead for a century and a half, more or less.

"Mind you, gentlemen," he murmured. "This document came to me entirely gratuitously and unsolicited. I really only glanced at it for a moment, not knowing why it was in my possession. Uh, gentlemen ... uh, why *was* it in my possession?"

He was not informed. Rather, deVille's recent near-scream dropped to an even more ominous growl. His scalp went incandescent.

"You're telling me, Whiffletree, that this document arrived in your office with no legatee designated and you're such a double-dyed shithead that you typed in this farmer's name? You went to all the trouble of a title search and then just guessed this name into place?"

"Oh, no. No, no! Certainly no. I can't even type. I wouldn't consider such an action. I'm a reputable officer of the courts, Mr. deVille. You know I wouldn't tamper with a legal document outside my competence."

"Everything's outside your competence," deVille explained to him in a slow, painfully guttural crusher. "How the hell did this name get typed in here while this document was in your possession? Your secretary got nothing to do but sit around typing names in wills. You've completely screwed up a beautiful business achievement that took months of preparation. The senator and I"—he nodded toward Ware, temporarily blinding both men—"have worked for weeks to get this one little detail set up, and you've blown the whole act. Now you will have to swear in court that you never saw this document, you never had it in your possession, you never heard of it ... you never. Uhn."

DeVille's invective had exhausted him. Finally, he added, "If the question ever comes up."

"It probably won't ever come up," Ware said. "I doubt if the Catton woman even knows she sent it. And nobody else does." He turned to Thos. S.

"But you beat me, Whif. Why you'd be so goddamned stupid as to look up the case and type in the guy's name before you'd had any instruction at all; that's just too mother-stuffin' stupid, even for you."

"If you ever get so much as a traffic ticket out of this town again, I'll have you disbarred for congenital idiocy."

"But I had nothing to *do* with it!" Thos. S. was toeing the slippery threshold of apoplexy. "And I can't possibly perjure myself. After all, I did *see* the document, although I must remind you that I didn't ask to see it. You know perfectly well that to act for a client an attorney must be instructed. I never received ..." He was shut off.

"You're instructed *now*," deVille instructed him. "If the question ever arises you never saw this sheet of paper, you never touched this sheet of paper, you never smelled this sheet of paper, you never heard of this sheet of paper, and you can't read or write anyway! You understand? And you can swear to it standing on the roof of a warehouse full of bibles with the American flag stuffed up your ass!"

Mr. Zeldinian had gone for a long walk.

DeVille's usual cold composure had been ripped apart by the misfiring of his long planned rural rape—and he really did think that Thos. S. Whiffletree had added the name to the putatively legateeless codicil, at least thirty-five Shaker Club diners were now far more aware of its existence than Mr. deVille might have wished. Some of them were trying to conceal their interest in the paper he was waving about, and they were precisely the ones whose minds were among the most devious in the membership.

DeVille had partially lost control, and control losing was the ultimate sin in his Decalogue.

Thos. S. Whiffletree was close to losing his mind.

And Senator Hadley Ware was a touch nervous himself. He had, of course, had an unusually disquieting week. It had, indeed, been only five days since his automobile, containing him, had departed vertically from Pearl Street, peaked out at about 13 inches, returned abruptly to the pavement and then—fortunately with him out of it—burned fiercely to a cinder, all this accompanied by smoke and loud noises.

Now the Senator dabbed at a bit of white sauce on the lapel of his blue pinstripe. Perhaps it was his cranial waggle, perhaps his boarding school upbringing, but he had never quite got the hang of conveying food all the way from plate to mouth without some minor loss. The negligible deprivation of nourishment this caused was of no consequence, but it did raise hell with his very expensive suits and cause other people to look away.

Returning that which, in a less arrogant man, would have been called his "attention" to his companions, he spoke, making more sense than deVille had expected.

"It doesn't really matter a helluva lot whose name is on the thing. We've got it. Shavaughn hasn't. We can't prove we own the land but neither can he show that he owns it. The only problem is the widow. If she can identify me, then we don't need her around. Otherwise, we just start a little litigation. Sue Shavaughn for having blue eyes or something. We spend a few thou, he spends a few thou, he goes broke. Then we buy his stupid farm for our price."

DeVille, whose arrogance is to Ware's as a medicine ball is to a goose-pimple, had difficulty hiding his admiration for this admirable program. Whiffletree seemed not to grasp the idea, but then his I.Q. does not tend to bring to mind the geranium. It was time, deVille saw, to dismiss Thos. S. Whiffletree.

"Whiffletree," he said, "you're dismissed. Sorry you didn't like your sandwich." Then, as a small sop—more accurately, call it a small bribe—he added, "Send the Senator a bill for your services. Commensurate *with* those services," he added pointedly. A paid lawyer, he knew, even an underpaid one, is always less trouble than an unpaid one.

Thos.S, who, like David W. Dimble, rarely cried in public, verged on breaking that rule, would perhaps have done so had he been able to decide quickly whether to cry over the catastrophe of his first—and probably only—lunch at the Shaker Club or to cry with joy at being dismissed without further threat of forced perjury.

He stood up, an action which is hardly discernible in a man of his stature, shook hands with the seated deVille and Ware, and backed off in a manner redolent of THE KING AND I. He got through the dining room door, and by the time he reached the lobby, his little legs were at full churn.

DeVille leaned back and made one of his invisible signs to an unseen staff, causing a black genie to materialize at his side. There was some sleight-of-hand with plates and flatware, coffee appeared, and the black magician evaporated. A whole new ambience of calm descended over the dining room. DeVille spoke into the hush.

"That Whiffletree is a menace. Next time you hire a gopher, get one who doesn't need a lobotomy. Do you want to instigate the tort proceedings, or shall I get an outsider." The question was more by way of instruction than interrogation.

Senator Ware had to give it some thought, however, and he already had a thought percolating in his skull. "I think I'll go out to Quandary Farm," he said, "and see if this Shavaughn even knows there's a possession question. And I'm not so sure about Whif. Even a dim bulb like him must have had *some* reason to put in the farmer's name and screw up the codicil. I'm not sure he even knew we were in the act until I phoned him and told him to bring it here. He jumped at the invitation, by the way." Ware finally got to deVille's rhetorical question. "It'd be better if you got somebody who does business with Shavaughn to sue him, somebody who can hoke up a business excuse for the suit. Just tell 'em to *do* it and shut up. They don't have to know why they're doing it.

DeVille already understood that perfectly well. "Think," he said, "before you rush out to the farm. Maybe it's a good idea and maybe it isn't. As of now, maybe the farmer doesn't even know we're about to dispossess him. Maybe he's never heard of us. It might be better to keep it that way!"

Thus did Senator Hadley Ware and Mr. Gilbert deVille push themselves back from the luncheon table, happy in their possession of the silly little sheet of paper, unhappy at the inclusion on that sheet of paper of Plug Shavaughn's right name, and quite remarkably ignorant of how the name got there. And thus, as that dour Scottish bard had insisted, do the best-laid plans of rats and men gang aft a-gley.

Jack F. Reynolds

This is an unretouched photo of the farm house as it stands today. It hasn't changed much since the mid-1950's.

VIII

We are instructed by numberless observers that April is the orgasm of months, the Kohinoor among these dozen segments into which our year is divided, the Rolls Royce of installment periods.

So legion and so persistent are these propagandists that we are in danger of being stampeded into a blind acceptance of April as the resident season in Adam's Eden.

Wrong!

April has its moments, of course. We're not here to vilify a decent enough month.

But May, magnificent May, the glorious month of May, is much more correctly identified as the time when God finally gets his act together, the month when the perfect day may occur.

It is on just such a May day as that that we find Senator Hadley Ware driving—very cautiously—up the long dirt road to Quandary Farm.

The air purred softly on a sunny zephyr, the sky was a diaphanous hemisphere of manic blue featuring a single drifting cloud of cotton white. The trees were in full, rustling leaf, as green as an Irish soul and alive with chirping birds and soft, silent squirrels. Nature smiled and chipmunks chortled. Even Senator Ware almost noticed.

He was chauffeuring himself, the outraged Giuseppe Diano having withdrawn his services. The vehicle was a brand new one, an altogether excessive Cadillac only marginally shorter than the New York, New Haven and Hartford Railroad. It was a vehicle designed to nourish megalomania and debilitate bankrolls, and for those purposes, it was a superb design job. But for driving up dirt farm roads the car was inappropriate. It was so sprung as to bottom out on the shallowest of declivities, and the road to Quandary Farm has no shallow declivities. Each is deeper than all the others. Senator Ware was, in fact, rather slowly scraping his way to his destination.

With perhaps as little as $150 damage to his brand new undersides he pulled gratefully into the drive beside the aged grey farmhouse, settling heavily into about three inches of native mud. It took him some moments to bring himself to step from the car into the soil he wished to steal.

Having once abandoned himself—and his top dollar Florsheims—to the task, he went manfully about it. Lifting his trouser legs as daintily as a maiden might lift her skirts, he made his way suckingly to the rear porch.

As he approached he was observed through the window by Midge, Able Mabel, and Zeke. It was the late breakfast shift; Plug was out jockeying the tractor.

Midge confirmed the visitor as the State Senator who had given her Farm Ladies League an education in legislative imbecility. Abel Mabel continued to knit, got in half-a-dozen stirs at the bubbling chili con carne, and wiped the window clean. Zeke agreed with Midge that it was, indeed, Hadley Ware. Then he strode out through the pantry door in search of Plug.

Senator Ware gave several moments to the cleaning of his shoes. He anticipated being invited into the farmhouse and felt that it would not be seemly to muddy a property he would soon own. He moved across the porch, stamping. With a final shuffle on the thick doormat, he raised his hand to knock. Before the blow could fall, the door was pulled away from him and he faced a short, spherical woman who seemed to be clicking thin little sticks between fat little fingers.

"Good morning, Madame," Ware said. He used his polite campaign voice, the one with the political semi-quaver. "Could you be Mrs. Shavaughn, perhaps?"

"I could if Fate was a little kinder. As it is, I'm just the family slave. You wanna see Mrs. Shavaughn?"

"Yes, yes I do. Or, perhaps, Mr. Shavaughn."

"Just a minute. I'll get 'em."

Ware was greatly piqued to be left standing on the porch of what was, practically, his own house.

Throughout this exchange, Midge had been standing by the stove. As the spherical body ceased to block the doorway, she moved forward, swept an arm in welcome and said, "C'mon in, c'mon in. No need to stand out there in a perfectly gorgeous May day when you can be in a hot, stuffy kitchen. I'm Midge

Shavaughn." And then, with her best mime of wide-eyed innocence, she asked, "And may I ask your name?"

Ware had not expected to arrive unknown. He never expected to arrive unknown. A major tenet of his canon was that *everyone* recognizes the Honorable Hadley Ware. Again, he was piqued: if not downright hurt.

"I, Mrs. Shavaughn, am Hadley Ware. *Senator* Hadley Ware. Your duly elected member of the Upper House of the Legislature of this wonderful State of Connecticut."

At this moment, a distant noise began to obtrude. It was the unignorable kind of noise that terminates conversations and then grows to set the walls into a defined rhythmic patter at about 3000 oscillations per minute (3K O/P/M, in scientific parlance), the kind of noise that will either cause madness or cease. In this fortunate case Plug switched off the tractor ignition and the noise ceased, its epicenter now just outside the door.

Senator Ware watched Plug descend from his perch by means of a series of anthropoid maneuvers, mount the porch and enter the kitchen. Ware, customarily less than observant, was, because of his own recent experience, further piqued to observe that Plug managed this transfer without picking up a single spot of mud.

Plug stood tall just inside the door, waiting to be introduced. Ware stood tall, expecting to be introduced, possibly to light applause. One hundred pounds of Midge peered up from beneath Ware's towering personage and winked at Plug. "Plug," she said, "we uns is hon-ered. This h'yer's Congersman Bear. He's come to visit a spell. Guess it mus' be 'lection time agin."

Senator Ware could not know, of course—indeed, he would have gone out of his way not to know—that Midge was a graduate in theater arts. But even he was surprised to find his constituency suddenly populated by hillbillies.

Plug, who had little histrionic talent, nevertheless went along and did his best. Gallantly he covered his catholic literacy taste and rather broad cultural range with his best shot at hoked hick.

"Waal, ain't thet great. Ah hopes yo' wins, Mayor!"

Senator Hadley was perhaps the only man in Connecticut thick enough to be taken by this charade. He did, of course, suffer from a kind of gold-plated tin ear.

"No, no. No. There's no election. And I'm *Senator* Bear, not Mayor Ware …" He stopped, resolutely. And started again. "Ware," he said, enunciating very slowly. "Senator Ware. With a 'w.' And an 's,' of course. And I'm not here to solicit your ballots. That will be next year. No, no. I've come to talk to you about this farm."

Plug warmed to his role. "Waal, naow, thet's mah-ty frien'ly, like. T'aint much uv a farm, course, but it's all we uns got. Would y' like to walk out t' the sty, Guv'ner, an' see the two-heded pig what got borned. That's interestin'"

"No, no. Not 'Governor.' Well, not yet. Perhaps, with time. But for now, just 'Senator'" As Ware was speaking he was also envisioning a two-headed pig and a walk through the mud. He blenched and, uninvited, sat down.

Midge came on. Her vaudeville bumpkin had become a black-faced minstrel.

"We all is sho nuf on-ahd, Suh, havin' a gen-u-ine Fus S'lekman comin' don h'yah t' d' ol' plantation. We don' get much im-po-tant folk h'ya."

Now, even Ware snapped a brain cell or two. From the pantry door, behind him, Zeke chimed in. "Sure and begorrah, it's a foine act whin the gintry come t' visit the poor, just as Holy Mither Church teaches us t' visit the sick an' the dyin an' comfort 'em, saints be praised." Then his voice dropped to its normal, reasonably well modulated tenor. "Or," he added, "whatever!"

Ware twisted his long, amazed body to see the source of this new confusion. He was, as we know, one of God's chosen takers, but he had certainly never mastered the art of taking a joke—nor, if fact, even recognizing one. He was simply flummoxed by the whole production.

Midge picked up the threads, her diction pure Katherine Hepburn. Like Miss Hepburn, she was a Hartford girl; their vocal deliveries were separated more by vocation than by dialect.

"As the newly appointed Fire Marshall, Mr. Hare, did you have a professional interest in Quandary Farm? Or is yours purely a sociological pursuit, a visit, perhaps, framed on one or another of the academic disciplines? Economics, Possibly?"

For the first time since he had initially grasped the importance of the money people kept giving him—he was about four at the time—Senator Ware felt out of place. Outnumbered. Outgunned. Out in left field. He stood up. It suddenly occurred to him that they might all be mad. And therefore dangerous. The gears of his mind ground.

He smiled. It was just about his best effort, and it would have soured a chocolate bar.

"You know, Mr. Shavaughn, I never have seen a two-headed pig. Let's just have a quick peek, shall we? Mustn't disturb the poor thing, of course." Bravely, he thought, he stepped past Plug, slipped through the door and positively bounded off the porch into three inches of the thickest and stickiest.

"On second thought," he cried over his shoulder, "I'm not feeling a bit well. I'll just sit here in my car for a moment. We can talk perfectly well out here, can't we?"

The Senator had come close to sprinting the last few feet to his lengthy refuge. His last words were spoken through a window open just a crack, his finger still on the button that would close it entirely. Then he relaxed a bit. He was of that ilk and generation that always felt secure while seated in a nineteen foot Cadillac. Even with a 60 horsepower John Deere drawn up alongside.

Secure, his mind returned to the business of stealing Quandary Farm.

Plug squidged through the mud to the Senator's side, placed his two huge hands on the car's roof and spoke to an open slit.

"I think you'll be perfectly safe to open the window, Senator Ware. And it'll be a lot easier to talk about the farm that way. Did you have anything special you wanted to say?"

"The fact is, Mr. Shavaughn," his voice quivered a bit with apprehension, but he went bravely ahead, "that a consortium with which I am associated would like to purchase this land. We have development plans that would be very beneficial to the State at large and to many, many young homemakers. Now, I'm no expert on agricultural matters, but I would guess that it is difficult getting a living out of this land. But …"

"What did he say?" The question came from Midge who was now approaching in a pair of Wellington boots. Plug responded.

"He says he's no expert on agriculture."

"Well, you've gotta believe him on that one!" Midge retorted. She leaned against the side of the car to hear the rest of the chat.

Senator Ware went on. "My colleagues and I could set you up in a very comfortable way of life."

Plug broke in. "The fact is, Senator, that if we wanted your kind of comfortable life we'd have gone another route a long time ago. We do this because this is what we wish to do. And, of course, we can't very well do it without the land. So I guess I'll have to disappoint you and the consortium. No sale!"

"You must be aware, Mr. Shavaughn, that title to some of this land lies in other hands." The Senator even opened his window an extra quarter inch for this thrust. "And I don't think faming would be at all viable here on two separate parcels of land."

"I wasn't aware, Senator, that there was any longer a question of ownership. Quite the contrary, in fact." Plug said this with the most uncharacteristic smugness.

"Then I must disabuse you."

Jack F. Reynolds

Even as Ware spoke, Zeke moved from the car, stomped onto the porch, stepped out of his boots into the kitchen, and in seconds he had Gemma on the phone. A few more seconds and she had the answer. The codicil was not where she had replaced it in Whiffletree's files!

Zeke was back at carside before negotiations had advanced much, but he did not arrive alone. As he was slipping back into his boots, a second alien automobile turned into the drive and rolled to a sticky stop behind Ware's landborned yacht.

From it, after a few moment's preparation, stepped a sartorially splendid David W. Dimble, his pear-shaped grey-suit molded to his pear-shaped self, his virgin pocket handkerchief starched at his breast, his black homburg set at just the correct angle and his feet, incongruously but wisely, stuffed into rubber boots. D.W.D., unlike Hadley Ware, had many years of experience of conniving, twisting, cheating, stealing, and lying on the scene—on the farms, empty lots and marshlands of Connecticut. He knew about mud and came prepared.

This unexpected appearance provided just the diversion Zeke needed to convey Gemma's news to Plug, who suddenly saw Senator Ware in a decreased buffoon, increased Mafioso role.

David W. Dimble wasn't able to spot that subtlety. In fact, although he was slightly acquainted with Ware on a socio-political level, he barely acknowledged the Senator's presence. But he did note the nineteen-foot Cadillac. It annoyed him. He had, in his own overstocked garage, an identical Cadillac. It just miffed him to see that Ware had one, too.

Exhibiting his usual business delicacy, he walked straight to Plug, ignoring everyone else, and said, "Mr. Shavaughn! I have astounding news. I have decided to accept your offer. My backers and I know full well that your price is ridiculously high, simply ludicrously high. But the nation's need for quality housing, *that* must be our first consideration, whatever the economic consequences to ourselves. I felt that I had to bring you this great good news in person, and I have brought along the instrument of intent for you to sign."

"What," Plug asked him, "offer?"

"Why, the offer you made me in Pearl Street a couple of weeks ago. That— really, really, quite—avaricious offer—of this farm—for that, that very HIGH figure." D.W.D.'s voice cracked. He could hardly bring himself to say "a million dollars" publicly under the best of circumstances. Now, with Ware sitting there he would have strangled himself with his own vocal chords had he attempted to vocalize the sacred phrase.

Also, he had chosen to ignore the part about two Bloomfield houses to be thrown in. He felt that, somehow, Plug would mentally mislay that part of the stipulation. At least he, David W. Dimble, could not stomach getting that close to an honest bargain.

"What figure was that?" Ware demanded through a suddenly wide-open car window.

The appearance of Dimble hadn't bothered him, hadn't even interested him. He felt that he had the farm in his pocket. But he was shocked to learn that other negotiations were already underway, that Plug had made an offer. He couldn't understand how the Great God who loved him could have allowed someone else to be bidding for something that he, Hadley Ware, The Honorable Hadley Ware, wanted. That wasn't the way it had ever worked!

"What figure did you set on this place, Shavaughn?"

"Ten million dollars," Plug told him. And he did it without so much as a twitch at the corner of his mouth. Absolutely straight-facedly Plug looked him directly in the eye and said, "ten million dollars."

Small woodland noises, chirps and gurgles and the like, came from the vicinity of David W. Dimble.

Hadley Ware could write checks for ten million dollars without even phoning his bank, so he took Plug seriously. "You're out of your mind," he said to everyone.

Then he finger-touched his window shut, started the Cadillac's engine, threw the car into reverse, and backed smartly into David W. Dimble's everyday Buick. Dimble was already a sick man. This caused a relapse.

The impact, after a passage of only two or three feet, was trivial. But the motion caused a great deal of mud to fly about, and the bump seemed much worse than it really was to an understandably jumpy Hadley Ware. It was mere days since the other large car in which he was feeling secure erupted.

Now, with thought only for escape, he threw open his door and leapt from the car, its engine still purring. In that mud-deep drive, his manifest destiny manifested itself. Zeke, heroically, stepped forward and lifted Senator Hadley Ware's face out of the mud, then helped drag him to his feet, a writhing column of the thick and sticky. By now, the Senator's pique had peaked.

And still the wheels of the Cadillac spun, and the mud continued to fly. The massive chrome bumper of the car went bumpety-bump, bumpety-bump bump bump in gentle taps against the Buick. David W. Dimble, transfixed and bespattered beyond recognition, reluctantly broke the rule of a lifetime and began to weep in public.

Jack F. Reynolds

Here are two men pumping fuel into the ancient biplane at a local airport.

IX

It will occur to the more sagacious reader that little of lasting commercial value would ensue from the circumstances just related, and little did.

Still, Senator Hadley Ware's decision to visit Quandary Farm allowed the various participants to know—very roughly—where they stood. It introduced, as it were, the good guys to the bad guys and provided the observation that, while keeping with tradition the latter far outnumber the former, at least the former are a united and loving front while the latter are a fragmented bunch of bastards.

Sadly, this situation changed, in part, that very day. An unfortunate amount of asunder-tearing occurred to the united and loving front in the following manner.

As we are well aware, all the world's a stage and all the men and women are merely players. What is less commonly understood is that it's a TV production stage, appointed to provide farcical entertainment for the several trillions of intelligent inhabitants of this galaxy, in residence out there on their various thousands of planets.

We, the players, are manipulated by the usual cadre of off-stage producers, directors, writers, sound mixers, videotape editors, script persons, grips, and arcane studio technicians. And it was one of these latter who pushed the wrong button that afternoon, causing Gemma Giordano's mother to drop dead in Chicopee Falls, Massachusetts.

In a production of this magnitude it's inevitable that these little glitches will occur. Nobody pretends that this is a convenience to, for instance, the late Mrs.

Barbara Santacroce of Chicopee Falls, but in the macrocosmic view there simply is not time to quibble with a basically very workable system.

And so it was that Gemma, hailed by phone by a very distraught aunt, hurriedly covered her IBM Executive, spoke a rushed word of explanation to an already frazzled Thos. S. Whiffletree, strode grimly to the Church Street parking garage, and was quickly over the river and headed north on Route 5. It was about four o'clock, and Zeke was scheduled to pick her up at her apartment at about six. Even in her dismay, she couldn't bring herself to contact him with the bad news; to draw him into family tragedy with a family he'd never met. She'd call him from Chicopee Falls.

But, that afternoon the studio technicians were having one of those days. *Nothing* would go right. It was a bit like those situations at Fenway Park in which the entire Red Sox outfield gathers at the centerfield wall and goes into its inimitable impression of the Ritz Brothers while the Toronto pitcher rounds third. Error compounds error.

And so it was that yet another technician punched up yet another scrambled sequence, causing an admittedly flustered and somewhat tearful Gemma to drive her aging Studebaker irresistibly into one of East Hartford's most immoveable objects, the abutment of the railroad underpass on north Main Street. This, in turn, brought about a series of concomitances, the only one of real interest to us being Gemma's swift ambulance ride to Hartford Hospital.

There, several hours later, she was resurrected from deep anesthesia. She had suffered only a broken wrist, not the kind of catastrophic trauma that calls for general anesthesia. A light local would have served admirably for the setting of a fractured ulna. But, up there in the studio nothing was going right that day. So, impelled by yet another digitally dopey technician, Actor/Doctor Leo Leonardis, usually an infallible whizbang with a needle, loaded our heroine as if for major aortic surgery. The guys kidded him about it for days.

Zeke Smithooski, however, was in no kidding mood by about seven p.m. He'd been mildly annoyed when Gemma had not answered her doorbell at six o'clock precisely. Not annoyed with her, of course. He knew perfectly well that she could do no wrong, and that some unseen force had detained her and it was at the unseen force that his annoyance was directed.

By seven, the annoyance had turned to worry, and when he looked at his watch and was told "eight o'clock" the worry turned to anguish. By eight-thirty, it had mutated into anger.

For those two-and-a-half hours, he had been conducting a kind of one-man parade between Gemma's front door and the corner oasis. Now, six beers, several unanswered phone calls, and quite a bit of hiking later, he had a manly thought. "She's stood me up!"

Anguish, after all, is not one of your durable emotions. It wears thin fast, and anger is a splendid surrogate, demanding little of its practitioner and heaping guilt upon its cause, usually with no discernible damage to the cause.

Zeke suffered a massive attack of recidivism. He backslid like a Hollywood mansion in the wet season, returning solidly to an earlier conviction that women were neither to be understood nor trusted. The reader has already been alerted to this Smithooskian deficiency, derived, probably, from the female lack of a differential gear or mag wheels. Whatever the cause, his fatal—sole, but fatal—character flaw now overtook him in a manner that would have pleased hell out of any competent Greek tragedian.

Your mechanically-minded macho misogynist is not one to think things through in a cool, calm, collected manner, nor one inclined to winnow out fact from fallacy, nor even much given to calling Hartford Hospital for an admissions update. Rather, he is apt, in moments of stress, to return once more to the corner oasis and become toxic.

Thus, at a few minutes after one in the morning the bartender was bemused to find that the big fellow at the end of the bar who had been tossing off boilermakers all evening was both unable to communicate orally and unable to stand up pedially. Experienced at his trade, the man shoulder-carried Zeke to a booth and divested him of his wallet. He then divested the wallet of ten dollars—fee for his services—phoned the number he found on the wallet's I.D. card, and returned the wallet to its rightful pocket. And waited.

Midge was not amused. Dragged from bed, she agreed to drive into town and retrieve the remains. She was disturbed, though. Zeke was certainly known to be capable of taking a drink now and again. But she had never known him to get smashed in a public bar. Too, she had no idea why he should have adopted such a posture. Naturally, no one at Quandary Farm had heard about the production glitches at the great control booth in the sky. They had no information about deceased Mrs. Santacroces or butted abutments or fractured Gemma's left-ulna or hyper-hypodermacists. They thought Zeke was out dating Gemma.

The following mid-morning, while half of Zeke was awake and suffering, Gemma was collected from Hartford Hospital by a distraught cousin and driven to the Oblinsky-Moriarty Funeral Parlors in Chicopee Falls. Untrained in the mysteries of mortuary science, there was little she could do in these environs except suffer the schlock compassion of Mr. Oblinsky, Mr. Moriarity, Jr., and someone named Grantz who had lately bought a piece of the funerary action.

A distraught uncle then drove her to her late mother's home where a distraught niece fainted as Gemma came through the front door with her arm in a sling. Distraught relatives were gathering in droves. The Cleveland branch arrived, distraught, about mid-afternoon, and even the Arizona outcast put in an appearance in late evening. Clergy were heavily in evidence, especially when Father Staphano checked in at five o'clock and about 350 pounds. He went directly to the kitchen where non-stop cooking was afoot. Altogether, it was a totally rotten two days for Gemma.

This nadir factor was underlined when, breaking away from a distraught florist, she locked herself in her late mother's room and tried to contact Zeke. John, as she much preferred to call him. Her brief, if intense, love affair with him had not yet included a visit to Quandary Farm; she knew of Able Mabel only by reputation. But it was that spherical dynamo who answered the phone, and she was busy. It was then that Gemma made her mistake. She asked for John.

"John? We ain't got no John. Well, we *have*. It's upstairs, and just about as far from my room as it could possibly be. Used to be out back, of course, but you must have the wrong number." She hung up.

A stoic Gemma grasped her error and started to dial the operator again. At that moment her presence was demanded, through the locked door, by the Reverend and distraught Father Giovanni. She had, for the moment, to abandon Zeke, but it really made no difference. Able Mabel's imperception was not the cause of the communications blackout. Zeke had left orders that "... if that broad calls, tell her to shove it!"

His remorse would set in as his hangover waned, but at the moment the order was issued he had meant every tragic syllable. Had Gemma asked for "Zeke," making the request comprehensible to Able Mabel, the latter would probably have followed Zeke's orders, though possibly not to the extent of using his language.

Gemma went out to console Father Giovanni, who was quite convinced that he was consoling her. For three more days she was locked in the embrace of consolation by unnumbered, often unknown relatives, all distraught. That she wanted to be locked in the embrace of Zeke Smithooski was unknown to these people—and just as well, really. None of those over forty would have approved of such a name. Paulo, Vincente, Fiorello? Okay. But Zeke? No way. And Smithooski didn't sound very Italian, either.

What with the consolation and Masses and a funeral and re-consolation and another Mass and a squalid little incident involving the Arizona outcast and a nubile third cousin, the days finally passed, and the gutted shell of Gemma at last escaped back to Hartford. She rode an almost empty Greyhound bus, her Studebaker still being severely bent, but the no-people-present ride was by far the best thing that had happened to her since the first hail on the phone by the distraught aunt, ever so long ago. And she still hadn't talked with John. He was never in when she called the farm, no matter what time she called. Much worse, he hadn't returned her calls.

He had, however, considered doing so. Remorse had set in, as advertised, and it had set in like a severe bout of gout. He hurt! But Zeke, manly to a fault, fought off the deep need to phone Gemma even after he knew where, if not why, she was. He even came to suspect that she had some perfectly good reason for her absence. But he was quite prepared to show *her*. If he and she were going to spend their lives together, and he had decided that they were, she would have to learn who was captain of the team. And she might as well learn now, no matter how effectively the lesson disemboweled him! He'd answer her calls when he was good and ready.

He was, in fact—during Gemma's hour-long bus ride—sitting at the kitchen table being damned good and ready and wondering why she didn't call now— with a damned good explanation—now that he *was* damned good and ready.

"Why don't *you* call *her*, you dingbat?" The query came from Midge who could almost read his thoughts. She was concerned about both the mental decline of Zeke and the unknown fate of Gemma, so much so that she was inclined to phone the girl herself. Still, one really shouldn't interfere, and Gemma might think she was interfering.

Gemma, rolling along beside the Connecticut River, gazing at the grey mist over the grey water, was giving deep thought to Zeke—John! Maybe it was all a mistake. It had, after all, started off pretty precipitately. Coldly viewed, she had been picked up in a bar! Right now, he was probably having a good giggle and looking around for his next conquest. He could certainly have returned her calls by now. Maybe she should call the farm and talk to Midge. But why would that happily married girl want to talk about Gemma's stupid indiscretions? And, anyway, Midge would only tell John she'd called. And he'd only giggle some more.

She arrived at Union Place, Hartford, thoroughly disenchanted and quite prepared to cancel the program. It had been her one slip in the four years since her divorce. There were no complications. Why not just scrub the whole scene and start again?

She stepped down from the bus and went directly to the pay phone. And phoned Nola Klim for a lunch date. She hadn't seen Nola in days—and there was so much to tell her. About mother. About the funeral. About her broken wrist. About the rotten little spiv from Arizona. So much to talk over, with Nola.

This is where Midge would pull the biplane with the tractor to the top of the hill. That would allow her to run the plane down the hill to get enough speed to take off.

X

In the nature of things, the sudden demise of Mrs. Barbara Santacroce of Chicopee Falls, Massachusetts, led to more than a family reunion of the distraught. No one even on this planet is limited to a single upshot—which, *inter alia*, may explain why we are plagued with the exponential excess of excitement that is always available to us!

Exempli gratia: Mrs. S. corked off. Her daughter drove northward to do the obligatory—and stopped suddenly, eyeball-to-eyeball with a bridge abutment. Hospital. Excessive anesthesia. Arm in cast. Relatives, funeral, consolation. All distraught. Perfectly normal.

But, all the while, Attorney Thos. S. Whiffletree, totally innocent of any involvement in any of these events, was deprived of his secretary—and keeper. Sad, unrelated upshot.

And, far worse, the good guys, among whom Att. Whiffletree would not, naturally, be mentioned, were deprived of their inside person in the camp of the bad guys, in, indeed, his office. Sadder, semi-related upshot.

And, also because of the events above—complicated by the boneheadedness of Zeke Smithooski—the romance of the century became a small pile of cool ashes.

And while all that tragedy was afoot, the bad guys were getting right on with their baddery. Unlike Plug & Co., they knew perfectly well where the codicil was, and, knowing that, didn't really give a damn that Plug's name had been cleverly inserted in it. They had been mildly inconvenienced, but in no way stymied.

In fact, it was at the very hour Gemma was being consoled out of her mind by a gaggle of graveside matrons, all distraught, that Gilbert deVille and Hadley Ware sat down in the chaste comfort of the Shaker Club to discuss personnel and tactics for turning Plug's farm into a few million dollars worth of highway and maybe a golf course of two.

DeVille, as we creep stealthily into the scene, is querying. "What the hell's Dimble doing? Far as I can find out, he hasn't got any other parcels on the roadbed. You figure he wants to put up office space way out there? Who'd be his client? I've got ears in every insurance boardroom in town, and it isn't one of them."

DeVille, though loathe to admit it, had been shaken by Ware's report that David W. Dimble was in the bidding for Quandary Farm. It had not occurred to him that anyone could, the opportunity being what it was, want the land for anything but resale to a superfatted highway department.

"I think he wants to get into housing," Ware replied.

"Stupid!" deVille opined. "You have to build the damned houses." The least effort for the most profit was his way, and brokering land certainly seemed faster and easier than building and marketing houses.

"You think the farmer was serious? Asking ten million?"

"Of course he was serious. You got to be serious when you use figures like that." The Senator, like David W. Dimble, was unable to grasp the idea of levity juxtaposed to money.

"Well," deVille said, "my people in highway tell me they're about ready to make firm proposals on the route. Of course, it goes right up our line. So we've gotta keep Dimble out of it for a while. I've got twenty companies arranged to sell the land—that ought to be enough to keep us out of sight. And I've got a suit against the farmer. One of my people has a plumbing firm that did some work out there about a year ago. No real specifications on the job, so they'll sue for non-payment—claim there's a big balance due. The plumber's scared witless but he'll behave."

"I reckon it'll cost a bunch of bucks, so I'm going to let one of my holding companies handle it—they've got staff lawyers. But it really shouldn't last long— these farmers never have anything in the bank. He'll probably be busted in a couple of weeks. You'll have to re-arrange the court calendar someplace, so we can move on it. Find a nice nit-picking judge and let me know where he sits so we can get started. What else are you doing to help the cause?"

Hadley Ware was musing, mentally running through his inventory of tame judges. There was a pause before he answered—he is not the sort of man who can do both A and B in one time span. Fully as crooked as deVille, of course, but less elastic between the ears.

Finally, he responded. "I spend my whole damned life keeping the highway department in line. They've got about a million people over there with pencils and big sheets of paper. They keep trying to change our route. One of 'em re-drew it so it missed three of our parcels completely, just for the sake of eliminating two little bridges. Thought he'd save the state some money. Damned idiot! I had to get his own union boss to get him back in line. His union's got some kind of tie with the welders and steel handlers. That bonehead would have cost them a lot of man-hours in overtime. It isn't easy keeping these highways bastards in line, you know. They don't understand anything!"

Originating in the misty region behind Senator Ware's eyebrows, this remark raised deVille's. He was always astonished if Ware said something intelligent. Over the years, deVille had been repeatedly frustrated by the inability of certain State employees to understand and participate in the most elementary profit ventures. Why it should be so difficult for these people to comprehend the most commonplace business practice—the bribe, the kickback, *anything*—he could never fathom. Now, he was surprised to hear Ware expound on the problem so lucidly. The simplest fraud, the most plausible swindle! They just don't understand anything. Still, on this occasion, he had a couple of rational, enterprising gentlemen correctly situated.

"Yes," he agreed with the Senator, "they never cease to amaze me. And you know, a lot of these guys barely earn enough to stay alive. They're starving to death working in the kitchen!"

The two men nodded sadly over the perplexing waywardness of hoi polloi and then adjourned to the Gold Room for an uplifting look at the bullion bar and refreshing pause at the wet bar. They could, after all, not save mankind from its own folly.

A week after the scene we have just crept stealthily back out of, Plug and Midge Shavaughn gave themselves a long anticipated evening out in celebration of eight years of wedded bliss. It was far away the most dismal celebratory since His Majesty's Hessian hirelings got together for a little Christmas drink-in back in 1776. Not that anyone came nipping over the Farmington River to lay the arm on the Shavaughns. Rather, the ambience of the day went along with them to the restaurant—and it had been a day memorable as a non-stop stinker.

First, Plug had suddenly and unexpectedly been sued for an over-due $10,000 pipe-laying bill—which he had paid more than a year before with a $375 check.

Plug had called Harry the Plumber to ask, "What the hell, Harry?" only to learn that Harry had suddenly and unexpectedly gone on vacation. But the summons told Plug to drop around to the courthouse the following Thursday morning.

Then, before the morning had aged significantly, Zeke had checked in from his weekend barreling-around-a-dirt-track. As a rule, he drove into the yard in a flatbed truck, waving a check and with his track car shining merrily on the flatbed. Today, he rode in, sitting up but seething, in an ambulance, the driver of which had to be given a check. By Plug. The money would come out of Zeke's bank account, but he wasn't doing his own check writing that day, what with the weight of the plaster and the awkwardness of the sling and all.

Without going into any printable detail, Zeke explained that the car was a write-off and it was all That Broad's fault because he had been thinking about her and not concentrating on what he was doing which turned out to be damned near killing himself. And if he ever got his hands on That Broad he'd do something which Plug didn't think could actually be done with a written-off automobile and a nice girl!

Midge, a natural opportunist, had seen Zeke's crash as a good excuse to contact Gemma, and did so. First, she called the Chicopee Falls number and was told that Gemma had gone back to Hartford but would be back up for the weekend. Then she called the law offices of Thos. S. Whiffletree and was told, by Gemma, that Gemma didn't want to talk to that insensitive lout and that she wouldn't mind if he died of his injuries. Then she burst into tears and hung up. And Thos.

J. Whiffletree phoned his doctor and asked for immediate delivery of something to sooth the Whiffletree neural complex!

Midge did not report the episode to Zeke, whose second masculine lapse was annoying her. What she did was try to find someone to replace him for several of the busiest weeks of the year. The kid from down the road found himself promoted to stand-in chief hired man and Plug found himself just that little bit overburdened with things that had to be done *now!*

Then the call came from Rhode Island. Aunt Gladys had been attacked in her kitchen the prior evening. The police were looking for the culprit but had no clues. And Aunt Gladys was doing well as could be expected in a Providence hospital.

So, in the restaurant that evening, when the waiter allowed an entire broiled shad to vault from tray to table to floor, the only comment was Plug's laconic observation, "Hell, I've seen those things jump twice as high at the Enfield dam."

Here is the famous Civil War Memorial Arch in the middle of Hartford.

XI

Midge was meticulous about getting the small tractor clear of the plane early the next morning. She and Plug were a little concerned about her flying the thing twice in so short a time, but she really had to do the dutiful by Aunt Gladys and there just wasn't time to drive to Rhode Island. She wanted to be back by noon to help Plug with the planting. Zeke was reassigned to one-handed chores.

At two regional airports she appeared on radar screens without causing undue alarm; the same was not true in Rhode Island where things had been tightened up a bit after a recent "incident." She had to leave the plane in the open, too, the barn being barred. And, she had not allowed for Catton Farm being aswarm with detectives—well, two, anyway.

Strangely, these gentlemen seemed wholly uninterested in her birdlike arrival, but they were very nosy about her presence, very eager to find clues. It was Midge's impression, based on her evaluation of their joint intelligence, that they were fortunate to have found the farm.

They wouldn't let her drive Aunt Gladys's car into Providence and they wouldn't drive her in themselves. "Busy, M'aam. Official." So she had to con a neighbor into driving her. Walking to neighbor's farm takes time. Conning neighbor takes time. Seeing rather pathetic old Aunt Gladys takes time. Getting a cab back to the farm takes time. It was just after two when she finally got airborne and she hadn't had lunch.

QUANDARY FARM

During her absence, an alerted Rhode Island State Trooper spotted wings crouching behind the Catton barn. He drove in and examined it. He was questioned by the jealous county detectives and questioned them back. And drove away to report that the missing plane looked okay but that its pilot had gone to a hospital in Providence.

Bureaucracy does not easily make simple sense out of this kind of information. So the Rhode Island authorities set out to find the injured pilot of the downed plane in a Providence hospital. They failed, and the next time they looked, they couldn't find the plane, either. They tried to trace it through its registration number, but the most cursory glance told them that the trooper had misread the number. Several weeks later the reprimand finally got to him—in triplicate, two copies of which he had to sign and return.

Midge banked sharply beyond the south rise at about 2:45, dropped steeply, pulled back hard and almost stalled at the crest, then allowed the nose to fall under power onto her nearly U-shaped landing zone. Within minutes, Plug was throwing the tarpaulin over the tail and an ashen faced trainee at Bradley Field was being calmed by his supervisor.

"Don't let it shake you, Maltz. We think it must be something atmospheric. When they seem to go down in that sector, it's best not to raise a rumpus. There've been several of them, but there's never been any wreckage. It's kinda spooky."

"Sorry, Darlin'," Midge told Plug. "You know how it is—nothing will actually go ahead and *happen* when you're in a hurry. Your Aunt's as okay as she can be, but some punk really sloshed her one. The doctor told me she must have a head of iron and I'm afraid I nodded pretty vigorously.

"Anyway, she walked into the kitchen night before last and found this guy standing there. So he belted her and took off. Says she could hear him drive away—but she hadn't heard him drive in. And she was able to phone the cops. Anyway, I'm glad I went over—she was pleased. Hey, did you notice?" She pointed to the point where their road, following earlier landings, had accumulated assorted uniformed personnel, all in seeming need of a hot cup of coffee or a cold up of gin. "No curious visitors!"

As she spoke, she transferred from her impromptu passenger's seat on the fender of the big John Deere to the rig behind, dragging several sacks of corn with her. Through the balance of the afternoon the two worked back to back, getting the seed corn into the ground where it could do some good. And in the lovely, attentive monotony of the action and the din of the hard engine they found silent tranquility within themselves, sealing off whatever apprehension lay beyond their labor.

Each was a bit surprised to find the other smiling when Plug pulled the tractor in beside the milking barn and dismounted to help the newly appointed stand-in chief hired man get the milk out of the cows. Midge went in to assist, too. They found the boy proudly getting on with it. They also found Zeke painstakingly trying to attach vacuum sockets to teats, one-handed. A man of maximum manual dexterity, he wasn't doing very well.

On Thursday, Plug went to court. This had at least the virtue of novelty, he having never been in a court before. But he soon came to feel that he preferred that prior dispensation. He learned quickly that it was against the rules to state a simple fact or introduce germane documents. More slowly, he grasped that he was being sued not by Harry the Plumber but by Intergalactic Macro-Conduit Companies, Inc., which owned Harry the Plumber. Harry the Plumber, of course, was not present.

Having come alone and armed only with truth, Plug was cause for considerable merriment among the large delegation doing the suing. When he spoke, they didn't so much object as banter. They took turns. Even Judge Groton was forced to crease his grim mask of judicial intensity. Plug's childlike behavior, his infantile faith in a cancelled check and an invoice stamped "PAID," these charmingly naïve traits finally broke a smile of almost beatific condescension across, so to speak, the bench's face.

A stern man—when instructed to be stern—but a merely smug man when left to his own devices, the judge halted proceedings before they could really have been said to proceed. And he gave Plug some advice.

"Mr. Shavaughn, every citizen has the right to retain trained, expert legal counsel when the need arises. In the situation in which you find yourself, I cannot overstate the wisdom that such a move would reflect upon your part. These gentlemen," and here he indicated the several thousand dollars worth of quality tailoring that represented Intergalactic Macro-Conduit, "come fully qualified and fully prepared. I think it would be only just, and I do favor justice, if you would give your own cause the same, the same advantage the plaintiff enjoys."

"You think," Plug interrupted, "I should hire six lawyers?"

"Oh, I do, Mr. Shavaughn. Most assuredly I do. I would not, of course, specify a number of counselors, but surely you should have counsel. I am prepared to adjourn this hearing until you have had time to consult counsel, if that is what you wish to do. Whatever the justice of the matter, and I certainly take no position on that as yet, it is perfectly possible that the plaintiff might receive judgment for this $10,000 debt of yours, along with very substantial court costs, if your case is not presented to its very best advantage. Let me tell you, in confidence, Mr. Shavaughn," and here Judge Groton leaned forward with decidedly confidential intent, "that within the legal profession it is said that a man who acts as his own attorney has a fool for a client. Ha, ha! Just a little lawyers' joke, Mr. Shavaughn, but there is surely a kernel of truth in that little witticism. What is you decision?"

Plug responded slowly. "Well, I can't really afford a lawyer, Your Honor. Matter of fact I can't see it would do these people much good to win because I haven't got $10,000 even if I did owe it to 'em, which I don't. But if you think I need a lawyer that bad, then I guess I'll have to dig into the penny bank."

"Yes. Very wise, Mr. Shavaughn. There is, of course, no way I can appoint a fee-paid public defender for a prosperous landowner like yourself. This hearing is adjourned until Tuesday next at this hour." And Judge Groton gave his gavel a tiny little tap on the polished bench.

The adjournment was well received by the corporate hit squad. Sent up from Intergalactic Macro-Conduit headquarters in Wall Street, none of them actually knew why they were there, but it quite obviously wasn't to collect ten thou. It cost the corporation more than that to *per diem* them for a couple of days. Anyway, now they could go home to Fairfield or Bucks County for the long weekend. With any luck, they might be able to drag this one on for weeks.

Plug found Catastrophobia right where he left her—one of the car's charms was that no one had tried to steal her—and headed back to the farm. He was wondering where to get the required lawyer. He could, in fact, pay a lawyer without having to cut the food budget, but he didn't want to. The only lawyer he'd ever dealt with, the fellow who got Uncle Selkirk's will through probate, had charged like the proverbial wounded buffalo. The whole arrangement stank. Why was it so damned hard to straighten out a simple billing error? Some stupid clerk just had the wrong bill for the wrong pipe at the wrong time in the wrong place. Or something!

In the kitchen, he found Zeke holding a skein of wool—that, he could manage with a cast—for Able Mabel, whose hands, winding the ball of wool, set up a nice cooling breeze in their immediate vicinity. Midge was doing something culinary at the counter.

"This damned thing is going to take longer than I want it to and the judge says I've got to hire a lawyer. Do we know a lawyer?"

"There's always good old Thos. S. Whiffletree," Zeke volunteered. He thought he was making a small joke, a minor pleasantry. Also, he had Gemma on his mind.

Plug and Midge took the suggestion straight. Able Mabel paid it no mind on principle; she did not engage in conversations about lawyers, harboring rather a strict moral code.

"You want to remember, though," Zeke went on, "that Gemma says he's a kind of cranial cripple."

"I don't think I need a *smart* lawyer, just a nice inexpensive one who knows the rules. It seems you can't just walk into court and tell it like it is, even with proof. You've got to do it by the book. Do you think Wafflebat knows what he's doing? And what does he charge? One thing, if we hire him we can get into his office."

"Sold," Midge said from the counter. "We buy Whiffletree." She laid down her knife and joined the group at the table. "We get into his office and we get to see Gemma. Suggest that she do a thorough search for the codicil. And maybe we can get this one's mind back on the track before he kills himself!"

No one bothered to notice, but Zeke offered no objection.

XII

Friday morning, Gemma left-handed herself into the office a few minutes before her employer arrived—her usual tactic. Her phone started ringing as she crossed the threshold. Seating herself on the edge of her desk and with her bag still over her shoulder, she picked up the talking tool and started the day's commerce.

"Good morning. Attorney Whiffletree's office."

"Hi, Gemma. This is Midge Shavaughn. Give me a candid answer, will you? Is your Whiffletree any good as a lawyer? I know it's a delicate question: if he's standing over your shoulder just say "yes" or "no.""

"Hello, Midge. No, he's not in yet. And, 'no,' he's no Oliver Wendell Holmes either. Well—that's probably not fair. I'm not the one to judge, really. All I know about law is what I've picked up around here, and the stuff that goes on here isn't exactly the kind of heroics you see on T.V. Double dull, to tell the truth. But he brings in the money, if that's any criterion. I keep his checkbook and I sure wish it was mine. It's just that he's a kind of a weirdo. Why do you ask?"

"Oh, Plug's got a legal problem. He's being sued for a bill we paid a year ago. It's an open-and-shut thing, but the judge wants him to have a lawyer."

"Open-and-shut I should think my weirdo could handle just fine. He does a lot of small damage cases, but mostly he seems to write up contracts for companies. Probably crooked as hell, for all I can tell.

"Could we get to see him soon? Like today, maybe?"

"Hang on," Gemma instructed. "I'll get his book."

She went into the Whiffletree inner sanctum, collected his appointments diary and picked up the phone on his desk.

"Midge? Hi. He's got some time open this afternoon, but he'll need part of that to clean up the paper on a hearing he's going to this morning. Would half an hour be any good to you, about three? He's got another at 3:30."

Midge's voice came back, sounding relieved. "Yeah, that's great. We'll all come trooping in to see you then. How's your arm, by the way?"

"Oh, I'm getting so I'm practically ambidextrous one-handed. The cast comes off in a week or so. Midge? How's ... how is John getting along?"

"I thought you'd never ask! He's great. He's too stupid to feel pain and too love sick to see straight. 'Course, he needs a keeper. We'll try to drag him along this afternoon. Don't hand him his head, huh? He needs to be petted and house-trained like a puppy."

Midge couldn't tell from the tremor in Gemma's voice whether see was chuckling or sobbing, but the message was clear. "Okay. If he doesn't kick me, I won't kick him! Hold it. Here comes Sir. We'll look for you at three. Bye-bye. Good morning, Mr. Whiffletree!"

"Good morning, Mrs. Giordano, good morning. Would you bring me the Vernon file, please, and order me a Yellow Cab for ten-fifteen sharp?" Thos. S. Whiffletree liked to start off each day in an orderly, businesslike manner, no matter how totally dismembered and dismaying he knew, from experience, that day would become. For all his squishy upper lip, he did have the virtue of optimism. Or, perhaps, a learning disability!

With that inevitability which has so impressed itself upon us over the eons, three o'clock slid into place precisely sixty seconds after two fifty-nine. And with it came, to the office of Thos. S. Whiffletree, Plug and Midge Shavaughn, looking serious, and Zeke Smithooski, alternating between the hangdog and the euphoric.

Gemma had briefed Thos. S. as fully as she could and shot the Shavaughns through to the inner sanctum with almost indecent promptness.

Then she turned around and stared at Zeke, saying nothing until the silence had him on the ropes. He broke the ice.

"You going to get down off your high horse?" he asked. The query lacked the kind of diplomatic finesse with which the State Department makes its thunderous blunders. What it had was a certain agrarian clumsiness.

"*My* high horse," Gemma said.

Well more accurately, "*MY HIGH HORSE,*" Gemma SHRIEKED!

Thos. S. had just closed the inner sanctum door, after welcoming his new clients. His hand was still on the knob. He pulled the door open again and peered out, said "Oh, dear," and closed the door once more. Inside, Midge explained that his secretary and their hired man were acquainted. Thos. S. pointed out that the woman was shrieking at the man and that both parties had their arms in casts.

"Yes," Midge told him, "they have a lot in common." Then she prodded Plug to get on with the saga of Harry the Plumber. There were further shrieks, but they became less frequent and less decibelic. By three-twenty-five, Attorney Whiffletree agreed to meet Plug at the court house on Tuesday morning, but had warned him that, having so little time for preparation, he would probably do no more than move for a further adjournment. He told Plug not to worry, that these errors were quite frequent and usually not too difficult to clear up. Attorney Whiffletree had, until a few minutes before, never heard of Intergalactic Macro-Conduit Companies, Inc., and Plug in his innocence had neglected to mention that Intergalactic, etc., had chosen to field half-a-million dollars in legal talent to collect a spurious debt of ten grand!

Thos S., optimistic or unteachable as always, felt that he had a simple commercial misunderstanding on his hands and he prided himself on simple, profitable settlements in such matters. Pride, as we all know, cometh before a prat-fall and Attorney Whiffletree was all puffed up for a ghastly Tuesday morning.

Anticipating his next appointment and satisfied that things were as they should be fore the nonce, he moved around his desk and pulled open the door, taking Midge by the elbow as the door swung away. Midge is as petite as he, and Thos. S. carried off the genteel gesture with perfect *élan*, for perhaps half a nanosecond. Then he spotted Gemma and Zeke in a clinch, which, his legal training told him, must be illegal. Not an innovator, he was reduced to a re-run of his prior observation. "Oh, dear!" he said. He got Midge out of the inner office with something very close to an ungenteel shove, beseeched Plug out with his eyes, and slammed the door. Then he tottered to his desk and buzzed Mrs. Giordano on the intercom.

It took a few moments for Gemma to pick up. "Yes, Mr. Whiffletree," she said in a voice that bespoke a heroic level of self-control.

"Please remember, Mrs. Giordano, that these are professional chambers. We cannot condone these animal exhibits."

Jack F. Reynolds

This unlikely statue stands in Bushnell Park in downtown Hartford. It commemorates the brave men who fought in the Spanish American War.

XIII

Came Tuesday, and the weather being delivered to the best of May specifications, Attorney Whiffletree decided to walk to court. He arrived just in time to meet his client as Plug emerged from Catastrophobia in front of the building. The attorney was taken aback by the vehicle; he should, perhaps, have recognized it as a harbinger, an omen. Even a Cassandra. Somehow, it made him nervous, but of course, everything did.

    Together, client and Attorney mounted the broad, sun-dappled courthouse steps, passed through the gigantic doors, and stepped into near blindness. The lobby was ill lit, in direct contradistinction to Mother Nature's lavish application of lumens outside. But, slowly, the optic adjustment took place and Plug guided his legal mentor to the correct room. He pulled open the heavy door, saw the familiar phalanx of last Thursday seated before the bench, and nudging Thos. S. ahead of him, went in.

    Whiffletree started smartly down the familiar aisle at full pedal churn. But, as he absorbed the scene before him the rapid motion slowed, and it slowed rapidly. Within ten steps he was stationary, suffering an acute attack of upper labial laxity. He felt like the Roman who had strolled confidently into the Forum for a friendly debate with colleagues, only to discover that he'd taken the wrong turning at the Coliseum and was in the lion's cage.

    Suddenly, confronted by the half dozen Savile Row Vikings, each of them a minimum of six feet tall, Thos. S. found that he was five feet tall, going on three. His adversaries were all peering over their shoulders at him, each displaying just the right amount of grey at the temple, each fingering a richly tooled briefcase bulging with richly tooled briefs. Thos. had expected Harry the Plumber to be represented by one local lawyer, possibly Pasquale Prossimmo or Stan Koslovski. Thos. was limp.

His rather talented impression of Ray Bolger as the Scarecrow was interrupted by a raucous voice telling the assemblage that Judge Groton would preside. Persistent old-movie buffs will recall that, in the epic, the Scarecrow repeatedly lamented his lack of a brain, and it was this aspect of the character that Whiffletree caught best. Mindless, he was also motionless until Plug gripped him by the elbow and more or less shoved him to stage center.

There, the little lawyer acknowledged the Judge, whom he knew, and was introduced to the hit squad from Intergalactic, whom he did not wish to know. These things are relative, of course, but it must be admitted that Thos. S. Whiffletree now had what may yet prove to be his finest hour. He didn't faint. Rather, he grimaced—or smirked or whatever that thing was—as the judge named the opposition. Of these gentlemen, each voiced an elocutionally perfect 'Good morning,' as the judge mentioned him, each speaking with either a seasoned tenor or an irreproachable bass. Finally, Thos. S. squeaked his alto greeting and the ordeal was almost over. He retained wit enough to open his escape hatch.

Turning to the bench, he asked the judge's leave to speak, received same, and moved that the case be adjourned for two weeks to allow him time to familiarize himself with his client's position. Like any lawyer who hasn't done his homework or has a golf date, Thos. S. had moved for adjournment many a hundred times, so he got through it without scrambling his sentences.

Plug was slightly perplexed. He'd been warned about the move for adjournment, but he hadn't realized that it would be for as long as two weeks. There was no sane reason why this foolishness should take more than two minutes. He rose and spoke, uninvited. "Do we have to wait that long, Your Honor? I can tell Mr. Whiffletree everything there is to know about this business in three minutes. And I've got a farm just getting pregnant—it won't wait. I've got an awful lot of things ..." He was interrupted by a rapid-fire gavel and told to sit down.

Whiffletree—it was a superhuman effort—rose. "I'm sorry, Your Honor. My client is inexperienced in court procedure." He turned and glared, insofar as an optical supplication can be characterized as a glare, at Plug.

"Motion granted. Plaintiff and defendant, with Counsel, will appear before this court two weeks from today at this same hour."

"All rise," said the raucous voice, too late. All had risen in concert with the Judge, who had skedaddled with a single sharp rap of his gavel.

Legs achurn, Thos. S. was half way up the aisle before any of the enemy could assemble his papers. The tooled ostrich and skived turtles cases were just clicking closed as he churned into the sunlight. Plug wasn't far behind and as he passed through the gigantic doors Thos. S. grabbed him by the arm and started pulling him along, the while berating him. "Mr. Shavaughn, you didn't tell me that the plaintiff was represented by a phalanx of Wall Street lawyers. You said that you were being sued by Harry the Plumber who had merged with a larger company. How much did you tell me they're suing you for?"

"Ten-thousand dollars—and I don't owe 'em a dime," Plug told him. "And why do we need two weeks. I've got the paid invoice right here. Can't we get this damned thing over so I can attend to my farm?"

Thos. S. kept dragging—he didn't want to even *see* the six-headed monster again—but he explained his lawyerly feeling as he dragged.

"There's something very peculiar in this, Mr. Shavaughn. I think there must be a great deal more to it than meets the eye. In any case, you need a much larger legal service than I can provide. You'll need a firm at least the size of Dwalgic, Framis, Karplewitz, Moog, and Welsh. You might well wish to retain a New York firm. I, of course, must withdraw my services. I couldn't possibly go into open court in opposition to that band of ... of ..." he let the pejorative die on his lips, remembering the sacred oath he had taken in law school never to tell the truth about a fellow lawyer. Or anything else.

Plug was rather confused. "Whaddaya mean you can't go into court in opposition? That's what I'm hiring you for, isn't it? All you've got to do is put the legal jargon on a few simple, demonstrable facts. It's an open and shut case!"

"No, no, Mr. Shavaughn. With that array of, er, talent suing you for a mere ten thousand dollars, it is not an open and shut case."

Thos. S. was, after all, a lawyer, not the smartest and certainly not the most courageous one, but a lawyer. And he could, therefore, see infinite complexity in any vacuum. He went on. "Your simple facts may bear some marginal relation to the case at hand, but I suspect they will be quite superfluous to the way that case goes in court. I would advise you to hire the largest, most expensive legal firm you can possibly afford."

"*You*," Plug informed him, "are the largest, most expensive law firm I can possibly afford!"

Thos said it once again. "Oh, dear."

They had arrived beside Catastrophobia and Thos. S. continued. "Nevertheless, I must, from this moment, withdraw my professional services. My best advice in the circumstance is that you accept the complaint and pay the $10,000.

There will undoubtedly be court costs, as well as heavy legal costs to the plaintiff. But that is probably your best bet, if you have any bets at all. Mr. Shavaughn, let me sincerely wish you the very best of luck."

And with that offering—distinctly ominous, in Plug's view—Attorney Thomas S. Whiffletree churned off down the street. His rapid passage caused smiles in several quarters, but Plug was not smiling.

Climbing into the car, he eased silently away from the curb and aimed for the farm. Attorney Whiffletree was, on reliable report from Gemma, supported by Zeke, prone to nervousness and, perhaps, a touch of gutlessness. Eccentric, like. But he didn't sound like a total fool. He had now uncorked Plug a small apprehension that had been, until this moment, well sealed as that bottled genie of Arabian Nights fame. Once out of the bottle, the thing instantly became a monster.

By the time he rolled into the farmyard, Plug was very apprehensive indeed, and just about on the boil with anger. He loomed large in the door of the kitchen, wherein his first team were busy with their various businesses, and announced:

"Some psychopathic sonofabitch is trying to drive us off this farm an I'm goin' to have his balls!"

Plug's everyday language was apt to be spattered with mild naughties acquired years before while he was assisting in the instruction of the German nation in the virtues of keeping their grubby little hands off of other people's liebestraum. But now, with the quoted prelude, he ran off a fifteen-minute paint-peeler that would have awed your average Billingsgate fish porter. By the time he cooled the flood, fire, and epidemic, Able Mabel was on her knees in full pray, Zeke was taking notes, and Midge, playing Jesuit to Able Mabel's Benedictine and Zeke's Franciscan, was handing Plug a very stiff Scotch and soda.

"The trouble is," Plug went on after several deep breaths and one deep draft, "I don't know who the no goo ..."

"Stop, stop, stop," Midge begged. "My eyeballs are bleeding. You just don't know who the no-good mother is, right?"

"Right, that's exactly what I don't know. But I'm damned sure Whiffletree hit the nail right on the thumb. That outfit is spending a lot more money to sue me than they can possibly recover if they win. Which they won't. BUT, big throat cutters like Intergalactic don't spend money like that. They invest it. They've got to be figuring to get the farm. That's all I've got that anybody could want, and *everybody* seems to want *it*. Dimble—Ware ..."

Zeke broke in, "Yeah, *and* every other real estate hood in the northeast. But they couldn't figure to get the farm by suing you for ten grand. You've already got an offer of a million from that nut, Dimble. At worst, you could take the million and run."

"Let us not even *mull* that *dumb* idea," Midge threw in.

"Right," Plug assented. "We don't want the goddam money, we want a farm. Anyway, answer me this; if Dimble actually put up a real million dollars for this place, how the hell would he make any money on the deal?"

"He'd build a bunch of houses and sell 'em. At fancy prices. That's not too hard to work out," Zeke told him.

Plug shook his head. "I don't think he could build enough houses on 215 acres to make a profit."

"He'd find a way," Midge muttered.

A sound, commanding because it was quite unknown in the human inventory of noises, came from Able Mabel. The others looked and saw that her pudgy little hand was pushing half-a-stub of pencil over the back of a calendar that had hung on the wall until moments before. The sound was correctly interpreted to mean, "Shut up while I calculate." They had seen her do her human adding machine routine before; it was awesome, especially in that day when the electronic computer had not yet appeared. Her head snapped up and she read.

"Allow thirty acres for roads and stuff; 185 acres left. Quarter of an acre per house, so 740 houses. At $30,000 each, gross $22,200,000. Guess the profit per house if $5000—so gross profit, $3,700,000. Take away the land cost, profit $2,700,000. Or, include the land cost in the original profit, guess. Back to gross profit $3,700,000."

"That sounds like a profit to me," Zeke opined. Plug simply said, "Jesus!"

Midge was impressed as well. "Dimble, or any of the rest of those guys, would peddle their mothers for that kind of money. Or for forty cents, for that matter. But Dimble just keeps upping his offer. Ware's different. He'd undoubtedly rather have a few thousand dollars worth of lawsuit to do the dirty work. He knows perfectly well that the only way we can afford long litigation is to sell the farm. Shall we draw straws to see who shoots Ware?"

"Don't bother. I'll volunteer!" It was hard to know whether Plug was kidding or not. He went on. "But how does Ware get this Intergalactic outfit to come in here spending big bucks so he can buy us out cheap. He's rich, but nobody's as rich as those conglomerates. Somebody in management there must be open to influence by our Senator."

Midge opened up again. "Ware said that he was part of an association of some kind. Maybe his association *is* Intergalactic—or maybe somebody with power in Intergalactic belongs to this association."

"He called it a consortium," Plug threw in. "But you could be right. Nobody actually owns these big outfits. They can have maybe twenty thousand stockholders, but ninety percent of the stock will be owned by maybe twenty or thirty people and the other ten percent will be divided up between the nineteen thousand, nine hundred and seventy five. The big owners don't talk to each other. So nobody's really the boss except the guys who manage 'em—for real big salaries and lots and lots of extras. Could be one of those management types is also in Ware's consortium."

"Yeah, I can see one of those characters using the corporate legal department for private gain. And if anybody ever asks any questions, he just apologizes for the big mistake." This was Zeke's contribution, and he added, "Maybe they'll just keep this suit alive until they reckon you're broke, then withdraw the whole thing."

Plug heard this with disgust and replied, "That'd be just about long enough, wouldn't it?"

"Well," Midge cut in, "if any of this cute little speculation happens to be accurate, what do we do about it? First, we've got to find out *if* Intergalactic is being used this way, then we've got to find out *who's* doing the using, then we've got to find a way to *stop* it. Do you think it would do any good to ask Ware to come back out here?—let him think we want to talk business. Then when he gets here, one of you big strong He-men could lean on him a little. There'd be no witnesses but us."

"I wouldn't bet on that. After that performance last time he'd probably come with an armed guard. Or not at all. I must say, though, that the idea of leaning on him does have great appeal."

For a little while, there was silence around the big kitchen table. The hush gave a kind of alarm quality to the telephone as it suddenly burred on the wall. A slightly sepulchral voice wanted to speak with Mr. William T. Shavaughn. Able Mabel handed over the phone to Plug. In a matter of seconds, he established that he was, indeed, the nephew, by marriage, of Mrs. Selkirk Catton of Catton Farm, Wampam Ridge, Rhode Island. The sepulchral voice then expressed official regret and told Plug that his Aunt Gladys had died of her injuries at about nine o'clock that morning.

QUANDARY FARM

Here is a photo of one of the barns located on Quandary Farm.

XIV

"How in hell would I know who the punk was? Just some brainless adolescent my people picked up in Providence. You can pick 'em up wholesale on any street corner in the world. He bungled the job, but the old lady died just the same. He got his money and shoved off for the golden west. Probably went to Las Vegas and by now he'll be panhandling. He's a moron, but it doesn't matter. He just has no way in the world to connect to me—even if he gets plastered and puts an ad in the paper saying he did it."

The speaker was Senator Ware and his head was making its characteristic bobbing motion as he gave Gilbert deVille the status report on the steps of the Shaker Club. The two men had arrived by cab but had made no reference to business in the cabby's presence. Now they paused for an open-air, or private, chat. DeVille's skull shone so in the brilliant sunlight that Ware was forced to move to his colleague's north side, and a couple of steps down.

"It was still a dumb move," deVille said. "These goddam kids have no sense of responsibility. If he blabs, now or in the future, he could be picked up and tell everything he knows!"

"Right," Ware responded. "And that's his big virtue; he doesn't know anything. He's an idiot. Forget him, he's gone."

DeVille was in one of his severe moods. "Don't ever take a serious action again without clearing it with me. People don't understand. They get all worked up over some useless old woman getting her skull smashed. These little details can cause trouble."

Senator Ware was getting tired of being berated. "Okay, forget it. It's done and there's no problem. The old lady was the only one who could possibly identify me and she's gone and the punk is gone and forget it. There's no problem. We've got the codicil. When we take over from Shavaughn we can write the acquisition description to include the center strip and just ignore the whole question. Who's to know?"

There was a distinct tension between the two men so Hadley Ware thought to ease things by adding a note of levity. "Oh, by the way, who do you think Shavaughn has retained to act for him? Whiffletree!"

DeVille's eyebrows rose far enough to diminish the glare. "Whiffletree? You get hold of that little runt and tell him to withdraw. As of last year! He has no idea of what's going on. *Has* he?"

"No, of course not. Groton told the farmer to get himself a lawyer and he came up with Whif."

"It's no good," deVille told him. "We want somebody who'll invoice the farmer like it was an antitrust case. Whiffletree probably charges according to Bar Association guidelines. Tell Groton to disqualify him and make the farmer hire an expensive lawyer—a whole firm of 'em. We haven't got forever on this deal. There's lots of other things going on in this world."

DeVille paused and decided that now might be as good a time as any to explain Hadley Ware's part in the next deVille coup. "Come on," he said, "let's go in and have a drink."

Once seated and served, deVille laid out his program with something like glee: no amount of accrued wealth, no sense of triumph in past or present swindles, could dampen his joy in tomorrow's fraud.

I'm going to establish an "Official" Fall-out-Shelter—sort of a patented arrangement. Got a plastics and concrete outfit out in Ohio that figures they can throw 'em out by the millions. We get governments to say that every family should have one. Every goddam park and backyard in America will be full of 'em. The only drawback is that we'll probably have to go through State legislatures and local governments. Nationally, we'd get too much static from the peaceniks. I say it'll be bigger than Geritol."

Even though his own wealth was largely hereditary, Hadley Ware knew a good speculation when he heard one. He actually smiled. "That's not bad," he mused as the idea sank in. "Every hick town council in the country will buy dozens of them if you can put a little something their way. Patriotic. Public well-being ..." his voice faded as he was inundated in a flood of poignant envy at the simple brilliance of the concept. Pre-fabbed plastic profit providers—that only a card-carrying commie could argue against! His grudging admiration showed, and Gilbert deVille sat back and sipped his cold tea in the euphoric smugness that the infliction of pain upon others so frequently brought to him.

Here are a few of the many storage sheds located on the farm.

XV

It will be seen that, at this stage of development, Senator Ware and Gilbert deVille were unaware that Attorney Thos. S. Whiffletree—for reasons wholly unrelated to *their* reasons—had already removed himself from the contest between Plug and Goliath. And, just as Plug had, as yet, no idea that Gilbert deVille was the power behind the expenditure of Intergalactic Macro-Conduit money for non-business reasons (deVille, a minor shareholder in the corporation, held certain papers which could have sent the firm's president to jail for several generations), so deVille had no idea that Plug had begun to pierce the veil; had, assisted by the scorned Thos. S. Whiffletree, grasped the fact that the law suit was a frame, not an error.

This fund of opposing ignorance may have contributed. Perhaps it was simply another goof by those technician clowns up there in the great studio in the sky. Maybe it was fate. Whatever the cause, things were about to change. Our French friends say, *"Plus ca change, plus c'est la meme chose,"* and maybe that works in Saint Symphorien d'Ozon or Chey, but in Connecticut things change. They may later revert, but they change!

E.g.! Zeke and Gemma. Just weeks before, unknown to one another. Then instantly, joyously in love and bed. Then sundered, as with a cleaver—including injuries! Now, reunited and trying desperately to make love in plaster casts. Not only do things change, but those stumblebums up there in the studio really have a helluva lot to answer for.

Jack F. Reynolds

Returning from that instructive little tangent we shall now see how some of these changes occurred—and to whom. And we shall do so keeping in mind that it's nearly half-past-book and the good guys have only a few score pages in which to triumph!

When last we saw Plug, his Aunt Gladys had just died, victim of an unknown assailant—unknown even to the bad guys who hired him to do the job. This led, of course, to several trips to Rhode Island for Midge and one for Plug. Able Mabel and Zeke stayed out of it, never having met the lady. Quandary Farm got by on good luck and heroic effort by everyone concerned.

Plug, meantime, figured out that he could wait the two weeks his case had been adjourned, then go back and explain to the judge that, through no fault of his own, he had no lawyer again. For the time being, this was costing him nothing and Intergalactic Macro-Conduit was feeding lawyers on the grand scale.

A further idea was suggested to him, unwittingly, by the bearded young lawyer who approached him immediately after the graveside service. This was a youth in a resplendent beard. The fur-faced one had the nerve to introduce himself as Attorney Attorno, and he came bearing what he regarded as good news.

Plug's Uncle Selkirk's legacy to his widow had been Catton Farm plus a surprising accumulation of life insurance policies. Getting jollier and jollier as he went along, the young man explained that the farm was entailed to Plug upon the death of his Aunt. "And," he said, "if there's anything left after I pay the burial expenses and any debts we find—and my whopping big bill—you'll get that, too." He laughed as he spoke these last words, so Plug decided that they were meant jokingly. At least, he hoped they were.

The bottom line, of course, was that he now owned two farms, or soon would. Contiguous farms make a splendid single farm. But farms in contiguous States, even tinies like Rhode Island and Connecticut, remain merely farms in contiguous States, constituting a kind of agricultural nightmare. Plug loved farming, but there are limits.

Solution? If Farm "B" is sixty-five miles form Farm "A," sell Farm "B." Quickly! *Unless* you're in danger of losing Farm "A" to the criminal machinations of a gigantic corporation, in which case keep Farm "B" salted away until the litigation is complete and the upshot has been fired. Meantime, try to winkle out the villains, the ones in Connecticut and the Rhode Island one who killed Aunt Gladys. Plug reflected that there did seem to be an excessive distribution of villains, suddenly, in southern New England.

In deference to the occasion, he and Midge had abandoned "Theplane" (too recently flown) and Catastrophobia (decidedly unsuitable for funerary processions) and driven to Rhode Island in the pick-up, going the final miles to the interment in the undertaker's limousine. Then, as now, there was no way to drive through the towns, villages, hamlets, burghs, and boroughs of northeastern Connecticut except slowly, so we rejoin them driving slowly home in their bucket.

Plug laid out his plan for innocent procrastination before the law and got Midge's enthusiastic approval. He also suggested that they might be able to find a series of Whiffletrees. This kind of logic is correctly adjectivized "Irrefutable."

They decided that while they had a respite from court and even though they most decidedly did not have respite from making the garden grow, they should try to find Harry the Plumber. Previously thought of only as a reasonably pleasant sort of clod who knew how to glue pipes together, Harry the P. was now viewed as a priority source of information. But absent. Plug had tried to get him in his office several times and had been told that Harry was on vacation, no one knew where.

"He's away," Plug told Midge. "How do you reckon we locate him?"

"Did you talk with his wife??"

"If *he's* on vacation, *she's* on vacation, I'd imagine."

Midge smiled. "You've never had Five-Handed Harry unload on you about his wife, have you? No, I don't think Harry would call it a vacation if she was along. When we get home we'll give her a call."

"And if she doesn't know where he is?"

"You try his mother. She lives in Middletown."

"And if Mother doesn't know?" Plug persisted. "You try his Mother-in-Law. Lives in Newington. If *she* doesn't know where he is, he is in Heaven and we won't find him!"

When they got home Plug phoned Harry the Plumber's wife. She also wanted to know where he was. He had told her he had to go away on business. As soon as she learned—a mild indiscretion by Plug—that her husband was, according to office, on vacation, she developed a piercing curiosity and a voice to match. Before he could get her off the phone, Plug had *almost* promised to tell her whatever he learned. He hung up and sought Harry's mother's number in the Middletown book. Before he could find it and dial, Mrs. Plombo was on the phone again.

"You find that dirty little whore-monger, you lemme know fast, right? Promise? Hey, ya promise? I got two brothers'll bring him home in a blotter if he's with some bimbo spending our money! Y'understan? The minute you know something, you let me know. Promise?"

Her last word was declarative. She was *telling Plug that he had promised!* *Plug chose to try to leave the question open. He only wanted to get some information* from Harry, not reassemble him for burial. He rather hoped that, when he found Harry, the poor guy would be alone. Isolated. Maybe living on top of a pillar.

He found Harry almost immediately. Harry's mother knew where he was. But he was not to be disturbed. There was some kind of law case.

Plug lied, right out loud on the telephone. "I don't know anything about law cases, Mrs. Plombo. But Harry's the only guy in the world who knows how my hydraulic milking rig works. I just need him to tell me one word about the machine." Plug hoped that Harry's mother knew nothing about milking rigs; "hydraulic" was kind of stupid, just the first thing that popped into his head.

Harry, it turned out, was upstairs in his mother's house, right there in Middletown. While the proud mother went to get the indispensable son, Plug pondered the hydraulically powered milking machine. He mused.

Harry's voice interrupted the musing, not very enthusiastically. "Who's this? My mother says you got a hydraulic milker. What kinda bullflop you pulling on her and who are you?"

Plug told him and Harry's enthusiasm decreased. There was a soundless pause, suggesting that Harry had his hand over the phone and was saying things to his mother, things that the eldest, smartest, best-looking son of the family should never say to his mother. Plug was afraid he'd hang up, so he shouted into the phone. "I KNOW WHERE YOU ARE, HARRY. HARRY? TALK TO ME."

"Yeah, whadda ya want Shavaughn. I'm supposed to be laying low and I can't talk about it. There's some big money guys involved. Why doncha gimme a break? I know your bill's all paid—everybody should pay so fast. But I got no choice in this one, so ya might as well lay off. My ass is in a sling—I can't help ya."

"Harry," Plug came back, and his voice had dropped about 200° Fahrenheit, "somebody is trying to screw me out of my farm and I'm going to have his balls and *you* are going to tell me who it is! What the hell have you got to do with this Intergalactic outfit and why the hell are they suing me? I never heard of 'em before now and I sure as hell don't owe 'em a dime, but their fancy lawyers are trying to work me over using your company's name and if you think your ass is in a sling now where do you think it'll be when I pull your tongue out through it and tie a bow knot?"

Plug's command of vocal vituperation was, as previously noted, right up there with the best of 'em, but suddenly he was startling himself. His fury and frustration suddenly exploded in Harry the Plumber's ear—and Plug wasn't even particularly angry with Harry, at least not yet, not until he knew what Harry's role was.

"How do these Intergalactic bastards even know I exist? Where do you get off dragging me into your goddam ..."

"Shavaughn, fer Chrissake! Listen, will ya? Anybody could know about you. Anybody could know I done work for ya! I got a list a' satisfied customers I show to every contract I try for. That's no crime—every contractor does it."

"Okay," Plug said, "let's slow down. Who's seen that list lately? And who told you to sue me? You had to be in on that because you're president of your company, even if Intergalactic bought it outright. Who saw the list and asked about me. Just tell me the name of every-goddam-body who's seen that list in the last year—say, since you re-laid that pipe for me. Start telling."

"Jesus, Shavaughn, I can't remember all the names offhand. Practically every builder in Connecticut. An' Western Mass, too. A bunch of real estate companies. And dozens of homeowners and businesses. But mostly biggish outfits. I started out just as a plumber, but I got into a lot of this pipe work—like I done for you—and that's where the money is. So I don't do much overflowing toilets no more. Mostly mains, conduits, heavy stuff."

All this autobiography was not what Plug was after and his anger was on the swell again. "Name some names, you sonovabitch." It was not polite, but it got the message across to Harry the Plumber.

"Shavaughn? Lemme go to my office tonight. After dark. I'll get the list I show with my bids, and the whole list a' bids I made all last year. You can look at the whole thing, honest. I got no idea why Intergalactic has got the gun on you. They just told me to get lost for a month and when I talked with 'em last week they told me to stay lost for another month. They're sending money to my wife while I'm away and they paid me two hundred gran' for that little jerk company a' mine. I don't ask no questions. Lately, I work less and make more, ya get me?"

"I get you. And speaking of your wife, she thinks you're shacking up some place. You oughta ..." Plug was screamed down.

"IMOGENE? Aw, shit, Shavaughn, that busts it. She's got two crazy brothers and every time she decides I'm getting a little on the side she sends these apes around to smash me up. All bets off—I'm leaving town and I won't be back until those gorillas are dead. I'm maybe no Joe Perfect, but nobody deserves my wife and her family!"

"Harry, you go to your office at nine o'clock tonight and I'll meet you there. Meantime, I'll talk to your wife and tell her I talked with you and you're on real business with no cutie-pies involved. But you leave town before I see that list and God and I will follow you with the gorillas helping! Nine o'clock, your place."

"Yeah, okay Shavaughn. Call Imogene quick. Get her to call off the gorillas. Lemme know tonight if she buys it."

This is one of the silos that used to stand around the farm.

XVI

Weekends, on farms, are like Wednesdays. Unless the staffing problem is solved by a huge family or neighborhood kibbutzim mentality, the same people do the same things at the same crack of dawn. So, in a strangely murky May Sunday dawn we find Plug shifting the milk from cow to cooler, aided by Able Mabel. Kids from down the road get Sunday off, rank notwithstanding. The cows, though crucial to the success of the operation, don't really do much. Occasionally, Old Mildred will try to kick the milker's head off, but on balance the great bovine blobs simply *are*, just standing there trying hard to think of anything.

For the milker, too, deep intellectual involvement is not a requirement, so Plug wasn't really neglecting his trade as he hooked and unhooked the milking apparatus and carried buckets of the warm and foamy. He just had his thoughts elsewhere.

His mind was surveying the peculiarity of recent events. His late Aunt Gladys, for instance, taking the trouble to find a long missing document and then mail it off to an unknown lawyer—just because some stranger told her to! Well, undeniably, *that* was Aunt Gladys. But somebody telling her to do it, that's the questionable part. The significant part of the question being, "Who?"

And Whiffletree being the recipient of the codicil that the unknown somebody conned Aunt Gladys into sending. How come him?

And Hadley Ware being in Whiffletree's office, then going out into Pearl Street and getting blown up. And then coming around to the farm a few days later and trying to buy the place. There was certainly no visible relationship between the events, but who knows? And that dingbat, David W. Dimble, offering a million dollars for the farm. Very likely a genuine offer, too—and the first time Plug had ever even given a thought to selling. At least the offer gave him a sense of security he'd never experienced before. And this goddamned lawsuit? What was that all about? Even if they won the suit, all they could collect would be ten thousand dollars in expenses, not the farm. And it did seem that all anybody in the world *wanted* was the farm. All *everybody* in the world wanted was the farm!

This pattern of useless interrogation became circular, going round and round in Plug's head until the last drop of milk had been fingered from udder to bucket. Able Mabel had already started the process of releasing the cows from their milking collars, and Plug set the last few free. All but one instinctively backed off and headed for the outdoors, making no great haste, but rather moving with a quiet patience that signaled a kind of deep religious certainty that the outdoors would still be there when they arrived, no matter when that might be.

The one recalcitrant was clobbered on the hipbone by Plug, who used a hefty steel milking stool for the blow. He did this by way of encouraging movement, but the cow clearly felt nothing. Indeed, the action was predestined to futility; it is well established in agricultural circles that cows react to almost nothing but irrelevant noise. Shouts and horn blowing directed at them go unheard, but the inadvertent sneeze can cause a stampede. The one other factor that may activate the bovine cerebrum is flies, flies landing on the cows' eyeballs, wearing golf shoes. That will occasionally get a reaction.

After a full, big-league windup, Plug laid another one on her. Nothing. At the third blow, Georgiana glanced slowly over her shoulder, showing only a kind of aggrieved wonderment at Plug's stupid waste of energy. It was cool at this hour, and Georgiana did not need the fanning.

Cows, generally speaking, would make great Christians, placidly turning the other cheek without ever getting a head knocked off. (Christians, on the other hand, have long since picked up on the catch in that cheek-turning ploy, and are once again increasing and multiplying!)

In frustration, Plug moved around to the cow's head, grabbed an ear, and by main force turned her head toward the door. Something seemed to click in Georgiana's mind; slowly the idea hacked its way through to the gearbox, slowly she shifted from "park" to "galumph" and slowly she passed along the length of the barn and out into the misty morning. By the time Plug had finished the chores in the milking barn—a little shoveling from the channel at the back of the stalls—a lot of cleaning and scrubbing of buckets and nozzles and fittings—one thing and another—Able Mabel had the kitchen asteam with early coffee and hot muffins, scrambled eggs and orange juice. Plug came gratefully to the table and found Midge and Zeke already seated and wearing large question marks all over their faces. Both had been in bed the prior night when he returned from his date with Harry the Plumber.

"So? What did you find out? Share the glad tidings?" This was Zeke; Midge always made an effort not to seem curious, but she was nodding her head in concert with Zeke's words.

"I found out either everything or nothing or something in between," Plug answered. "Harry finally arrived about half an hour late and we spent more than two hours going over his last year. He's in a nice way of business, by the way. It turns out this Intergalactic outfit is going around the country buying out successful local plumbing firms. They pay a good price and they leave the local head man in charge, except that they handle all the pricing and bookkeeping.

Harry didn't know that when he sold out—they let him think he was a special case. Still, he's not unhappy with the deal so far. But he has noticed that two of his former competitors are no longer in business. Intergalactic is pushing prices up a little at a time, and even pulling prices down when competition demands. It's just that pretty soon there won't be any competition."

"Is that legal," Midge asked. "Aren't there antitrust laws or something?"

Plug shook his head. "Apparently nobody's asked any questions so far. And the way those antitrust cases go in the courts, every living operator and his grandson will be a zillionaire before anything could be done. Anyway, my own recent legal history suggests that the management at Intergalactic doesn't lose any sleep over legal technicalities. They just *use* legal technicalities!"

"Anyway," he went on, "all that's not why I went. I went to find out who could have known Harry did a job for me last year. And he's absolutely right. Practically anybody could know. The Intergalactic people have total access to all his records. But why the hell should they want to sue me? And my name is on a list of "satisfied customers" that Harry shows to everybody he tries to get a contract with. Which is a lot of people. Mind you, he never asked me if I was satisfied and he never asked permission to use my name, but I guess that's just quibbling."

"All that doesn't explain much, does it?" Midge opined. "*If* Intergalactic just picked your name off Harry's list, *why* did they just pick your name off Harry's list? Are they interested in farming or are they just out to monopolize the pipes and sewers business? They can't be for real suing us for ten thousand dollars. They've got ten thousand dollars ten thousand times over …"

"That'd only be ten million dollars," Able Mabel blurted out. "They got lots more than that." She had rather a literal turn of mind.

Midge nodded, but said no more. Her chain of questions didn't seem to be getting anywhere with or without interruptions.

For a little while, everyone shut up and ate, although Able Mabel did her eating at the stove where she was deep into the preparation for lunch.

Finally, Zeke came back with more questions. "Didn't Harry have any idea why they packed him off to oblivion and started suing you? He must have had some clue?"

"The only thing I could deduce," Plug told him, "is that Harry is scared. He didn't say that right out, except in the case of his brothers-in-law. He wasn't a bit backward about telling me how scared he is of them. *And* his wife, who operates the brother-in-law like her private goon squads. But you could sense that he's really scared of Intergalactic. He's just doing what they tell him even though they have no right to tell him anything. Except how to run his own company.

"When I was through with him, he told me he was shoving off for the west coast—maybe the west coast of Africa! But I got the impression he was running from the corporation, not from the in-laws.

"The upshot of the whole thing is that I still don't know who's doing what or how or why? And considering how early I got up this morning I got in too late last night and I'm going to take a nap!"

With this most uncharacteristic declaration, Plug tossed back his orange juice and pointed himself toward the living room couch.

XVII

The building isn't there anymore, but in the late fifties it was a paradigm of corporate shlock. Already sixteen or seventeen years old and fast approaching that antiquity which marks Manhattan structures for destruction, the huge tower sported genteel brass plaques on either side of the cathedralesque front doors. These informed us that this was world headquarters for Intergalactic Macro-Conduits, Inc.

Those who entered—very high-powered executives, very high-bosomed secretaries and paunchy balding delicatessen delivery boys, for the most part—found themselves first in THE LOBBY. This, like the rest of the edifice, had been openly plagiarized by the architectural firm of Stemtalent, Outonyer, Kiester, and

J.K.F. Friedbaumeister; originality being in the enlargement of the space by just over fifty percent, in keeping with the expressed wishes of Intergalactic's old parent firm, The Penny Pipe Company, which commissioned the structure. It was built in the late thirties for opening in 1940, and anyone who was around then will recall that in those days you could buy a really big bunch of ostentation for the kind of bucks that Penny Pipe laid out.

Midmorning, just ten days after we were first introduced to the cast at Quandary Farm, a very middle-class looking person entered that LOBBY. His name was Gordon Gilbey, and this was not his first visit to what corporate insiders liked to call Intmac Central. He was, in fact, entering to face the music about the results of his first visit, nearly a month before. He was most uncomfortable, not because of the intimidating magnitude of the space around him—this time around he was barely aware of that—but because the result of his first visit had been ignominious failure.

Gordon Gilbey had not slept well the night before, and he was tired. By the time he had traversed the entire LOBBY to the wall of elevators he was exhausted. He was also very nervous for a man who made his living killing people. One expects such careerists to be tireless and nerveless, as well as mindless.

He was quickly elevated to the penultimate floor and just as quickly whisked along a cavernous corridor to the private elevators, one of which wafted him suddenly UP, up to the very top floor where the important people worked their wills on destiny. He was, of course, expected; other, unexpected, types—salesmen and other such supplicants—had spent hundreds of thousands of cumulative hours waiting to make just that quick, easy ascent. Often, in vain.

The mid-thirties Miss America who greeted him coolly as the elevator door slid silently open appeared to be a ceramic creation, porcelain where the skin showed, Meissenware elsewhere. It is a measure of Gordon Gilbey's frame of mind that he failed to notice her.

She led him to the central, and by far the largest, of a group of doors, behind which, as Gilbey already knew, labored the most important person in the tower. Maybe in the world. Gilbey, who thought nothing of shooting people through the head from long distances with high-powered, telescopically equipped rifles, or placing massive exploding devices in the private limousines of State Senators, was just at the brink of trembling.

Miss Wedgewood knocked gently on the door, which opened immediately. Far away, at the furthest end of a quite remarkably large room, Gordon Gilbey could see his host, his client, if you will, the Chairman of the Board, President and Chief Executive Officer of Intergalactic Macro-Conduits Companies, Inc.,

D.P. Gee.

The bulging linebacker who opened the door ran his hands quickly over Gordon Gilbey's person and then allowed him to enter the room. Far away, D.P. Gee condescended to rise to greet his hired, but failed, assassin.

As is usual with such persons, D.P. Gee had not attained his present station by wasting words. Only people. Wasting no time on "hello," or brief observations on the meteorological situation, he closed the door, with Miss Wedgewood on its other side.

"You screwed it up very badly, Gilbey. You've still got our five thousand dollars. You can still get the other five if you finish the job. Do you think you're capable of finishing the job?"

Gordon Gilbey suddenly looked upon the distant D. P. Gee with the eyes of a child being interviewed by Santa Claus. When he spoke, the relief was audible. He had been terrified that his client would want his money back, and he would have been hard pressed to produce it, being a man of expensive hobbies.

"I sure can. Sir. With a bullet right through the skull. And this time there won't be any stupid hero cops around to save him. He shoulda been roasted in that car."

A slight movement of D.P. Gee's head told Gilbey to shut up. And get on with it. "You don't," Gee managed to express silently, "get ahead in this world by wasting time."

"You'd probably better put *several* bullets in his head," Mr. Gee said icily. "By a week from today. We'll be watching your performance. Remember, you've got *two* on your list." And that was the end of the interview.

The linebacker opened the huge door, and Gordon Gilbey passed gratefully through it on his was to kill Senator Hadley Ware. *And Gilbert deVille.*

Miss Wedgewood rose from her Hepplewhite desk and guided a newly lighthearted Gordon Gilbey to the elevator. Now he noticed her—and spoke with his usual suave delicacy.

"Jesus, Baby, you're some dish. You doin' anything for lunch?"

She spoke, the only words other than "Good Morning" that she had uttered to him in their three, very brief, prior meetings. "Do shut up," she said as the elevator door slid silently across his face.

Back in D.P. Gee's baronial hangar, as his gigantic door swung shut, the Chairman spoke to the linebacker. "Keep an eye on him. Get pictures."

The linebacker nodded and sprinted through a side door directly into an elevator even more private than the one from which Gordon Gilbey was changing to the express on the floor below. By the time Gilbey reached THE LOBBY, the linebacker was waiting for him. In the entirety of the ensuing week, Gordon Gil-bey never discovered that he was almost constantly under observation by the linebacker or his teammate, under observation and occasionally photographed, cinematically.

Back in the fifties, train riding to Connecticut had become a dismal activity, rather on a par with burning at the stake or listening to lieder singers. Still, business is business and Gordon Gilbey was nothing if not a businessman, albeit specialized. Doggedly then, after a very good lunch, he boarded the old New York, New Haven, and Hades Railroad and rode back to Hartford, dutifully changing in New Haven from a coach that hadn't been cleaned since 1920 to one that hadn't been cleaned since 1820. Perhaps surprisingly, he arrived. And, after renting a car, drove to the little motel on the Turnpike where he'd been living for a month.

This was ordinarily a rooms-by-the-half-hour operation, its owner being motivated by common commercial zeal and periodic attacks of voyeurism. For all the wonderful things he'd seen, however, he would have been greatly shocked to see the contents of the heavy, and heavily locked, "sample cases" the guy in 109 had deposited with him for lock-and-key safekeeping. "Calibrating instruments," Gil-bey had told him when he deposited the cases. The owner didn't have the foggiest idea what a calibrating instrument might be, so he dropped the subject.

The actual contents of one of these cases was, as the Drill Instructors used to say, "United States Rifle, Caliber 30, M1, a clip fed, gas operated, semi-automatic shoulder weapon," thoughtfully left over from those days when Plug Shavaughn and sixteen million other guys were instructing the Germans and Japanese to stay home. This, really quite efficient, little nine-pounder was augmented by the kind of nifty telescopic gunsight that makes National Rifle Association members drool. If they aren't already doing so.

Barrel, bolt and stock were disassembled for packing, the shape of the squarish case giving no hint of the contents. Gordon Gilbey may have been clone to a mental defective, but he handled his professional life well. He had, in fact, been one of the sixteen million, and he was among the relatively few who actually did, as the recruiting posters had promised, learn a trade in the army. And he'd learned it well. With his M1, at a hundred yards, he could take an unwanted wart from the back of your hand and from five hundred yards, he had once taken an unwanted husband off the hands of an ever-so-grateful young heir-ess. Through a very small porthole! He understood explosives, too, and was a dab hand with a knife, although he much preferred to work at a distance.

The motel owner was spared being greatly shocked. Gordon Gilbey actively and aggressively failed to show him the contents of the sample case when he reclaimed it. The case and its contents, all of the above plus several clips of marksman's ammunition, weighed in excess of thirty pounds, so Gilbey was grateful to the big fellow who held the door for him as he lugged the case out of the motel office and headed for 109. It didn't register that this was the same guy who had been standing beside him, dealing with the second clerk at the car rental counter.

Back in his now familiar little room, Gilbey made sure that the door was firmly locked, then hauled his burden into the bathroom. Here he opened the case and removed the components, fitting them together with a quick and practiced hand until he was armed with a Garand Rifle cum-telescopic sight. He twined his arm into the sling in approved military manner and struck a pose, aiming his weapon through the bathroom door and the window beyond, locking his pose rigid as he lined up the cross hairs on the "o" of a motel sign. He felt right at home.

He mumbled to himself, "Just about 300 yards." Then he picked a small triangulation device from the case—a kind of hand-held theodolite of the kind sometimes sneakily used by naughty golfers. He put this to his eye and again sighted on the motel sign. The rough vernier registered at 305 yards, and Gordon Gilbey felt slightly smug. Then he drew from the case and unfolded a loose-fitting, zippered bag into which he slipped the rifle and then put the whole between mattress and box spring. He felt that the next day or the day after would be the right time to open fire on Senator Hadley Ware and Mr. Gilbert deVille. His plans laid, he went out into the soft May evening to see if he could do as well for himself.

Farms like Quandary Farm have need of many various types of trucks. Here are a few of them on the farm currently.

XVIII

We tell ourselves that, in our time, the assassination of public figures has lost its novelty, has snowballed into a major modern industry, and that this is different from past circumstances.

Let us scrub this absurd idea. Assassination is always very novel to the guy who gets assassinated, albeit not for long. But it has never had any novelty value for anyone else. Cain laid it on Abel, and the habit stuck. Proportionately, there are probably no more assassinations today than ever there were, just a great many more people. What does appear to exist is a slippage in the quality of the average victim, again, simply because there are so many of them.

Abel was a big man in his day—one of only three in existence! No one could possibly make such a claim about Senator Hadley Ware. On average, State Senators might be expected to bring about a dollar a gross when the market is hot, but of course, Ware is not average. If there were a gross of him—and God forbid—it would be difficult to predict a market so volatile as to wring forty cents out of the wildest spendthrift.

He must, therefore, be viewed as a minor or sub-minor public figure, even a negligible one, in all matters exclusive of his inherited pile. Still, in any statistical analysis he would have to be classed as a public figure. (This kind of arbitrary classification goes far to explain why statistics are both infallible and foolish!) And, beyond doubt, the effort was afoot to assassinate him, and had, indeed, already been made, albeit thwarted by a particularly gusty cop and the dumb chance of the cop's presence.

Senator Hadley Ware having, in intellectual matters, the denseness of a black hole, he had not perceived that someone was trying to kill him. Why should anyone? But the police are not so sanguine in such matters.

Any little street explosion tends to draw their attention, and this wasn't just any little street explosion. This was a whingdoolie of a street explosion. The police laboratory people had no trouble showing that the explosion was no accident, that it had been caused by a quite large amount of dynamite secured very close to the fuel tank and set off from a distance, probably by a timer activated by radio, shortly before the bang.

Having determined this, they sent one of their lads around to share the news with the senator, to warn him of possible sequels and to pump him about who might stoop to such antisocial behavior. Ware had no idea.

And his unrelenting denseness wasn't the sole reason for that. He could hardly be expected to understand that a man in New York, a man whom he had never met and had barely heard of, was paying to have him assassinated simply because he was associated with Gilbert deVille.

Any competent debater could make a case for the proposition, "Resolved, that association with Gilbert deVille is sufficient grounds for assassination." But Ware was not a competent debater, and he had just never got around to thinking along those lines.

He viewed the young detective as alarmist, but he couldn't wholly brush off the memory of the deplorable condition of his limousine just milliseconds after he was dragged out of it. Still, he was expert at putting from his mind whatever seemed unadapted to profit taking.

Lunching with deVille—perhaps "caballing" with deVille would be more apt—he had mentioned the warning from the police. DeVille had, from the moment, presumed that the Pearl Street incident was an assassination attempt: it seemed to him wholly natural that someone should wish to kill his friend and colleague, Hadley Ware. If only to cut back on the world's oversupply of stupidity. He did not say this, however, and he was just as far away from making the connection with D.P. Gee as was Ware. Unlike Ware, he had a personal connection with Gee, but he knew Ware didn't know Gee. Himself, although he did not take time to think about the matter right now, *he* had D.P. Gee over a barrel.

DeVille, in fact, had never so much as hinted of his connection to D.P. Gee and Intergalactic to Hadley Ware. Only potential gain tended to cause deVille to confide, and he saw nothing to be gained by telling the senator that a New York corporation czar was scattering his company's expensive lawyers around the countryside as a result of blackmail. Gilbert deVille, of course, could not see the sequence as blackmail, but rather as a simple deal. D.P. Gee spent a good many thousands of his company's dollars doing deVille's dirty work. And deVille kept up his end of the deal by not divulging things about D.P. Gee which, apparently,

D.P. Gee wished to keep undivulged. What could be fairer? Simple. Straightforward. Businesslike. Especially, businesslike!

The two sat for many minutes before Ware's ill-concealed impatience gave way to his bad manners, and he blurted out the one question uppermost in his— well, we really must say "mind." Since he'd first heard of it, the bomb shelters idea had been skipping around inside him like an inebriated bacillus.

"How far," he asked expectantly, "have you got with the bomb shelter thing?"

DeVille did not wish to speak of bomb shelters, not just at this moment.

"Not far. That'll keep. The question is, how far have *you* got on the Shavaughn thing? Time keeps going by. Nothing gets fitted together. It's a week since Whif gave us the middle of the farm, but we're no closer to the two big parts. They keep having adjournments in the court suit, and Shavaughn isn't spending anything on it. The House'll pass the acquisition resolution the instant it's tabled. We've gotta move this thing!"

"So what do you want me to do, hold Shavaughn up with a pistol and make him hand over his farm? You've got to have a little patience, Gil. Anyway, the court suit was your idea. And it'll probably do the trick. But you've got to give it a little time."

"I'm fed up to here with waiting for that farmer to smarten up. We're going to go out there and just plain lean on him!"

This was a whole new Gilbert deVille in the eyes of Hadley Ware, who had not been privy to the intramural action when deVille had been strolling on the faces of his relatives in quest of his present, supreme, position in the family insurance company. Ware had never heard the screams in the night nor watched the avuncular heads roll across the parquet flooring. He hadn't even heard deVille denounce his older brother to the State Insurance Commissioner for some little tricks that Gilbert himself had performed. In his brother's name, of course.

"You thought it would be stupid when *I* went up there," Ware told him. "How come *you* suddenly want to go?"

"When you went, it might well have *been* stupid. When *we* go, it will prove very useful."

And it was through these few casual, if slightly surprising, words that we come to the procession of the following day. "Procession" is the only word, although the moving line of vehicles and personnel did lack the sound organization and strict liturgy associated with more formal processional events.

In fact, in this event, most of the participants were unaware that most of the other participants were participating.

It all started the following morning when Gordon Gilbey, sitting in his rented car with his cleaned, oiled and loaded M1 laid out under a motel blanket on the floor of the back seat, spotted his prey. He was sitting there, half a block from Hadley Ware's splendiferous home, for just that purpose. Ware's car, a huge limousine lately supplied in the stead of the one Gilbey had destroyed, went left and was aimed for Hartford by the newly hired replacement for the indignant Giuseppe Diano. Gilbey had his engine running instantly and took off in pursuit. He had no intention of shooting the senator right out in public, but intended simply to see where he was going and work out a plan.

To his surprise, the limousine slowed after only a couple of minutes and turned into a huge circular driveway, but Gilbey knew the site. The drive fronted the home of Gilbert deVille, the other name on his list, and had been cased by him some weeks before.

As a good little hit man, Gilbey had asked nosy questions about the men he was sent to exterminate. He had been given their names and addresses and a touch of socioeconomic background, i.e., deVille was an insurance executive and Ware was a State Senator. He knew little else about them. Certainly not that deVille was really his prime target and that Ware was fingered only because D.P. Gee knew that the senator was a sometime associate of deVille's.

He drove very slowly past the house and saw deVille come out the front door. Then his view was blocked by the near forest that surrounded all but the road side of the mansion. He pulled over and waited, and in moments, the limousine debouched from the driveway and tuned off in the direction from which it had just come.

This was of no great consequence to him; there was plenty of road room for a leisurely U turn. But it was slightly awkward for the car that had been following *him*. This one, with D.P. Gee's linebacker and a teammate plus a late model 16mm camera aboard, had to allow both the limo and Gilbey to pass and then get turned around fast without looking too much like a car trying to get turned around fast. As it happened, no one up ahead noticed. No one had the foggiest idea he was being followed.

The maneuver was even *more* awkward for the young State Police officer who had been assigned to keep a protective eye on Senator Hadley Ware, at least for a few days while the department had no abnormal pressures. When Ware's limo had first come out of its own drive, this young man had been parked on the opposite side of the road, several hundred yards away and facing the wrong way, well slouched down in his car. He had had to get himself together, get turned around in the wake of the car in the wake of Ware's car, and without ramming the car that had suddenly appeared from a driveway and appeared to be closing fast on the second car. He managed the turn, only to have to reverse field minutes later. And, at the end of the procession he was able to determine that that second car seemed to be tailing the Senator. Which is what he was there for. And the tail seemed to have a tail. Nobody had told him about that.

With the assemblage finally all together and moving at roughly the same speed and at neatly spaced intervals, we had a true procession. And a pretty one it was, too. A large black-and-shiny limo full of important people. A medium sized Buick of rather natty maroon hue full of Gordon Gilbey and Garand, a green Chevy equipped with the Gee Team camera, and a dark grey Ford bearing one young State cop. As long as he could see the limo up ahead, the young officer made no effort to jump the line and thus remained un-noted by either the teammates or Gilbey.

And so, of a mild May morn, our quiet little procession proceeded. The watchwords seemed to be "Quandary Farm, Ho!" although only Ware and deVille knew that. Even Ware's new chauffeur was simply turning right here and turning left there as the instruction occurred, but after a while, his rear view mirror made him conscious that he was not alone. There was a maroon car, then a green car, then a rather grimy grey car and they were all following the same instruction, although it seemed unlikely that their drivers could hear Senator Ware's directions. He felt duty bound to mention this to his employer.

Ware and deVille both spun in their seats and quickly confirmed the chauffeur's observation. Ware had a sudden vision of that young policeman telling him that he had been a victim of an assassination attempt. DeVille suddenly and unpleasantly found himself in the same—followed—limousine with a man who was manifestly prime meat for assassination. Both shouted at the driver, instructing him to drive like hell to the nearest police station.

The driver had no idea where the nearest police station might be, but he willingly speeded up: he knew about the indignation of Giuseppe Diano, and how this job had become available.

The cars behind speeded up, too, and our quiet little procession became a rushing little race, flashing down that staid old College Highway with a liveliness that Route 10 hadn't seen since the twenties when rumble-seated coupés full of beaver-coated Yalies used to ream off to Mount Holyoke and Smith weekends, intent upon spreading the Gospels of Freud and Kraft-Ebbing.

Alertness spreads quickly in such moments. In seconds, Gordon Gilbey realized that not only he but the car behind him had speeded up in response to the limousine's sudden haste. The driving member of the photographic teammates, now rushing down the road at a speed he really didn't care for, realized that the little grey car behind him was also in the chase.

Suddenly, up ahead, the limousine swerved off the road and into the forecourt of a gas station. Standing on the brakes the chauffeur brought the huge vehicle to a shuddering stop, leapt out and ran awkwardly into the little station, his hands held high above his head. He had had a sudden change of heart about being a chauffeur and associating with persons whose cars were followed and sometimes blown up. He now hoped that the three cars full of homicidal maniacs would accept his peaceful surrender and do what they might with his passengers.

Totally confused by the maneuver ahead of him, Gordon Gilbey could only slow down a bit and drive on by the gas station, feigning indifference to the limousine parked therein. This left the teammates little choice but to slow down, too, and continue following Gordon Gilbey.

The lone cop in the Ford pulled in behind the limousine, just as confused as everyone else. Ware and deVille, both befuddled by the chauffeur's behavior, peered out the window of the limousine as the maroon car, which had been their immediate successor in the procession, whizzed on down Route 10. Although its speed was diminishing, the car was past them so suddenly that neither even caught a glimpse of the driver.

By now, it had occurred to the chauffeur that he might make use of the telephone so conveniently sitting on the counter behind which he was crouched. The garage keeper came out of the service bay into his little office just in time to note that, contrary to his expectation, there was nobody there—and then see a hand appear from behind his counter and lift the phone out of sight.

"Hey," he hollered, nearly as indignant as Giuseppe Diano, "there's a pay phone right outside. That's a business phone—no freebies!"

The chauffeur remained where he was. "Get down," he hissed. There's going to be shooting. I'm trying to call the cops."

The garage keeper did not believe this. There was never any shooting in his gas station, but there were lots of telephone freeloaders. He was about to remonstrate with the freeloader behind his counter when the door opened and another figure appeared. The garage keeper could not know that this person, in very plain clothes, was, in fact, a State Trooper. Neither could the chauffeur. "Okay," the latter shouted from his sanctuary, "I won't call the cops. But ya don't need to shoot me. I won't call anybody or tell anybody nothin', so help me. I got a wife and kids …"

The young police officer said, "Give me the phone, please, I've got to get some help." He'd been in radio contact with his barracks right along; now he wanted local help as well. He asked the operator for local police.

The trooper explained what had happened, assured the recipient of this information that the Senator and his guest were okay, gave the license number of the green Chevy, the only one he'd approached close enough to read, and ended by commenting that the chauffeur had made a very intelligent move—*if, in fact, the other cars really contained assassins.*

Sitting in the limousine, Ware and deVille were babbling at one another. Ware: *"That's driver's a pretty smart cookie. If* those cars were really following us. *That* fella doesn't seem to be following us, he's just here to use the phone. I don't think they were really following us. Just coincidence. Nobody'd want to ..." DeVille, *over* Ware, neither man hearing a word the other spoke: "They might have killed *me*! They're out to get you and they might have shot *me*. Who's *that* guy," as the State Trooper strode past the limousine with just a glance inside. "Do you realize that they might have injured *me*? And that damned driver just deserted us, He could have got me killed. I'll have his license lifted."

This little exchange of drivel went on in nervous incessation for minutes until the policeman came out of the office and approached the limousine. Fear—let us call it, instead, 'flat-out panic'—was rekindled. DeVille tried to push past Ware and get out of the limousine by the left hand door as the plainclothes cop approached the right side.

Ware screamed, "Don't open that door. They're locked good. He can't get in. the cop knocked on the glass and Senator Ware shook his head in a violent negative at the man. "Go away," he shouted, "the police will be here in a minute."

The man shouted back, "I *am* the police," and he held his badge against the glass to convince the occupants of his bona fides.

Slowly, Senator Hadley Ware became convinced. But Gilbert deVille's misgiving misgave again and again, and now there was a standoff both between the officer and the occupants of the limousine, and intramurally between the occupants.

Finally, the chauffeur was coaxed back into the scene and his presence reassured even deVille that it was once again safe to mingle with mankind. Reinforcing this decision was the arrival of uniformed police protection in the form of a lonely, non-dieting, officer of the local force with the magic word "police" on both sides of his car. This person never really did find out what was going on. In reporting back to his chief, he relied heavily on the garage keeper who had even less idea of what was happening, although he continued to harbor the idea that the chauffeur was just trying to chisel a free phone call—probably long distance.

On down the road the efficiency level was a bit higher, with ironic effect. Gordon Gilbey, ever professional, was quickly sure that the car that remained behind him was no coincidence and before he was out of sight of the gas station he was thinking of ways of losing it. That State Police efficiency did this job for him.

His pursuers were surprised when he suddenly reduced speed, but they followed suit. And only then did they see why he had slowed; a State Police patrol car was parked up ahead on the shoulder of the three-lane road. They couldn't know it, but its driver had the description and registration number of their car, radioed from the officer tailing Ware to the barracks to him.

Almost decelerated to legal driving speed, Gilbey rolled past the police vehicle without interference, but as the Teammates came alongside in their green Chevy, the police car's top light suddenly came on, and its siren set up a wail.

The trooper spun onto the highway in pursuit, quite obviously of the Teammates, not of Gordon Gilbey, who had never even been mentioned to him. In less than a minute, he had followed his received instructions.

The Teammates saw no reason to try to run. They could earnestly claim coincidence in all their actions, and there's no law against carrying a 16mm movie camera. As they were slowing down they also agreed a policy of knowing nothing whatever about the car that was, just then, running off Route 10 and down an eastbound side road. They pulled over and stopped. The trooper pulled over, stopped behind them, and then, through a bullhorn, asked them to please get out of their car. They got out.

The trooper still sat with his gun under his hand in the seat beside him. One never knows. These problems always arise suddenly. And yet, already he was beginning to breathe easier. "If you'd stand right there for just a moment, please." With this, he made radio contact with his unit and reported the apprehension, his eyes never leaving the two up front. Now he asked what he was supposed to do with the two guys and what were they wanted for? These things take time and detail can be boring. The teammates were released within the hour with apologies for the inconvenience and without the indignity of formal arrest.

Gordon Gilbey had, for about the third time that morning, stood on his brakes when he had spotted the patrol car on the shoulder of Route 10. He hadn't quite got down to legal speed as he went by the trooper, and he wondered if he would be stopped—and should he run for it, with the rifle sitting on the floor behind. But this trooper was feeling occupied. He was watching for a green

Chevy thought to be moving his way—and which just happened to be coming up next.

Gilbey checked his mirror to see if he was being chased and wondered if he'd be able to dump the rifle before he stopped. He then had revealed behind him the incredible picture of the police car screaming onto the roadbed, lights and siren awhirl—and stopping the car that was pursuing him!

He still didn't feel out of the limelight. He was now quite sure that other cops must be in search of him—he wondered what had transpired back at the gas station. And he was befogged by that other car. Who were they? And why had the police stopped them?

Never a man to philosophize when he could hit, kick, shoot, or speed, Gilbey sped. At least, he moved as quickly as discretion allowed, and in a matter of minutes, he found himself driving into the grey old industrial city of New Britain, then as now, one of the great places to get lost.

Gordon Gilbey didn't know that on arrival, but he was quickly lost and quickly learned. He found an unoccupied parking meter, slid around into the back seat of the car, and without ever lowering his eyes from their constant scanning of the neighborhood, disassembled his rifle.

Rolling the pieces of rifle and gunsight into their covering blanket, he made an innocent enough package, albeit a heavy one, climbed out of the car and asked the first passerby for direction to the bus station. It took three more tries, but he finally found a local who knew where the bus station was. Within the hour, he was back in Hartford reporting the theft of his rented car to the car's owners, and estimating the time of the theft at two or so hours before he had abandoned it. He had to fill out some forms, which he did with an easy lack of candor about several details, but he did tell the rental people that he'd been in New Britain at the time—this in the hope that they'd find it soon and forget the incident sooner. On his side, unknown to him, was the fact that customers are forever reporting "stolen" cars that are merely parked in an unremembered place.

Then he rented another car from the rivals down the street. It was just coming lunchtime when he cleared the second rental car transaction, so he fed himself and then headed back out to his Highview Drive stakeout. He was really becoming quite tired of this job, and just a little frightened of it.

XIX

While Gordon Gilbey was having his morning frustration and escape therefrom, Senator Hadley Ware and Gilbert deVille were getting on with their planned program, a visit to Quandary Farm. This took a little doing.

As we have seen, the senator's brand new chauffeur had informally resigned. Either of his passengers could have driven the vehicle, of course, but neither was much inclined to do so, and Gilbert deVille wasn't even much inclined to get in it!

But even the humble working man is subject to fits of vanity. So when the State Police officer repeated to the Senator his prior observation that the chauffeur had made a very intelligent move, the senator, having made the same observation himself, agreed. And the chauffeur overheard. That person—his name was Waldo, so he naturally preferred to be called Peter and we shall allow him that privilege—when that person, Peter, heard the policeman's remark, he was much pleased. Now, with the repeat of the remark by the cop and with his employer taking up this laudatory view, Peter's quickly developed distaste for further involvement just as quickly evaporated. He did his best to be modest—it was a rotten best, he positively preened—and allowed it to be believed that he had driven into the gas station as a ploy, rather than as an act of overt cowardice. Indeed, he quickly believed it himself and was just as quickly back behind the wheel.

And so off they went one more time, now with the State Policeman's assignment known to them and his slightly grimy Ford directly behind their magnificent limousine.

The mud of May was still very prevalent as they passed over the last half-mile or so to Quandary Farm, but the sun glowed brilliantly in its ever-popular way. Making every effort to appear superficially, if not underlyingly, above their recent excitement, the two leaders of this threatening expedition left Peter in the solitude of his glass-enclosed driver's compartment and consulted about strategy. I.e., deVille instructed Ware. "If we've got that cop of yours hanging around, we won't be able to put any real pressure on that damn farmer. The cop's supposed to be guarding you, so you take him for a walk in the country or something. Show him the beautiful view. They got any kind of view up there? Then I can let Shavaughn know that we're for real and that what he really wants to do is sell out—fast. That bonehead, Dimble, has offered him a bundle, but I'll tell him Dimble is an escaped mental case, which he may be. And I'll try an offer like a couple of hundred thou—then work up a little, if necessary. But I'll let him know it's not a choice matter. He's going to sell or get hurt. He's got a wife, too, hasn't he? You just have to keep that cop out of my hair." DeVille totally failed to appreciate his own non-sequitur. So did Ware.

Never so fastidious as Senator Ware, and always a little quicker off the mark, deVille hopped out of the limousine without waiting for Peter to do his duty. Right into three or four inches of mud! The senator, now practiced, had taken the precaution of wearing rubbers, which, until this moment, had seemed a bit eccentric to deVille. Feeling somehow cheated, but ever willing to sacrifice a pair of hundred dollar shoes for a million dollar farm, he strode manfully up to the front door—no back doors for deVille—and looked for a button to push.

The farmhouse at Quandary Farm has no doorbell. What it has is a front door that is firmly locked from September 15th until June 15th and left wide open during the summer months. Even then, weeks can pass without any person passing through it. One simply does not use front doors, which don't actually go anywhere that one wishes to go. If one is leaving the house there must be a reason. Barn? Car? Motorcycle? Silo? None of these is propinquitous to the front door.

In-bound, deVille beat vigorously upon it. Through the neatly draped curtain that straddled the glass pane he saw materialize a short and rotund personage, decidedly feminine, who fitted perfectly his preconception of what a farmer's wife should look like. So, when Able Mabel got the door open—it took a bit of unlocking—he greeted her as "Mrs. Shavaughn."

He was, of course, standing in the bright sun of a bright day and she was really unable to determine what his facial fixtures might be, the glare of his pate being what it always was. But she dutifully assured him that she was not Mrs. Shavaughn, actively neglected to tell him who she was, and demanded to know who he was? And what he wanted? And what did he think he was doing using this door before June 15th. As she spoke, Senator Hadley Ware appeared behind deVille, and him she knew. She thought he was a bit strange, but she knew who he was. Right behind him came the State cop, in his very plain clothes. Again, she had no idea who he might be. DeVille told her, in his usual cheerfully arrogant way, that he was Gilbert deVille, Board Chairman, President and Chief Executive Officer of the Rejuvenation Assurance Society.

Able Mabel told him that she didn't want to buy any insurance, and she didn't think Mrs. Shavaughn would, either. DeVille disabused her of the misapprehension and said he wished to see Mr. Shavaughn on other matters. Able Mabel noted the mud on his feet and told him to walk around the house to the barnyard. Mr. Shavaughn was "out back" somewhere. But he wouldn't want to buy any insurance, either!

Almost gallantly, for him, deVille nodded agreement, turned, and strode off toward the barnyard. The sudden flash of his skull caught the young officer off guard, and left him with the fear that he might have a permanently damaged optic nerve.

Arriving at the back of the house, deVille found that Able Mabel had beaten him by several seconds, taking the short, dry, inside route. Now she stood on the back porch and pointed out the architectural splendors of the farm. "That's the milkin' barn. He probably ain't in there—it ain't milkin' time. Try the tractor barn. I don't hear nothin' out in the fields, so maybe he's in there."

At this moment Midge appeared on the porch, recognized Ware and greeted him, not as one would greet a long, lost friend, but more as one would greet a not-long-enough-lost Senator Hadley Ware. Politely. But without the joyous smiles and loud "huzzahs" Ware always confidently expected, however rarely they materialized.

Ware greeted Midge and introduced her to "… my good friend and colleague, President Gilbert deVille of the Rejuvenation Assurance Society."

"I already told 'em we don't want any insurance," Abel Mabel said to Midge. Midge acknowledged the introduction, noticed the chauffeur sitting in the huge car at the front of the house, and was slightly surprised not to be introduced to the third figure in the Ware/deVille party (who seemed to melt into the scenery). Then she told Ware that, if he were looking for Plug, he would probably find him in the tractor barn, adding, "that's the middle one, the one with the stone foundation."

"It is my colleague who wishes to speak with your husband, Madam. Perhaps you wouldn't mind if I remained here, out of the mud!" Ware said this with manifest glee, and watched appreciatively as deVille sludged off into the deep pondlets of ooze that led to the tractor barn.

We will leave Midge, Ware, Able Mabel, and the almost invisible State cop on the porch and follow the beacon atop Gilbert deVille in quest of Plug, stepping daintily above the muck as only he can.

DeVille's experience of barns was about on a par with Mary Magdalene's experience of igloos. He squelched to the great black orifice that implied "entry," stood in the brilliant sunlight, and spoke into the ebony shade beyond, his voice somehow chilled by the funereal ambience against which his eyeballs were leaning hard but ineffectually.

"Mr. Shavaughn?" Even to himself, he sounded gelded. He cleared his throat and tried again. "Mr. Shavaughn?" This was a bit better, but still had a kind of goosed-alto quality. By now, he could see a foot or two into the lessening darkness. He wasn't actually afraid of the dark, he was just a congenital conservative, quite willing to let the passage of time, milliseconds or eons, as required, remove the element of chance.

"Mr. Shavaughn?" This was reasonably loud and much more resembled his normal or ungoosed alto tone. It bore fruit.

"Yeah. What can I do for you?" The response came from a couple of yards in front of and a couple of yards below his busily adjusting eyes. Plug lay on the barn floor straddled by a green machine, which was just coming into Gilbert deVille's focal plane. Plug was doing a little elementary tractor fixing, although then or later that fact never occurred to deVille. He simply accepted that farmers were prone to proneness, and got on with the important thing.

"Ah! Mr. Shavaughn. There you are. I have come to buy your farm."

"Can't help ya," Plug told him, still prone. "I've already sold it."

This was the kind of information, which, in the ordinary way, might have silenced and discouraged some men. Not Gilbert deVille. He had come to buy the farm because he wanted the farm. Ergo, prior sales didn't count.

"Are the contracts signed?" he queried.

Naturally, Plug had not actually sold the farm. In recent days he'd hardly had time to nip to the john. He also hadn't the foggiest idea whom he was talking with, only that the case didn't know enough to come in out of the mud. But he had decided, by way of fighting off the crowds, to report to all comers that the farm had been sold.

"Nope," he answered. "We've got to have lawyers for that. Sorry to waste your time." He thought the latter a bit pointed, but being excessively busy, he also thought it would be nice if his visitor would go away.

"Good, good," said a suddenly genial deVille. "That makes things so much simpler. May I ask what the intended buyer was prepared to pay? Indeed, may I ask who was the intended buyer?"

DeVille was a bit put out by Plug's answer. "Nope!"

The master of the manse snapped a spring-loaded grease nipple into place, felt about on the concrete floor for his grease gun, gave the nipple a good blast of fine gooey, and pulled himself out from under the tractor. From his prone position he hauled himself upright with one hand, a procedure which did not miss but did disturb, deVille.

The latter had come to threaten Plug into selling his farm. He had, of course, no intention of doing any strongarm work himself, merely of suggesting the possibilities. Still, the size and structure and strength of his intended threatenee did cause pause. From a reservoir of talents deep within and well hidden, he produced a reasonable facsimile of *politesse, which started to work rather well. But then he smiled, and the deVille smile has been known to kill puppies.*

Still not knowing with whom he has conversationally engaged, Plug Shavaughn—who liked pretty much everybody until disabused—came up with an immediate distaste for the Gilbert deVille behind that grotesque grimace. Midge had, after all, often noted Plug's occasional similarity to a puppy.

In a sense, the two men squared off. Neither had the slightest idea of violence, but a very aggressive—one could fairly say 'offensive'—deVille stood there wearing his padrionic paunch and cranial coruscation, determined to frighten Plug into selling the farm, while Plug, somehow looking far more threatening, felt a growing need to show his visitor out onto the highway. This inclination was reinforced by the self-introduction of the insistent Mr. deVille. Plug knew the name.

They talked. DeVille cajoled, offered, counter-offered, raised his price and even his voice, and was finally driven to the verge of outright threat. Still—his offer never got above five hundred thousand and Plug was sitting on an offer of one million from David W. Dimble, and feeling oversupplied with farms.

He also had the sudden perception that this deVille guy, even though he wouldn't come close to matching the Dimble offer, really wanted the place. Which put deVille in an interesting perspective from Plug's viewpoint. Plug raised his hand. DeVille paused. Plug asked, "How do you relate to Intergalactic Macro-Conduits?"

DeVille was startled—and reacted intuitively. "What's that?" he lied.

And Plug knew instantly that he was lying. "Just asked," he said quietly.

The two resumed walking toward the house. Plug watched the group on the porch until he was sure that neither Ware nor the stranger was looking his way. Then his large right foot flicked between Gilbert deVille's muddy size nines.

Padronic paunch first, face following, deVille swanned heavily into the slough. Plug accepted the minor shower of mud that followed and strolled along toward the porch. There, all eyes turned toward the large "splash." Midge gave Plug a slow, sage nod of approval.

Reluctantly the State cop moved off the porch to assist the down and dirty deVille. Able Mabel, never one to kid around in an emergency, trotted smartly along to where the garden hose lay coiled, turned on the faucet and without invitation proceeded to hose down deVille, now erect but hardly upright, especially in the matter of language. But he hadn't pinpointed Plug's guilt.

The hullabaloo was sufficient that Peter the chauffeur was roused from his snooze in the privacy of the limo's front office. He started his engine, just in case. Able Mabel, an authoritative ministering angel, issued orders to deVille.

"Turn around, lemme get yer stomach again. You're still all muddy in front, and there's probably some cow flop in there, too."

That aspect of his trauma had not, until that moment, been part of his very non-agricultural perception of the matter, but once the thought had occurred to deVille, he turned as ordered and seemed almost to welcome the ministration.

Midge sidled up to Plug. "That," she observed, "was naughty! But I liked the way you never broke stride."

"I think," Plug told her, "he's the sub-something bucket of pigpuss behind Intergalactic. In the circumstances, I think my restraint should win me a Nobel Prize." He nodded at the State Cop. "Who's the guy in the twelve dollar suit?"

"I don't know," Midge admitted. "He seems to keep evaporating. Came with these two, but nobody introduced me."

Plug walked over to the cop and asked him who he was. Ever diplomatic, the young policeman identified himself and his duty, and then added gratuitously that he had not actually seen Mr. deVille fall, so he couldn't be a witness if the latter should decide to sue. Plug said, "Thanks." He hadn't gotten as far as law suits.

Doubly shocked—the Intergalactic query and the mud bath together were a bit much for a man as perpetually cosseted as deVille—that lanky column of moisture was toweling his head back to its normal incandescence with a kitchen towel thoughtfully provided by Able Mabel. She had turned to pulling weeds from the herb bed. DeVille looked at Ware. "Hadley," he said, "I think we'd better go back home. I really must change." Nobody gave him an argument.

Here is a current photo of the bridge mentioned in the story.

XX

While we have a brief break in the action (a sodden Gilbert deVille is in transit to his home and some clean, dry clothing, accompanied by Senator Hadley Ware, driven by Peter and followed by the evanescent State cop; the residents of Quandary Farm are working and thinking; Gordon Gilbey is waiting for deVille and Ware, and, unwittingly, being overseen by D.P. Gee's Team; Gemma Giordano is single-handedly brewing black tea for a frazzled Thos S. Whiffletree; Zeke Smithooski is with kindly old Dr. Cheflentoskowitz, impatiently having his heavy cast replaced by a lighter model; David W. Dimble is cheating a blind widow in South Glastonbury; and Harry the Plumber is holding a newspaper in front of his face at Bradley Field while he waits for his Chicago plane to be called) let us recapitulate the current ghastly situation.

Dear old Aunt Gladys is dead, her killer gone like the snows of yesteryear.

A codicil to the particular will of Uncle Selkirk Catton has been modified to will a central strip of Quandary Farm to Plug—but the bad guys have stolen the codicil!

In a moment of psychic angst, David W. Dimble has offered Plug $1,000,000 for Quandary Farm. Meantime, Plug has inherited Catton Farm in Rhode Island.

Plug is being fraudulently sued for $10,000 by D.P.Gee/Intergalactic under blackmail by Gilbert deVille. So far the suit has been repeatedly postponed at no significant cost to Plug.

Found, lost, and refound, the love of Gemma & Zeke is alive but in limbo.

Got all that? Then, what happened next was, in a certain view, predictable.

Peter the chauffeur, under instruction, dropped Hadley Ware off at his mansion, then proceeded to the deVille palace. There, a still wringing-wet Gilbert deVille stepped from the large limo, mounted his shallow portico, and leaned irritably on the bell.

The ever-alert reader will recall that Gordon Gilbey, after giving himself a change of automobiles, had driven self and rifle back to Avon to await the return of deVille and/or Ware. Having had bad luck with his first attempt on Ware, he thought he'd give deVille a shot (no serious play on words intended!).

He found a convenient and moderately secluded spot between a couple of enthusiastic mountain laurel bushes, so positioned on the road shoulder that he might, but probably would not, be seen by passing drivers and could depart in haste if such a move were to prove appropriate. He had a nice field of fire to Gilbert deVille's large and rather ostentatious front door. Indeed, for the job in hand, the only thing he didn't have was the total lack of third-party attention which, deep down inside, was really his heart's greatest desire.

For, although Gordon Gilbey still didn't know that they existed, D.P. Gee's little team of scrutinizers had never lost their interest in him. They had lost *him*, briefly, when they wrong-guessed his departure route from the car rental lot, but they immediately right-guessed him and were actually waiting in the woods when he positioned himself across the road from the deVille door.

Gordon was perhaps 240–250 yards from the door as the crow—or the .30 caliber slug—flies, while the Gee-Team was a mere thirty yards further, pleasantly embowered in the leafy greenery of the season, their car a quarter mile distant. With two camp chairs and one 16mm movie camera, theirs was really quite a pleasant little stake out, until interrupted by the stately arrival of the inexplicably moist—it had been sunny all day—Gilbert deVille.

The driveway approach, deVille's hasty exit from the limousine and his aggrieved stomp up the stairs, even the short moment while he waited for the giant door to be opened, together these gave Gordon Gilbey plenty of time to position his ready rifle, draw a careful bead on his gleaming target through the nifty little Lyman gunsight, and squeeze off one round—the Gee Team filming all the way!

Still, man does not live—nor even die—by bead alone. We must forever remember that we are merely players, with our exits and our entrances, Big William had that spot-on, but as we have seen before, he hadn't really grasped the cosmic structure of the thing. How, after all, could he? Elizabethan London may have been a fun town, but it gave him no exposure to TV production studios, intricate, computer-generated wipes and all that stuff. He had no better access to the facts of big league theatrical production than St. Augustine had to the techniques of autobiographical confession, and for the same reason. How could a first millennial Saint be expected to understand such matters without an extensive apprenticeship on a good, hard-hitting supermarket slandersheet? Really, some of those old timers did very well indeed, considering their debilitating lack of facilities.

Please excuse the digression!

Gordon Gilbey fired!

But, as you may have guessed, those fumbling stumblebums out there in the cosmic production studio goofed again. Gordon missed!

Missing was not a common fault with Gordon Gilbey, certainly not among his major social weaknesses. But, when an assistant celestial/studio manager sits in at the console and hits the wrong switch, what can a mere mundane assassin do? Gordon, as we say, missed, as would any one of us if some clumsy oaf of an apprentice switcher had carelessly hit the sudden-insufferable-nose-itch switch.

Gordon was amazed. Then incensed. He could have spit!

But he could also have been arrested had he chose to clutter up the area much longer. He tossed the rifle over his shoulder, slammed the car into first, and roared away ... a little bit!

We say "a little bit" because, although he was pressing very authoritatively on the accelerator, it was precisely that moment that the grimy little dark grey Ford suddenly nosed into the shoulder just ahead of him. There was a certain amount of scraping and a great deal of screeching, and the two cars went into a kind of embrace beneath a spreading laurel bush.

Gordon, his weapon out of reach behind him, felt the ignominy of looking down the barrel of the State cop's large service revolver. Gordon was nothing if not a respecter of large service revolvers, especially when such equipage was in the hands of youngish looking, uniformed persons, whom Gordon always suspected of being nervous. He just *hated nervous gun-handlers.*

While all this noisy violence was going on, the Gee Team was quietly walking away through the far side of their leafy bower, content that they had a film that would take all the prizes without having to go near Cannes or Venice. They even felt that D.P. Gee, despite his reputation for thrift, wouldn't mind the abandonment of a couple of cheap, expense-account deck chairs. And, while they were circumspect in their routing, they managed to be positively hasty in their departure.

Less organized and far less satisfied was Peter the chauffeur. He was quite sure that he had heard a shot and even more sure that a shot had passed over the bow of his yacht-sized limousine. He had locked himself into the chauffeur's compartment and was scrunched down on the floor, one hand stuck up like a goose's neck, blowing the horn nonstop.

Wet right through to his psyche, Gilbert deVille saw the great door swing open, saw his svelte little boom-boom of a wife seeing *him* in disbelief, and heard the shot, in that order. He understood the door. It would be gross flattery to say that he understood his wife, although he deserved her, and it is probably quite true to say that he really did not understand that an actual bullet had passed an inch over his gleaming head. Still, with gentle explanation, he became a believer, especially after the pellet had been dug from its lodging place in the pink and puce wall of the foyer. (Mrs. deVille's decorator was suffering a pink-and-puce period; in certain respects the Eisenhower years were *very trying*.)

It was a couple of local policemen, dressed up as detectives, who took revenge on the pink and puce wallpaper. They started with a jackknife, but soon resorted to a long screwdriver and finally tore the bullet lose with a garden trowel. It's surprising how large a hole a .30 caliber bullet can make when augmented by a couple of eager country cops.

Shown the battered slug, Gilbert deVille became convinced that he had been shot at, but the most skillful cross questioning by two deadly serious—but, of course, respectful—country cops could not get deVille to admit that there was anyone on earth who could possibly wish him harm. He mentioned his assorted ingrate relatives but dismissed them in the same breath as too gutless, and he genuinely never thought of D.P. Gee. Gee, to the certain knowledge of Gilbert deVille, was totally cowed by a little elementary blackmail. Measured in both his dimensions, deVille was a plotter but also a plodder; a stinker, not a thinker.

It was about an hour after the shooting that a State cruiser rolled into the mud at Quandary Farm. Two troopers had come to check on the day's movements of the intended victim. They had no thought that *any*one at the farm was responsible for the shooting—one of their men had collared the thwarted killer almost as the bullet was fired. They just wanted to know what the universally beloved Mr. deVille had been doing all day.

Plug Shavaughn is one of nature's noblemen, which includes a total inability to deceive, conceal, or mislead. He told the troopers what he knew about Mr. deVille and what he thought of Mr. deVille. Though he did dissemble to the extent of letting the cops think that Mr. deVille had adroitly tripped himself into the mud, Plug explained in detail about his presumption of a connection between the excessively bald Mr. deVille and Intergalactic Macro-Conduit and Harry the Plumber. And that #@$%*!@ lawsuit. The more Plug talked about these entities, the more the two leathery old cops developed blisters on their ear canals. One finally broke in. "Mr. Shavaughn, I think we'll have to take a written statement from you, but could ya' please tone it down a bit. On paper, this could put us all in jail for blasphemy and peelin' the paint."

Able Mabel got out the old Smith Corona and Plug re-told his story without the color and in about half the time. Able Mabel's little pudgies flew over the keys, one of the cops read the deposition, Plug signed it after swearing with his right hand raised, and the cops went away.

They were hardly out of the driveway, however, before they were reporting the gist of this thing to the barracks, and within the hour a couple of New York policemen were walking through the awesome lobby of Intergalactic Macro-Conduits, Inc. "Jesus," one of these gentlemen observed. "I never have been in here before. It's biggern' Gran' Cen'tral. Like haf again." His partner nodded. "Yeah. Bewtaful, huh?"

It took a while, but they were finally shown into the legal department where it developed that nobody knew anything. They talked to a dozen different people from the dishy-poo with the English accent at the front desk, upwards through junior lawyers whose individual annual salaries would have paid both the cops between leap years, middle grade attorneys who shook *serious* money out of the corporate tree and senior legal counsels whose incomes were obscene. Not a single one of these people knew anything whatever about anything. The two reps from New York's finest were finally instructed that if they wanted questions answered they'd have to put them in writing, preferably through the office of the District Attorney, and have the questions accompanied by a court order or a warrant.

"Look," the lobby aesthete finally said in exasperation, "all we wanna know is do you guys have a lawsuit goin' up in Connecticut against somebody named …" he read this, slowly, "William Thackeray Shavaughn?"

Twenty faces looked at him, cumulatively showing the bright-eyed mental vigor of a bunch of balloons. But one bored young man at the back of the office looked at the two cops from behind his colleagues, closed his eyes, and slowly nodded an affirmative.

"Okay," said the talking cop. "We'll writcha a letta."

The law strolled back to their precinct station and reported that Intergalactic lawyers were tough, but that they had found out that there was a lawsuit. Et cetera!

Meanwhile, somebody in the legal department sent a quick memo up to D.P. Gee reporting the nosy Blues. Miss Wedgewood slipped the memo into Mr. Gee's "In" basket next time she had occasion to enter the sanctum.

Minutes later—it was that hour when most of Manhattan was leaving offices and flowing off to improbable places like Mamaroneck or the corner of 4th and 11th streets—D.P. Gee spotted the chit "from the desk of", read it, reread it, and actually changed from his normal sick-sallow complexion to a nasty shade of fish-belly green; the sort of color that might, during that trying period, have turned up on the palette of Mrs. deVille's decorator.

D.P. Gee was not amused by the idea of anybody, particularly policemen, dropping by to ask about a silly little Connecticut lawsuit that didn't happen to relate to the corporate bottom line. He was instantly on the phone with the memo writer who, at his salary scale, does not flow off to improbable places like Mamaroneck or the corner of 4th Street and 11th Street and most especially does not do with the 5 P.M. or clock-watching clique.

Gee simply issued instructions. "*Terminate* that cost recovery suit up in Hartford. Apologize. Eat the costs. Tell 'em it was just a bookkeeping balls-up. If the farmer gives ya any chat, slip him something for his trouble." As a businessman's knee-jerk afterthought he added, "get a receipt!"

Mr. Gee had no idea how he was going to square his problem with that bastard, deVille, but he anticipated that it wouldn't need squaring. If that bastard, Gilbey, would just get on with his job.

Gee tried Gordon Gilbey's motel in Connecticut. "Mr. Gilbey isn't in," he was told. This, of course, was not technically true. Mr. Gilbey was in, but what he was in was the calaboose, waiting transfer to a state prison.

Meanwhile, southbound on the Merritt Parkway, the Gee Team were rolling along in high spirits, having come far enough to assume that they were not being followed. They had a camera full of fascinating film, film showing that Gordon Gilbey had failed to do what the boss commanded while they had succeeded in doing what the boss commanded. They could hardly wait to tell the boss!

A fly on their windshield would have heard this chit chat.

"What the hell d'ya s'pose got inta Gilbey, anyway? He ain't supposed to miss nothin'"

"Yeah. But he *missed*," his colleague told him gleefully. "We oughta phone Mr. Gee, shouldn' we?" He really couldn't wait to tell the boss!

"The sooner the better," agreed the driver and then, to cover his own eagerness added, "He likes to know things even before they happen. I'll pull into the next station. Ya got any dimes?"

The fly on the windscreen would, by now, have been bored out of his mind by this recondite crosstalk, so we'll leave the Gee Team peering into the greenery ahead in search of a filling station with its complement of phone booths, and we'll leap back to mid-town Manhattan.

D.P. Gee, like any red hot Chief Executive Officer of any gigantic corporation, rarely left the office before eight or nine at night, returning by seven-thirty in the morning. He was thus the last out and first in, making it difficult for any of his trusted personnel to spend any solo time with the books. If anybody was going to have his hand in the cookie jar, it was going to be Old Ambidextrous, himself!

At the moment we leapt back to midtown Manhattan, Old A., himself, was still of that fish-belly pallor and doing a creditable neural impression of Thos. S. Whiffletree.

Usually a very cool vendor, (for the erudite among us, we might say that he was the absolute *raison d'etre* for that old Roman saw, *caveat emptor*) he found himself suddenly, ... well, nervous! In the ordinary way it would be a breeze to lose one lousy little lawsuit in the shuffle of briefs, abstracts and litigatory lies that occupied his huge legal department. But right at the moment the advertising agency guys were hanging around the place all day, every day, trying to piece together the many elements that would comprise the actual printed version of the Annual Report, and the auditors were juggling the figures that would be set in type for that purpose, and there were at least two untrustworthy bastards on the Board who were out to fry his go ... well, you know how it is in the business when the least little thing is visible to outsiders. So, D.P. Gee was nervous.

And besides, he couldn't locate that bastard, Gilbey, *or those two stupid bastards who were supposed to be tailing Gilbey! Nobody could ever get the simplest little thing right!*

The perceptive reader will understand, then, why D.P. Gee—who was usually an Eight on any Unpleasantness Scale of Ten to his employees—greeted the call from a phone booth on the Merritt-Parkway in Stamford with profound gentility. "Great," he exploded. "Get your asses in here fast and don't lose that film!" By him, that was profound gentility.

And here we will leave D.P. Gee to await his happy team and their detailed report, since we in our privileged wisdom already know the content of that report. We will nip back to Connecticut where ... well, déjà vu and his cousin, Emory, if it isn't ... Plug and Midge Shavaughn, complete with Zeke Smithooski and Able Mabel, all gathered 'round the tall and icy silver can while Plug zestfully stirs the too-cold and too-dry! Not everything in this world is miserable and businesslike!

XXI

Come eighteen hundred hours or thereabouts, every evening brings that span of minutes defined by America's last great literary gentleman, Bernard DeVoto, as "The Lavender Hour," that ritual respite when one may rationally receive the merciful *coup de grace* at the base of the skull, be that coup a fist full of iced Scotch whisky or a crisp, crystalline martini.

Not notably a religious family, the William Thackeray Shavaughn's and whomever else may be so fortunate as to share their devotions—nevertheless wear this ritual pretty much every afternoon, frequently getting it mixed up with cow milking, twenty-hour harvesting days, dark and chilled winter snow plowing, and whatever other depredations the day may bring.

This day, despite interruptions of an almost continuous nature—seemingly endless visits from lanky and loony State Senators and covetous insurance salesmen and State cops—in shifts—as well as dried out tractor lubricants, testy cows and the still non-functioning, albeit much lighter, broken arm of Zeke Smith-ooski—*this* day the ritual was observed as usual, and in that sense at least it was just a day, like any other.

What you and I can know, reader, but what the ritual celebrants could not know was that on this day their small part of the world was going through one of those improbable periods when things come out right, one of those periods pointedly unmentioned by that dour Scot with the weird syntax (the one who talked to mice), one of those days when crime profits little and decency shows signs of survival.

So, there they sat, cooling their hands and warming their hearts and staring at the walls with a bit of glaze on—all but Able Mabel, who was cooling her hands and warming her heart and preparing dinner while cleaning Plug's barn boots and periodically darting into the pantry to perform some arcane chore beneficial to a severely bent fox she had found complaining in the hay barn that morning.

It was a quiet group, reflective rather than glum, and everyone was ready to stoke up the conversation when Plug finally broke the sipping silence.

"Somebody took a shot at the subhuman bucket of camel whatsit, and they *missed*? How often does anybody get an opportunity like that? The guy with the gun must be a *true* cubic cue ball."

"A little dab of sympathy," Midge urged. "He was probably blinded by the deVille cranium, which you will admit is a little different." She was anti-killing anybody, even if the anybody was Gilbert deVille, whom she had learned not to love at first sight.

Zeke wanted to know how the cops had been so quick to pick up the guy who should've but didn't.

"The cops who came and took my statement said their guy was right smack on the spot. I know the cop who was here; then was tailing Ware, sort of guarding him, ever since our loopy Senator got blown up practically right under our little noses." Plug paused to sip. "Apparently the two of 'em are close neighbors up in the big-bucks suburbs!"

Able Mabel rolled in from a visit to her bushy-tailed patient. "Jes' said on the radio that the man who missed the insurance salesman won't say a word to the cops. Says he's waitin' for his lawyer, but he ain't called one!"

The tipplers around the table looked at one another and Midge voiced their joint deduction. "That must mean something, but not to me!"

What it meant, of course, was that Gordon Gilbey was all cut up about missing his target, but confidently expected that sooner or later an Intergalactic lawyer would be along to spring him. Somehow! He knew that he was in trouble several ways, but he was quite confident that D.P. Gee wouldn't want to be mentioned in dispatches. Somehow, there *would* be a defense lawyer! It was very odd that a man of Mr. Gilbey's vocation didn't grasp the ramifications thereof.

Still, as he expected there *was a lawyer the next morning. By then, Gordon Gilbey was the new Star Boarder at the Westmunk State Prison. The lawyer was shown into the Gilbey cell at about 11:00 a.m., carrying a briefcase, which he opened at the cell door for inspection by the two guards. Evidently the dynamite was in his jacket pocket.*

He left at about 11:30 and the "BOOM" was heard, for several blocks, at about 11:35. Gordon Gilbey was fairly evenly distributed over the east and south walls of his cell. The attorney for the defense changed vehicles once about fifteen seconds before the blast and again about two minutes after. Strangely, the excitement in the prison was such that no one even started to search for him until he was in his fourth vehicle and second county. (It is of no significance to our story, but about two years later, he was struck in the head by a vicious four-wood on the Fifteenth at the Azalea Cove Links in Oregon. He never recovered consciousness, and the event was unrelated to his biggest coup!)

Even with all the fast footwork, however, D.P. Gee was not wholly dissociated from the events in and around Hartford. His instructions to his legal department were, of course, followed in full haste. When next the matter of "Harry the Plumber vs W.T. Shavaughn" came up before Judge Groton, so did one lonely little lawyer who apologized profusely, moved dismissal of the case, explained that his client was deeply embarrassed by the inexplicable error in the booking department and graciously offered to pay costs for all parties. Judge Groton made the necessary notes, thanked the tiny attorney for his corporation's forthright admission of error and upright acceptance of financial responsibility and, privately, made a mental note never to buy stock in Intergalactic Macro-Circuits, Inc. There was, he felt, something fishy there. But it was none of his business to go fishing.

Long before that court appearance, of course—indeed, just over an hour and a quarter after the event—the One O'clock News carried the tale of the explosion and apparent murder in Westmunk State Prison. The radio was on at the farm.

"*Jesus Christ*," shouted Plug Shavaughn, "they blew him up—*in jail!*"

"Yes," responded his wife. "I keep reading how the safest place to be is in a commercial airliner. But, like you say, *Jesus Christ!*" She was astonished!

Able Mabel, just in from burying the fox and busy changing the dressing on her fox bite, opined that you'd never get *her* in a commercial airplane.

"How about a nice safe State Prison?" Plug asked. He was wide-eyed and semi-dazed by the news. "That poor bastard just didn't have *anything* going for him, did he?" "Couldn't hit the side of a crystal ball with an M1, and now he gets blown to dust in *jail*! Jesus! Talk about 'some days ya shouldn't get out of bed?'"

The One o'clock News was auditioned in many quarters, naturally; not the least of them the homes of Senator Hadley Ware and Gilbert deVille. The latter had the radio on, the expensive new black and white TV on, the morning's Hartford Courant, New York Times and Springfield Union spread all over the room, and he was on the phone.

Mostly, he was on the phone—his eighth call; with a series of bemused people who were quite unable to tell him why anyone would wish to shoot him. Some were jokers, his broker; "Geez, Gil, he musta found out about you and his teenage daughter ... heh ... heh ..." Some were serious; his youngest nephew, the one member of the family who knew which side his bread was buttered on, regularly ate both sides, and fantasized an endeavour to feed his uncle a crushed-glass quiche; "He's gotta be crazy, Uncle Gilbert. You know, a real clinical case. Probably broke out of some nuthouse, somewhere." Some were unctuous, his wife's priest; "Ah, Mr. deVille. I'm so glad to hear you sounding so well, so ... firm! I read about this appalling business in the morning paper. God's ways are indeed mysterious, are they not? But we can thank Him for your safe delivery." And some, businesslike, his doctor; "I'm very pleased that you're alright, Gilbert, at least superficially. But I think it would be the better part of valor if you were to come in this afternoon for a thorough going-over. I know you weren't *hit* by this lunatic, but there can be some fairly severe ancillary trauma associated with this kind of experience."

DeVille was just ringing off from businesslike ol' Doc Hennessey when the newscaster's voice broke through to him. "... and a prison spokesman has said that the prisoner, Gordon Gilbey, the prime suspect in yesterday's attempt on the life of insurance tycoon Gilbert deVille, was killed instantly by the blast which devastated his cell. Extensive damage was done to adjacent cells and at least one other inmate, as yet unnamed, received injuries. Police are seeking Gilbey's attorney, who was visiting his client just minutes before the explosion. We'll have follow-up details on the Westmunk Prison blast, as they break, from our man *on the spot!* In other news, the Shekokan Valley Strawberry Festival gets under way in just a couple of hours when Assistant Deputy Commissioner Frank Bettucii cuts ..."

As suggested earlier, Gilbert deVille was a stinker but not a thinker. And yet, even *he* was brought to a contemplative pause by this news. Considerably experienced though he was at plotting, strategizing and scheming, the distantly related art of contemplation was rather off his beat. The sensation frightened him; at least, *something* frightened him! He thought of making more calls but he couldn't think of anyone else to call. He was doing a mental inventory of his acquaintances—it did not occur to him that he had no friends—when the neural Rolodex flipped up the name "Gee," D.P. Gee. Gilbert deVille slowly put two and two together and came up a generation older.

That a man upon whose groin he was stomping might object, might even hit back, was a new idea for him, and he was a conservative. He had stomped a goodly many over the years. None had ever struck back before, but of course they were mostly relatives.

He rose from his seat at the telephone table and walked, almost shuffled, out to the foyer and had a long, hard stare at the big hole in the pink and puce wallpaper, the hole from which had been extracted the .30 caliber slug intended for his skull by—Gordon Gilbey? "Who the hell is—was—Gordon Gilbey?" he asked himself for the severalth time. But on the prior occasions of questioning he had expected that, ultimately, he would find out. Now that seemed much less likely. And even Gilbert deVille could appreciate that the danger—D.P. Gee?— was still out there in the big world where shooters and bombers were readily available in the marketplace.

He shuffled back to his telephone and fingered it for a moment or two. Then he put it down and went to his room to dress for the outside world. Dressed, you might say, to kill, and with pate aglow he drove himself along to Hadley Ware's little palace of ostentation, had a short consultative chat with the Senator, and then drove off to make his next phone call from a difficult-to-pinpoint phone booth in the Wethersfield shopping center. He dialed the Providence connection Ware had supplied.

This was a person named Eloise Cecchinni, not so much by choice as because she was the widow of a personage name Ercole "Choo-Choo" Cecchinni who had died in the course of a prison riot, which had been orchestrated by Mrs. Cecchinni specifically to facilitate her widowhood.

Before becoming associated with Mr. Cecchinni she had been Eloise Shea, which she much preferred, and broke, which she hated. After she had orchestrated the association into legal marriage she stopped being broke, but she never really became accustomed to the name. Ercole! Or, Choo-Choo, for that matter.

When her husband was sent along to do a quick two years on a racketeering rap—he figured he'd be in for about five months, or $150,000 a month, not bad for a common soldato—she instantly saw that her orchestrating skills were being positively wasted in his absence. And talent was ubiquitous, inside as well as out.

The trouble with this sort of arrangement, as Eloise quickly found, was that her limited circle of Italianate associates were all very musical. No one, naturally, cared much about the termination of a nient' like Choo-Choo, but they all know a downbeat when they heard one. Eloise inherited a nice little nest egg, but for the two or three years while her looks held out, she spent an awful lot of time on her back. Thereafter, she was a soldato herself. Leaving town was hard to do.

When the phone rang, she was in the bath—she spent a lot of time in the bath. She didn't know deVille, but she knew Ware, albeit only as "a guy in Hartford" or, as her current friend called him, "a gyne Hu'fred." Mincing words, DeVille told her he needed a no-fault hit man. The whole conversation lasted only three or four minutes. Arrangements were made for an expert to plant D.P. Gee within twenty-four hours. "Usual" guarantees were made, which added to Gilbert deVille's growing fear, but he had no real choice in the matter, or so he felt very strongly. In fact, he was in way over his head! Eloise felt the tension and subsequently thought the price was really pretty good.

XXII

We have suggested, along this narrative path, that the vernal climate of Connecticut is of a beneficent and genial temper, appropriately kind to the five million or so sane and sagacious souls who inhabit this most salubrious of sites. Far too good for the wicked few, of course! But by and large aptly smooth, mellow, soothing, and of a dulcet dispensation conducive to civilized comfort and creativity.

Summer can be different. July 15th *was*.

Thunderstorms, as a rule, are brief afternoon phenomena, but this blackhearted monster blasted in around four in the morning, raged on until well after lunchtime, and just would not let go. Darkness enshrouded the entire center of the State for hours after dawn, the frightening opacity broken only by chains of fire in the sky, suddenly turning entire landscapes into blue-lit, momentary silhouettes. The rain raised wide rivers by inches in hours, and low-lying roads were just extraneous riverbeds. It was, as Plug announced, holding the kitchen door closed with his foot while he peeled himself out of his sodden clothes, "… one sonofabitch of a shower out there."

His first hay crop had been safely in the barn for many days. His number one hired man was back to working full time like a number one hired horse. Failing this one day, the weather had been a farmer's dream. He had received formal notice from the State that the lawsuit against him had been dropped and all costs assumed by 'Harry the Plumber.' (He still couldn't figure that one, but he certainly wasn't buying the 'error in bookkeeping' tale.) And he'd had a note from the redbearded lawyer in Rhode Island telling him that, "with luck" the probate work on Uncle Selkirk's will would probably be cleared up in less than eighteen months. In fact, ever since the still unidentified Gordon Gilbey (the FBI fingerprint people had told the world that the man was Gordon Gilbey, which didn't advance the cause much) had been dispatched, the world had been bob-bob-bobbin' along much like the roseate robin of sing-along memory.

There *was* David W. Dimble, of course. And Senator Ware. But at least that insurance company clown with the shimmering skull hadn't been around. All in all, it had been a pretty good season. So far! This rotten storm could set things back. If it went on in current mode, he'd have drowned cows! Not to mention drowned hay still in the field, hay that would take weeks longer to dry and might never make it at all. Still!

Able Mabel brought him a cup of coffee and asked what time he wanted lunch. Midge strolled in, commented on the degree of wet one guy could achieve if he were tenacious and really worked at it, and asked him what time he wanted lunch. Zeke, who was wisely doing dry things in the back shed, stuck his head in and asked what time lunch was.

"Here I am," Plug moaned to the walls, "trapped on an isolated farm with three gluttons who can't think of anything but lunch. It's dangerous; *I* could become a comestible! Don't any of you people ever think of anything but lunch?"

"Yeah, I got to!" said Able Mabel from the stove. "What time you want dinner tonight?"

Plug shrugged in defeat, and the motion turned his head enough so that he saw the car coming up the drive. He hadn't heard it. The meteorological crash-bang outside was such that a large tank could have driven up with all guns blazing and he wouldn't have heard it.

"Now here," Plug advised the assembly, "is the all time, long distance world's champion salesman. I don't care *what* he's selling, I'm gonna buy one! Any guy who would drive out here in this kind of celestial garbage..."

He rose to answer the knock he expected and in doing so saw through the thick screen of rain that the car was the well-identified property of the local police department. A second of the same was pulling in behind it.

Moments later, four—count 'em, four—cops in black raincoats blazoned with orange Day-Glo stripes and matching, broad-brimmed rain hats were spread around the back porch. One advanced and knocked. Plug pulled the door open and said, "Swim on in." He recognized the officer—and at the same time spotted a third car drawing up opposite the front door path. "Hello, Klizwicz," he said. "What the hell brings you guys out in THIS?"

The policeman, showing gratitude for the invitation and embarrassment at both his errand and his supersaturated condition—he had been maybe 15 seconds in the deluge and was thoroughly drenched—moved into the kitchen and said, "Hi, Plug. Hiya, Mrs. Shavaughn! Hawarya, Mabel? Look, Plug, this is gonna surprise ya. I'm still kinda knocked out, myself. But you're under arrest!"

"Sure," said Midge. "And I, as the old saying goes, am Marie of Romania! What *are* you on about, Stash?"

"Like I say. I'm sorry. But I gotta take Plug in. He's under arrest. I got a warrant right here. And I have to tell you your rights. You wanna listen?"

"Arrest," Plug gasped. "What the hell have I done that I didn't even know enough to enjoy while I was doing it?"

"Yeah. Well. I'm afraid this is serious, Plug. That's why I got practic'ly the whole force with me. But I told 'em you wouldn't pull nothin'. So, please don't pull nothing. Anyway, the warrant says … actually, it *specifies* … 'suspicion of homicide of the person of Dorset P. Gee.' You know Dorset Gee? I hope you didn't kill 'im!"

"Jesus, no. I haven't killed anybody and I don't *know* anybody named Dorset Gee and where the hell did all this idiocy come from?"

"Hay, Plug, c'mon, wha' do I know? I jus' get these things handed to me. Usually the Sheriff's office serves 'em, but on a—you know, a serious charge ah … like this …"

Plug shook his head and looked at Midge. "Okay, it's a rotten day, anyway. I suppose I'd better go along before the whole damned police force drowns out there." He noted that the car parked by the front door had its lights on; he could *just* see the glow through the downpour. The other three cops were now standing on the porch, out of the savage rain—and two of them were holding guns. "Christ, Stash, your whole army got guns?"

"Sure," Klizwicz told him. "You know we all carry." Suddenly, the policeman was very serious. "Aw, Plug, come off it. Nobody's gonna shoot ya!"

"Thanks a lot," Plug told him. "Lemme get some wet gear on—like, maybe, a scuba suit!"

Midge observed, "God! Here I am living with Al Capone and I didn't even know it." She was nervous. "I'll call Marilyn, Plug, and see what's going on!" Marilyn was a neighbor and on the Town Council.

"Right. And you can send me a cake with a file in, too. I understand that's S.O.P." He was nervous, too. "Anyway, when this lets up"—he shook his head at the cascade outside—"c'mon down and bail me out, or whatever ya do in these situations." He was struck with an afterthought. "Stash, did you guys have any trouble getting up the bottom road?"

"Yeah. Well, as a matter of fact we came through eight—ten inches a' water. It was really movin', too. Tell ya the truth, I'm not real sure we'll get back."

And thus, for the first and only time in his life, William Thackeray Shavaughn was whisked—well, slowly forded—off to jail for murder. As they drove he kept asking officer Stanley Klizwicz, "Who the goddamhell is Dorset P. Gee?"

The small convoy of police cars proceeded slowly down the road toward the highway, Plug's vehicle being driven by a nervous young cop he didn't know. The youngster had his wipers going full blast but could see little more than shades of grey ahead. Suddenly he braked, sliding a bit, and looking at Klizwicz sitting sideways in the front passenger seat. "Where does the road go?" Sergeant Klizwicz wiped a space on his segment of windscreen, peered out at a minor sea, and shook his head. "Plug?" he asked. Plug leaned over the front seat and slowly figured out where they were. "There should be a couple of big lilac bushes. Go right between 'em." The young cop looked at Klizwicz and asked, "He straight?" "Go between the bushes," Klizwicz told him. "If you can see any bushes!"

They moved ahead, very cautiously. And again the young driver stopped suddenly. "What's that?" he asked. Plug leaned forward again, stared, and spoke more to Klizwicz than the driver, "Hey, I think it's going to *rain*! *Don't* go any further," he told the driver. "That's the bottom bridge. Wow!"

A hundred yards or so along the farm road, inward from the highway, was a low, short, iron bridge, carried over the narrow stream by two short arches.

Plug defined the situation. "That goddam brook's gotta be three or four *feet* over its banks. We're either walking or swimming, but don't even *think* about driving down there. You'll need a periscope!"

So, with a major natural disaster unloading on the town, one innocent homicide suspect, five of the town's policemen and three of the town's seven police cars were neatly tied up on the wrong side of an impassable stream. Klizwicz immediately understood that he—and, fortunately, his boss—had made a tactical boo-boo. He and his guys should be on emergency duty downtown, not chauffeuring innocent Plug Shavaughns around in the best little monsoon since Noah. He consulted with his prisoner.

"Can we get out the other side of your property, Plug? You're right on the town border, aren't cha?"

"Yeah. You go a few miles east, you'll be in the Connecticut River. In fact, you hang around a while and the River may join us here. But if we can get backed-up and turned around, we can go back by my place and eventually come to the Old State Route, and you can either go north or south and pick up a road back to your cop shop. It's the long way around, but no bridges!"

And so it happened that what is normally a twenty-minute run from Quandary Farm to the town Police Station became a two hour hegira through the culmination of the wildest storm the State had seen in years. The three police cars pulled into the station parking lot Indian file, reflecting some cute following by the second and third cars that had been barely able to see the lead vehicle for at least half the journey. It is fair comment on the way God manages these matters that, as they arrived, the sun, which was pretty close to straight overhead, but totally blacked out, could be seen streaking the western sky while the eastern sky remained a dirty shade of black. The distant roll of thunder was even still discernible.

Plug was booked. On suspicion of homicide.

Once indoors out of the bizarre weather, he was able to give some attention to that little problem. His rights were read to him, and he was told that he could call a lawyer. He told the assembled law that he was fed to the teeth with call lawyers, and that all lawyers seemed to be bonebrains. And who the hell was this guy he was supposed to have killed?

"Dorset P. Gee," the duty officer read to him, "is President and Chief Executive officer of Intergalactic Macro-Circuits, Incorporated. Or, *was*! Do you want to tell us anything about his death?"

"Not a word," Plug responded. "You tell *me* anything about it. At least, now I know who, who the hell he is—was. That outfit was trying to chisel me out of ten grand over a thousand dollar bill I paid Harry the Plombo over a year ago. You guys know Plomb? 'Harry the Plumber.' His company was taken over by this ..." he stopped his lectures. He perceived that the policemen had all picked up on something. "What's up?" he asked.

The desk man said, "Mr. Plombo disappeared several weeks ago. What do you know about him. You got mentioned when his wife reported his disappearance, but we didn't pursue you then. We figured it was just a domestic." Another policeman cut in with a chuckle in his voice. "He's got a couple of ... difficult ... in-laws."

The desk man spoke again. "You wanna get yourself a lawyer? I would, if I were you. Why did this Gee guy have the needle in you?"

"Beats hell out of me," Plug told him. "I never even heard his name before this afternoon. Lousy afternoon, huh? I just had his legal beagles and this dumb lawsuit. I could easily prove that the bill had been paid, but the lawyer I got for *that* said that there must be more to it than Harry the Plumber's bill. He just didn't tell me *what*!"

"About a lawyer," Plug went on. "My wife is coming down as soon as she can get out of our road. She'll dig up a lawyer. I take it Harry is still missing?"

"Harry Plombo is still missing. Much more important to you, Dorset Gee is still dead, and you are still under suspicion of murder!"

"Yeah, but I'm innocent until proven guilty, aren't I?"

"Yep. But you're also under arrest until proven innocent. Or until you make bail, if a hearing judge allows bail. And today, I don't think you'll get to *see* a hearing judge. Everybody's pretty busy. If I was you I'd get a lawyer the fastest possible."

Plug was pondering the advice when the great front door opened, the great outdoors howled for moments, the great front door was forced shut again, and Midge stood there, only moderately soaked after her dash from the car. She looked at her husband and seemed to relax a bit.

"Good old bureaucracy; they haven't got around to shooting you yet! I talked …"

Plug interrupted. "How'd you get here so fast? The road's double-flooded in spades!"

"I just followed your little parade. When you came back by the house I could just see the lights, but it sure figured that the road was a-little moist. Anyway, I talked to Marilyn, and she made a couple of phone calls, all while you and these gentle men were exploring the upper reaches of the Amazon. She says that this Dorset Gee is head man at … wait for it … Intergalactic!" she was disappointed that Plug already knew. "And he is totally dead, as advertised. But in New York. We should have thousands of witnesses that you haven't been in New York since the last time you took me to the theater, which would be the week before God was born! Marilyn says the New York Police asked for you to be picked up. Funny. I always thought they were on our side. Anyway, I got you what we have learned, right or wrong, to call a lawyer. Named Thos. S. Whiffletree, your favorite and mine. But I couldn't think of anybody else and Gemma INSTRUCTED him to act. I could hear her leaning on him over the phone. She told me he was having a fit of the frenzies over the storm, but she goosed him. He should be along pretty soon, in fact. She told me she'd order him a cab."

She paused just an instant, then continued. "AND, just by the way, the wedding is Sunday after next. Would you believe that fathead, Zeke, didn't even *tell* us?"

Plug re-engaged mental gears, then smiled. "Oh, he told us. He told *me*! I will quote you verbatim what he said. He said 'Save Sunday after next, we're havin' a party!'" Zeke is not one for ostentation.

"That's *all* he said? No mention of nuptials. No clues, like when, where. What time, what do I wear? He also didn't tell you you're best man, did he? Gemma said they just decided last night, but you would think that mindless clod ... anyway, Gemma is rushing out invitations. One of her sisters is going to stand up for her." Midge sounded a tad disappointed.

Sitting around country police stations, even when there's a whizbang of a storm tapering off outside, gets an upscale rating on the dumb-activities chart.

This undoubtedly contributed to the fact that Plug and Midge were both genuinely pleased to see Thos. S. Whiffletree suddenly blown in the door. Unlike them, he didn't look the slightest bit pleased, but he did look wet enough for several people his size.

"Uh," he said in acknowledgement of their presence. "Mrs. Giordano told me that you were here. I ... I rushed right over. Could you brief me on the circumstances?"

Thos. S. Whiffletree came very close to fainting when the word "homicide" drifted into the conversation. As we know, his specialties are title searching, devious corporate agreements and serpentine contracts. He immediately started his retreat but Midge wasn't having any, even when Attorney Whiffletree had a severe dizzy spell on learning that the dead party was CEO of Intergalactic, the corporation with the phalanx of Ivy League hit men in Judge Groton's court.

Cold bloodedly, Thos. S. Whiffletree is not *exactly* Earl Warren or John Marshal, but at least he does know the jargon of the lawyer's swindle and which buttons to push. A few phone calls established that the N.Y.P.D. wanted to ask Plug a great many questions about the person one of their own wags was calling 'The Gee Man,' but they weren't seriously considering plugging his chair into a wall socket. They just wanted to be very, very, very sure that he wasn't suddenly called away on business in Tibet. And, of course, there always was just that tiny possibility that Mr. Shavaughn ...

Connecticut jurisprudence is sufficiently prudent that even Thos. S. was able to arrange for Plug to sleep in his own bed that night, although the set bail seemed—at least to the family Shavaughn—utterly excessive at $50,000.

Jack F. Reynolds

This is a current photo of the stream mentioned in the story.

XXIII

Nothing of any great interest happened in the period of run-up to the marriage of Gemma and John (she was taking a firmish stand on his being called "John") except that the $50,000 lien against Quandary Farm was released after Plug had spent one entire day in a room in the town lock-up being quizzed, queried and questioned by a two-man team of nosy-Parkers from the office of the District Attorney of New York County. Well, *one* little disturbance occurred!

Attorney Whiffletree sat in on this inquisition and after a timorous start got slowly into the spirit of the thing. Indeed, by mid-way in the proceedings Plug was seriously considering *hitting* eager, well-intentioned, waffle-worded Thos. S., who just would not shut up. Every time Plug answered a long, complex, heavily booby-trapped question with a simple "yeah," "no way," or "forget it," Whiffletree would leap in with five minutes of interpretation. This interpretation was wholly meaningless, but the New Yorkers were both lawyers, too. They ate it up. In the end, Plug just made like he really wasn't there.

Finally, the horrors were over, the whole day's yakity-yak was reduced to about six pages of typescript by a woman who seemed to have about twenty-three fingers, all electrically charged. Whiffletree read it and Plug signed it—right under the part where it said that he, Plug, had read it and understood it, which he hadn't and therefore probably didn't.

Jack F. Reynolds

The day had one reward for Plug. In the later hours, he came to realize that Whiffletree was positively enjoying himself. As they parted at the big front door of the police station, the little attorney wrung Plug's huge right hand with both of his smaller ones, beamed upward at his client and told him "... how thoroughly I have enjoyed today's little, uh—adversarial—ah—struggle. I know that this kind of thing can be very unpleasant from your viewpoint, but professionally it is most uplifting, both to provide client support and to achieve such complete domination of the proceedings." Plug had somehow failed to notice that level of incompetence on the part of the D.A.'s men, but he still came away feeling virtuous.

Within minutes, he was driving happily up the road to Quandary Farm with the car radio delivering "Strictly Sports" with Bob Steele. He strode into the kitchen with a cheery "bang" of the screen door and aimed for the bar cabinet.

Able Mabel had an extended message for him. "Midge had to go into Hartford to help Zeke's woman get her troo-sew fixed up. She said don't wait on dinner. Zeke's gone for some car parts. We still gotta do the milkin', but the kid's got all the cows in the barn. We're havin' cold stuff for dinner and it's all ready, so you want me to come milkin' with ya? Zeke should be back pretty soon."

Plug absorbed this and got out some cold beer instead of the anticipated bracer, and waved Mabel to follow him. Secretly, it vexed him a bit that she could empty cows at a rate of about 2.3 to one against Zeke and himself, both very proficient lads in the field, but he fully understood the utility of the arrangement.

Zeke drove in while they were still working and joined Plug in the sterilizing room. Finally, all the pails and nozzles and hoses and paraphernalia were sterile and stacked, and the big churns of milk stood in the cooling chest awaiting pick up by the contractor the following morning. The big stupids were all driven out to sleep under the stars and the troughs were shoveled and washed down, and all the unending detail of dairying was done—for twelve hours or so. People slowly assembled in the kitchen, and Plug played sorcerer over the gin and lemon and whatnot; after a hot session with the cows, everyone had opted for the chilling balm of Thomas the Collins.

Able Mabel was washing and picking over what looked to be about a ton of blueberries preparatory to freezing them. She was also putting and taking things from the oven, but broke off long enough to disappear into the living room and come back with the day's mail. "Mos'ly blish," she said as she tossed the little stack on the table. After several years of association Plug still had no accurate translation for "blish," but he knew that he—even he—should never use the word in polite company.

Piece by piece he opened the stack, setting aside a couple of bills to be paid and turning a few cubic inches of paper into about a cubic foot of rubbish. The very last one was a little strange, even by the standards of junk mail. It came in a plain white envelope with no return address. Inside was a plain white card with no address, but with a short message.

"Farms can be burnt down
with people and cows"

Plug was enough of an amateur semanticist to get the meaning even though he had difficulty envisioning 180 acres of topsoil ablaze.

He handed the card to Zeke, asking, "How's that grab you?"

Zeke read, then said, "It could be, I say *could* be, somebody going to try to sell you fire insurance."

"But it isn't, huh?" Plug appended.

"Yeah. I guess it isn't."

They passed the card back and forth between them, examining it carefully. Neither found anything that hadn't been instantly apparent.

"A threat is a threat is a threat," said Plug.

"It sure as hell isn't a rose," Zeke conceded. "But why would anybody be threatening the cows?"

"Well," Plug philosophized, "they add very little to the cultural ambience of the place, but every bloody one comes with a big dollar sign in front!"

The card kept going back and forth, as if neither wanted to keep it. At last, Plug said quietly, "Don't say anything to Midge for a while. I'll have a little talk with one of my new fans down at the cop shop."

Able Mabel's voice came from the vicinity of the oven. "Whatcha got? Naughty pictures? Leave 'em lying around, accidentally, so I can have a peak later."

She went right on sticking straws in cakes and packing blueberries into little foil packets she created as she went along.

Plug divided the remaining Tom Collins and told her, "Naw. I'm going to burn 'em. You're too young for this sort of thing. Couple of generations down the road I'll tell you about birds and bees and whips and leather pants and stuff." He jammed the nasty little postcard into his hip pocket, just as Midge swung her tired little car into the slot beside his. She now being among those present, he manufactured a whole new batch of Collinses.

Everyone sipped and told everyone else about his/her day and ate six kinds of salads plus strawberry shortcake with whipped cream designed to drive your cardiologist out of his mind.

Against the odds, Plug tried to describe a happy, gratified Thos. S. Whiffletree. Zeke tried to apprise the assembled ignoramuses about the greatest thing that ever happened in the way of a fixed-jet carburetor with the wildest venture design in history. Able Mabel tried to make people understand that the blueberries down by the lick were the best, and the most she'd ever seen, and she figured she had near thirty pints of 'em a-freezin.' Midge informed a heavily un-style-conscious aggregation that Gemma was going to be a storybook-beautiful bride in a street length silk sheath just off cream color. "I don't know how you fell in for this one Smithooski, but that girl has without a doubt the most sensational figure ever seen by God or animals like you two. And her face is angelic; I could learn to hate her! She's going to be just *lovely* Sunday."

"Yeah, I know," Zeke concurred, and his attention seemed to float away from the glorious table of Able Mabel.

It's always hard to believe, but after a single night of doing absolutely nothing under the stars, the great stupid cows were screaming to be emptied again at six o'clock in the morning. Plug and Zeke emptied 'em, then got on with a few hundred other things that have to be done to keep Mother Nature turning over. Subconsciously, Plug was waiting for Jerry the mailman to come second-gearing down the hill.

He came, bringing a stack of postal goodies very like yesterday's, including the plain white envelope with the plain white card inside. Plug managed to beat Able Mabel to the mailman and snaffled the white envelope before handing her the pile to go inside. He went around behind the tractor barn and read,

"Sell,

Or yours will!"

Zeke came edging around the barn, obviously with the same subject on his mind. Plug had no comment. He just handed the card to Zeke. It was a quick read. Plug said, "I'm going to run down to the police station right now. Tell Midge I developed a sudden need for left-handed grommets or something." Zeke just nodded.

Plug made a return trip to the gend-armory where a nameless familiar face told him that most people, once they're out, tend to not come back, but of course there was no accounting for tastes. This was all said with a smile, but Plug rather quashed the morning's ration of humor.

"You got any detectives or chief inspectors or anything of that type, or is everybody a traffic warden? I've got a little problem, and I think it's a police problem."

The desk man sent him along to the Chief; in small towns it's easier to go right to the top. This gentleman, Plug had not run into before, but he turned out to be named Fine and seemed competent. Plug showed him the cards. Chief Fine asked for all the background Plug could give, probed a bit, and then got on the phone. He talked to someone he seemed to know slightly in the F.B.I. office in New Haven. He read the cards and gave a little of Plug's report listened a little and hung up. "That," he said, "is the regional F.B.I. office. They're sending a man up now—he should be here within an hour. You want to hang around? I can fill him in and then send him up to the farm, if you'd rather."

Plug chose the "... go back and get on with it—there are a million things to do ..." option. He left the evidential cards with the Chief, promising to try to find the first plain white envelope, which had been carelessly thrown out. And he drove off to Quandary Farm wondering what had made the Chief get the FBI in the act? He, himself, hadn't even thought of going that far up the hierarchy of law and order, but he felt rather buoyed by the involvement of FBI expertise, even though he was normally suspicious of some of the Bureau's claims.

It must be remembered that, back in those nineteen fifties, the FBI still had a good reputation not only among knee-jerk patriots but even among ordinary citizens who didn't happen to slip outside the constrained tastes of that ultimate own personal national police force, years to go proclaiming democracy and hobbling dissidents, promulgating the work ethic and breaking unions, living with a man and damning deviants, heralding equality and harassing blacks, championing representative government and terrorizing Congress.

Years later the dead John Edgar was seen to have been the maniacal manipulator he had, in fact, been, but in the fifties nobody in American government dared question anything, *anything*, Mr. Hoover chose to do. By then, he chose mainly to do only two things, constantly reinforce the impregnability of the Bureau of which he alone might be master, and heroically expose the thousands upon thousands of wicked, debauched and cunning communists whom he knew to have infiltrated the very fabric of Free American Democracy. He did very well on the empire-building side.

Still, his little chunk of the Justice Department had a big chunk of the Department's budget, and was perfectly capable of doing good police work. Every year, many first-rate young lawyers and accountants joined the Bureau and many of them accomplished much that was good for law enforcement. Presumably, they joined sharing the national reverence for the Bureau, but a good many left with a bad taste lingering. For Plug's little problem, of course, they had the facilities that Chief Fine hadn't.

Plug knew nothing of these later revelations, but he knew he had to let Midge in on the threats before the G-Man arrived. He rolled up the farm road, nipped Catastrophobia into its place, strolled into the kitchen to find Able Mabel high on a jerry-built scaffold re-wiring a ceiling light, and asked for Midge's latest known coordinates. Directed to the back shed, he found his spouse and without preamble told her, "We've got a G-man coming to visit. Lemme fill you in."

She laid aside what she was doing and observed, "You're getting altogether too chummy with the law. My mother always used to say that really good people never got to know any policemen. Why are we entertaining the Feds? Mother didn't ask that last part, that's my own contribution."

Plug told his tale, explained that he couldn't show her the cards because the police Chief had them and committed himself to the idea that with the FBI involved the problem, if there was a problem, was more or less pre-solved. He didn't believe that anymore than Midge did, but there are times when a man has to say something to his wife. Then he asked her to help him find the missing envelope.

Able Mabel had thrown out the little mound of scrap that Plug had created in opening the prior day's mail. They got her into the search, and she explained that everything in all the wastebaskets had gone into the incinerator that morning. Burning the rubbish was how she whiled away the time between chores. "That the envelope the dirty pictures came in?" she asked. Over the years, Midge had developed a sort of instinct about observations of this kind: she didn't even ask!

In their different places, they both heard the car coming up the drive, and both went to meet their visitors at the door. Plug noted that Midge had put on a dress for the occasion. Chief Fine had come along, and he made three because there were two, not one, representatives of the Federal Bureau of Investigation. Both were in the middle thirties and affable, but serious. Fortunately, neither had a square jaw or dark, wavy hair. Indeed, the one named Fuss was in fairly big trouble for any hair at all, although he was good enough not to mimic Gilbert deVille's astonishing domal incandescence. Plug thought that "Fuss" was a strange name until he was introduced to the second agent, Mr. Fury. The Messrs. Fuss and Fury had evidently lived with that little problem for some time, and the joke got very small play.

They produced the two plain white cards and the one extant plain white envelope, all now encased in cellophane. Midge had her first look at the evidence, and it was apparent that she found it distasteful.

Able Mabel and Zeke were corralled for a little meeting with the law and were instructed to be careful, take note of anything that happened, save all evidence however insignificant, and call the FBI office *and* Chief Fine—Plug thought that showed a nice sense of inter-jurisdictional diplomacy—in the event of any unpleasantness. Also, they were to run, not fight, in the event of confrontation.

Plug and Zeke both had mixed reactions to that: it seemed like a good idea; it seemed like a bad idea!

The visitors had a superficial look around the premises. Chief Fine admitted that he'd never been on a farm before and remarked that it was a nice layout. Plug agreed, but stressed his words when he noted that it needed "... a lot of *work* right now." After a while, Fine, Fuss, and Fury drove off into what was not yet, but all too soon would be, the sunset.

The agrarians got back to it, the two men cutting huge acreage of high ground hay before trudging into the barn to empty the big stupids again. Happily, the kid had brought the cows in for them; all that remained was the work. By eight o'clock, they were finally regrouped around the evening pitcher. On a farm, the long, long days of summer are short.

XXIV

It had taken a little peer pressure—everyone the Shavaughns and Gemma knew—but Zeke had, in fine, been brought around to the idea that even though his arm was 'practically perfect'; and he was the possessor of a wholly rebuilt track car including a sensational new fixed-jet carburetor with the wildest venturi design in history, he should forego the dirt track race meet in New York State next week and attend his own honeymoon.

This, of course, was preceded by the Sunday wedding. And Party. Midge's prediction was almost accurate but, if possible, Gemma was even more gloriously beautiful than Midge had foretold. Privately, after the quiet ceremony, Midge said as much to her. Gemma looked straight at her with slightly moistened eyes and said, "Thank you, Midge. I hope John thinks so. I can tell you it helps to be happy—really happy—for a change."

The small affair, ceremony and all, was held in the home of one of Gemma's sisters; no churching, she had been married before—in the church—and it hadn't caught on. More of her younger than older relatives turned up, which made it a manageable crowd, and a hot one as the day turned out. There was no pinning of money on her dress as there had been at her first, wholly Italianate, wedding, but a few older males of the familia managed to slip her hundred dollar bills that one wouldn't have thought they had to spare. In the late afternoon, Midge saw Zeke being sheep-dogged toward the front door by one of the sisters. Gemma appeared on the narrow stairs in different, sportier garb. There was restrained excitement, a thrown bouquet and a dash for the door as rice and confetti cascaded from heaven knows where. With Zeke at the wheel, a ready-and-waiting car flashed out of the suburban side street, and they were gone.

Plug and Midge drove the forty odd miles back to the farm—and emptied the cows.

Early to bed and psychopathic to rise, they found themselves doing the same damned thing twelve hours later. Able Mabel waded in, and the kid showed up to help finish the job, but it was obviously going to be a no-loafing time span until Zeke/John came back.

It had been decided that Gemma and he would keep his apartment and give up hers, and she had told Midge to reclaim the spare room John used at the farm; he would be coming home nights! But that, as the reader will remember, is not the way farms work and in subsequent time, until, in fact, John, Jr. climbed out screaming, Gemma herself became a part time farmer and co-occupant of the spare room. But that is another, if parallel, tale.

Mid-August happened, and there seemed to be a riverine flow to the days. Zeke came back. The full work load was more than two guys could handle, but they did it—with a lot of help from Midge, Able Mabel and a surprised Gemma who learned to drive a tractor by moonlight and tow a binder by headlight. She was scared silly, but later admitted that in that wondrous summer everything had been new and delicious and frightening and exciting and, in retrospect, as close to heaven as she had ever thought to get, notwithstanding days with Thos. S. Whiffletree.

Nothing is perfect, of course.

David W. Dimble came by. And telephoned. And wrote. And finally hired a billboard directly opposite the point where the farm road debouched onto the highway.

Senator Hadley Ware came by—and telephoned and wrote—and tried to get David W. Dimble's billboard declared an illegal eyesore.

Gilbert deVille sent emissaries and telephoned and wrote and became very angry when told of David W. Dimble's enterprising billboard.

And three more plain white cards came, in plain white envelopes.

Plug forwarded them immediately to Fuss and Fury by way of Fine, on the theory that police Chiefs had more time and staff for errand-running than summer farmers.

All of the interested enforcers of law and order were well acquainted with the history of commercial interest in the farm, and Plug had the impression—after a telephone conversation with Mr. Fuss—that all of the recent expressors of such interest, plus all past expressors of such interest, and maybe all of the real estate developers in the world, in their capacities as potential expressors of such interest, had been engaged in conversation by the FBI. Nobody was admitting to the sending of unpleasant plain white postcards.

Also, nothing else seemed to be happening. The days and the nights flowed, and then we were up to the twenty-second night of August. That was the night the blish hit the fan.

Public wisdom notwithstanding, fiction can sometimes be just as strange as fact. E. (as the old Latin contraction has it) g., not one, not two, but three different land-grabbers chose the night of August twenty-second to "approach" Quandary Farm.

This dubious coincidence can undoubtedly be explained by some simple set of circumstances: perhaps there was nothing of interest on television that night; maybe there was some strange conjunction of heavenly bodies in the astrological sky; or maybe those celestial studio goons were having another bad run!

Who knows why these glitches occur? Just keep in mind that, in the fifties world population hit two and a half billion people, which is rather a lot of opportunities for interactive mishmash. (As this memoir is compiled, we have hit five billion. Gentle reader, does that tell you something about the triumph of nookie over knowledge? And please stop shoving!)

Whatever the reason, the position is that on the night of August twenty-second, Quandary Farm was in for visitation on a threefold scale. Not all of the callers had identical programs, of course; that *would* be pushing coincidence! We shall examine their various agendas one at a time, starting with the most totally sinister.

For a bunch of baddies, they chose rather a good meeting place—the old Honiss Fish House, a Hartford eatery with a history reaching back to the oil lamp and candle days and at one time or another visited by everyone from Mark Twain (many times) to Buffalo Bill. Indeed, one of the reasons why it was a good place for four villains to meet was that everybody else was there, too. In the cellared recesses of Honiss's, surrounded by overhead steam pipes and sidewall photographs of just about every personality who had ever faced a footlight or milked a microphone in Hartford, Senator Hadley Ware could sit down to fine food in unpretentious circumstances, and there brief his three hired hoods. As we know, the Senator was tallish, and his head had this unfortunate tendency to wobble, making him conspicuous. He looked not unlike a bored potentate perpetually nodding to his subjects, and that may well be what he thought he was. In any case, conspicuousness was okay with him.

The three hoods, unacquainted nominees of Eloise Cecchinni lately arrived from disparate and distant places, were all well dressed; given an acceptance of the white-on-white necktie-and-shirt school of sartorial splendor. Together, they did look a little like those anonymous signori who stand around watching bocci games in Torre Annunciata, but their deportment was beyond reproach, and of the quartet, only the Senator managed to dribble wine on his tie. Happily, that cravat was of a rich burgundy hue and immune to error.

It was Senator Ware's plan to have Quandary Farm burned down by his dinner guests.

It was their plan to do the job and get back to Tucson, Toledo and Tacoma by hasty but varied transport. Each thought that the hiring of three men was ostentatious overkill, but each was perfectly happy to have the company. And, over the past forty-eight hours the three had been given intense geography lessons in Quandary Farm including, that morning, a leisurely airplane ride over the property.

One automobile, one pickup truck, and one motorcycle completed their preparation, except for the gallonage of inflammable liquids stored in the pickup.

Short, patient, splayfooted waiters in white shirts, black vest and long white aprons shuffled about supplying that huge variety of seafood that makes visitors to New England angry with envy. Tacoma chose to sample a Maine lobster; he'd never had one. Tucson really came from Woonsocket originally and knew all about lobsters; scrod for him: and Toledo thought he hated seafood until he was talked into a plateful of deep fried Niantic scallops, after which he considered moving east. Everybody had a splendid meal and then nearly drove their short, patient, splayfooted waiter mad with praise while cash customers waited for seating. After which three blithe arsonists went off into the night—there were still streaks of light in the western sky when they emerged into State Street—leaving Senator Hadley Ware, his head bobbing, in conversation with a surprised journalist from the Courant, a man who had never before found the Senator to be the slightest bit chummy.

While all this overt gourmandizing was getting under way, David W. Dimble was strolling along a nearly deserted Main Street, subconsciously estimating foot-frontage rates. On impulse, he made a decision. He would nip out to Quandary Farm and have another try; persistence, he knew, was the secret of all success. Also, he wanted to have another look at his billboard, which quite pleased him. But first he would have dinner. There was no point in driving all the way home to Suffield and then all the way back down to the farm. Happily, the least expensive of the few good restaurants in town was right around the corner. For David W. Dimble, too, it was hi-ho Honiss.

As a loner, he was seated at a table for two in the middle of all the movement. The bentwood chair didn't fit his pear shape nearly so well as his suit, but the position offered him the possibility of seeing someone to whom he could sell something. He dined, without ever seeing Senator Hadley Ware.

This was just as well because he disliked the Senator intensely—free, open, entrepreneurial competition was not his forte—and his pleasant repast could have been ruined by the sighting.

He did, however, see the Senator as they were both departing. It was a kind of omen for the evening, one might think. Standing at the cashier's desk, tossing back the mint pillows (he didn't much like mints, but they were free) he became aware of a tall presence at his side. The cashier handed him his change and he made a move. Ware, shaking hands with one of his departing incendiaries, moved at the same moment. Dimble's heel came down on Ware's toe. This hurt Ware. Dimble stumbled, spilling his handful of change. This hurt Dimble. The contretemps would have been a draw, but DWD unhesitatingly bent to recover his money and ceased to hurt. It is worth remarking that he was able to perform the required contortions without affecting the meticulous drape of his suit; his tailor might bear investigation.

Senator Ware limped to the bottom of the stairs, where he paused and greeted a man coming down. The limp made DWD happy. Ware glared at Dimble. Dimble had a glare at Ware. Then he walked warily around the senator and up the stairs to State Street where he blundered into a fearsome trio of men in white neckties, themselves just up from the restaurant. He apologized and jumped quickly away, but they didn't seem to notice him.

For David W. Dimble, the moment provided as much excitement as one day should be allowed to provide. He walked—a tad more rapidly than was his custom—to the parking garage and claimed his long, long Cadillac. Secure therein, he pushed buttons and rolled smoothly off toward Quandary Farm.

XXV

Readers with long memories will recall that there were three visitations promised for the farm this night. The third was already in progress while these prandial incidents were unfolding.

Having made no headway with emissaries, and having decided that working in hand with his imbecile colleague, Senator Ware, was futile, Gilbert deVille had independently become part of the evening's coincidental infestation of Quandary Farm.

He had, since the day of the attempt on his life, been no less interested in acquiring Plug's land, but a great deal more diffident than had previously been his style; diffident, one might say, to the point of coyness. He was positively shy about being seen in public. Qualities of modesty and bashfulness which none of his acquaintances—especially his relatives—would ever have suspected, were now his most manifested traits.

He had employed a new, gun-toting chauffeur and two gun-toting bodyguards. The latter had, thus far, been rather underemployed, since the CEO of Rejuvenation Assurance Society spent his time either locked in his study at home or locked in the innermost reaches of the corporate palazzo.

For public consumption, an ever image-conscious Gilbert deVille managed to look confident and forthright, but there was almost no public to see and appreciate this performance.

In short, your average pillar-resident and ascetic hermit was, as compared with the post-attempt-on-his-life-Mr.-deVille, an egregiously extroverted Rotarian.

The deVille scalp still outshone the standard second magnitude star, but it did so with all the wasted voltage of Diogenes lantern.

And he did so want Plug's farm. He did. He *did*. He *did*! Poor devil, he had no idea that his erstwhile henchman, Hadley Ware, in the anguish of *his desire to acquire, had turned to the very threats which Gilbert deVille himself had so secretly advocated.*

That, in a less driven personality, would have been a little like bravery, Gilbert deVille had ordered up the car as he left the office on that evening of the twenty-second and, to the surprise of his armed staff, specified a trip to Quandary Farm rather than the accustomed dash home.

There were reasons for this. Our Gilbert was not given to whim. Or rashness. Especially lately. But the General Assembly was in recess, the Highway Department was in summer mode, a majority of the regional executive muscle was in Maine (State of) or Maine (Province de) or just "at the beach." Things were quiet and this always made Gilbert deVille suspicious. With nothing much going on, some sneaky S.O.B. was bound to pull a fast one, and Chairman deVille instinctively knew that he was the anointed for that job. And, to make it all come together, he had to get Plug's farm, even if it meant going out in public where the madmen could shoot at him.

So, while Hadley Ware and his hoods were settling in at Honiss's and while David W.D. was deciding to dine in the same place, Gilbert deVille, one chauffeur, two bodyguards, and three revolvers were driving up the farm road. Their timing was excellent. Nobody was glad to see them, but Plug was just pouring and always a gentleman, so Gilbert got to pretend that he was having a drink with them. He wouldn't actually touch the stuff, but ... and the working stiffs were turned off cold by their nervous employer. Thereafter, they simply practiced that old street-corner art of standing around.

Perhaps there's really nothing in it, but upon arrival he, too, had one of those little portents of a heavy night to come. At the very spot where, just a few weeks before, he had been propelled by Plug's booted foot, nose-first and tummy-to-follow into a minor sea of the thickest and slimiest, he now came to rest—hard—on his coccyx, the inevitable result of reaching for the support of an open limousine door which had just closed, while stepping over a full grown rut. His pratfall lacked the drama of the mud episode, but he got a good bust in the butt. Everyone tried not to laugh, and it speaks well for the civilizing effect of a weekly pay packet that none of his own entourage did!

The Lavender Hour passed. In truth, it had turned a yucky grey and pretty much evaporated when Gilbert and Goons arrived. Able Mabel tried to figure out how to feed nine instead of five, but loaves and fishes were not on the menu, and she was brinking on one of her very rare stoppages when deVille—ever the heavyweight executive—grasped the nature of the social bind and solved it.

He sportingly proclaimed that neither he nor any of his staff was hungry, that they'd have dinner later, and that the Shavaughns and their guests should go right ahead. He really didn't want a single thing—except the farm. He was obnoxious enough to say this last *with* the chuckle, and yet the entire negotiation—and that's all it was up till then—had been civil. He added that they should all go into the dining room and his people would stay right here in the kitchen. He'd just tag along to work out the details.

Midge explained that "right here in the kitchen" was precisely where they proposed to dine and that there were no details to work out because there was no sale in the offing. The Shavaughns were going to *keep* the farm! "Emphasize 'keep'," she said.

"I understood from your husband that he'd already sold it once, but I guess you had a change of heart on that?" deVille said. "So here I am with a really splendid offer, an offer you can't refuse, as they say on television. Heh, heh." This was the very first hint of threat. Until now there had been no suggestion of armaments or other coercion.

There was chat back and forth. Plug, Midge, Able Mabel and Zeke all stated, each in his or her own way, that the farm was not for sale. Gemma didn't really feel qualified to get into the conversation, but finally she couldn't stand it anymore and said, "I'm sorry, Sir. I haven't been in on your prior meetings, so perhaps I shouldn't interfere, but I'm not sure you're getting the message my friends are trying to convey. I *know* I can hear them *saying* 'no,' as in 'niente,' or as President Eisenhower would say, 'negative.' 'Nothing doing,' 'not on,' 'no way,' and 'N'-'O'!" She was really getting a little warm.

"Ah, Young Lady," said Gilbert deVille. "You are very lovely, but I don't think you understand. It is *important* that I own this land. I ..."

He was interrupted by Plug, almost shouting. "It is important that *I* own this land, which I *do*. And I am *not* going to sell it!"

Plug came half to his feet as he rolled that one off. DeVille motioned to one of his bodyguards, much as he was accustomed to motion to the waiter in the Gold Room. The man moved forward, drawing a large, remarkably long-barreled gun from under his left arm.

Plug slid into his seat again. "Jesus," he said at deVille. "You're the bastard who's been sending those shitty cards. The cops are all over that, the FBI and everybody!"

"I have sent no cards, Mr. Shavaughn. Only sterile—apparently sterile—documentation to facilitate the sale. I am going to *have* this land. You will be very well compensated, and I hope that we can remain friends after the arrangements have been consummated. But I am going to have this land!" He was now icy.

Plug sat on his anger and said, very slowly, "There is no way you can get this land, Mr. deVille. It would take days of lawyers to arrange this sale. Everybody knows I do not want to sell it, including all the police forces in America."

"I have all the required lawyers' work with me, Mr. Shavaughn, completed and needing only your signature—yours and Mrs. Shavaughn's. You can readily change your mind about wanting to sell, and it would be very difficult to convince anyone that you had really been against selling while you're walking around with a check for a million dollars in your pocket. Even the press would simply think you were having a belated fit of greed and trying to up the price."

"Maybe, but I'm not signing any papers. And Midge can't write—never got beyond an M.A. in Dramatic Arts." Plug was almost in tears with rage.

"Mrs. Shavaughn will sign after you have done so. Meanwhile, she will be going along with one of my—associates—to await the completion of our business. As will this other young lady, Mrs ... Smith? I believe.

Zeke came to his feet at that, and the armed man took another step forward; he also signaled to Gilbert deVille and looked puzzled. The second bodyguard was brought forward, and deVille looked puzzled. DeVille went out onto the porch with the bodyguard who had hand-signaled him.

"Look, Mr. deVille," the man said. "I signed on to protect you, after somebody took a shot at you. But I'm not getting into any pushing around. I take those women so much as half a block down the street, and I could be up on a kidnapping charge. I never been inside, and I'm staying that way."

"Don't be so damned stupid," deVille told him. "I don't want legal trouble any more than you do. Just keep the women out here and silent, while I get this hayseed to sign the papers. Let him think you're taking them to China, if he wants, but you don't have to go anywhere but right here."

The man looked doubtful, but he also looked diagnosably stupid. "Okay, but no rough stuff—unless you need to be protected, of course! That's okay. Is it—is it all legal, what you're doing?"

"My God, Man," said deVille, who could hardly see the subtlety of difference himself, "I'm *paying* him a million dollars for this—this—this mud hole!" Mr. deVille was not a forgiving man.

Back in the kitchen deVille waved the two wives out toward the porch. "Where the hell do you think you're sending them?" Zeke demanded.

"Please be still, Mr. Smith. Relax. They probably won't be going far, not unless it should become absolutely necessary. If it will ease your mind, it might be just as well for you to go along with them while Mr. Shavaughn and I complete our arrangements." He turned his attention to Able Mabel. "You, too," he added, "may wish to step out into the cool night air. It's really very pleasant out there."

She got the hint and followed Gemma, quietly picking up a paring knife as she left the kitchen counter. A girl never knows when she will want a paring knife.

The three women, Zeke, the armed chauffeur and the law-abiding bodyguard formed a pretty good crowd on the small back porch, but a strangely silent one. Zeke caught Gemma around the waist, but neither spoke.

Even a Gilbert deVille calls one right once in a while. It was, as he had suggested, really very pleasant out there. The night was not yet truly cool, but the oppressive heat of the day was gone, as were the last streaks of daylight in the western sky. A linear glow on the northern horizon indicated the distant highway. Otherwise, the break between rolling countryside and skyline was barely perceptible at first. Mingling leaves on a nearby red maple gave a constant rustle, but beyond that, there was almost no sound except the occasional plaint of an insomniac cow, far across the meadows. There was bright light through the curtained kitchen window, but everyone's eyes slowly adjusted to the darkness beyond. Zeke whispered to Gemma, but his words had nothing to do with the drama under enactment. Midge and Able Mabel were seated on the old glider, while the law-abiding bodyguard lounged against the railing. Ten feet away, the chauffeur stalked back and forth along the length of his limousine. One by one, then dozens by dozens, stars glimmered into view and then suddenly the first of the August evening's shooting stars showered a huge arc across the sky. Gemma's head was on Zeke's shoulder, but her eyes were open, and she was facing the bit of cosmic rubble as it burst into atmospheric flame. She gasped, the first sound in minutes. The law-abiding bodyguard rose about four inches, coming down with his long barreled gun already in hand and a Charlie Brown smile of embarrassment developing on his face. He hadn't seen the meteor, and slowly decided that the gasp must have been a product of young love. It occurred to Zeke that the man showed a certain nervousness.

XXVI

Inside the house, things were a little more tense. The cast was smaller, but the light was harsher and so were the words. Number two bodyguard was standing in the corner of the living room, holding an outsized gun in his hand. Plug was sitting on the couch with a briefcase-full of papers spread out on the coffee table in front of him. Gilbert deVille was standing, not unlike a lighthouse, what with his shining pate, but he was shedding more heat than light.

Plug didn't care much for the guy with the gun, but he really didn't think the man would shoot him. DeVille kept insisting that Plug go ahead and sign where all the little "x" marks were. Plug kept telling him that no court on earth would allow such a document to carry legal weight. He also kept wondering how he could get to his feet with deVille between himself and the gunman. DeVille was, after all, older and more delicate. Plug had been brought up in the conviction that it was a social no-no to punch out your elders, but he was more than willing to make an exception in the deVille instance. Except for that niggling question of the man with the damned big gun. Plug thought he'd try the direct approach.

He addressed himself to the bodyguard. "Hey, Friend! Would you put that gun down for a minute and tell your employer that this whole exercise is ridiculous? Contracts made at gunpoint don't work."

The man had seemed alert enough, but now he appeared to respond rather slowly.

"I don' know 'bout no contracks," he said, "Somebody tried to assassinate Mr. Devil, so I got hired to be his bodyguard. At least, one of 'em. So I jus' do what he says. I don't have to do no contracks or nothin.' But if you just sign 'em, like he says, we could prob'ly go an' eat!"

Plug looked straight at the oaf and said, "Thank you for that persuasive discourse."

To himself, he said, "The man's an institutional case and they let him carry a twenty pound gun around." To deVille he said, "Your man's a remarkable negotiator." He had decided to sign now and fight later. Again, to deVille, "If you'll show me again where to sign …" And to himself, "Nobody in the *world* can *possibly* take these contracts seriously. And if I just don't cash the stupid check, there's no deal anyway!" He felt better doing *something!*

Gilbert deVille had no high opinion of his employees, but he was a little startled by this man's manifestation of imbecility. The clod had almost never spoken in his presence, but he did think he'd bought better than that. In the same instant, though, he was much braced by the results obtained. He nodded to the man and said, "Thank you, Cecil," and bent to show Plug where to start. From behind him came "'At's okay, Boss. Any time."

It took Plug about ninety seconds to sign his name in eleven places, which isn't bad for a name of that span. Then deVille issued more orders.

"Alright, Mr. Shavaughn. Now if you'll go out onto the porch and ask Mrs. Shavaughn to come in, please …" He turned to the happy Cretin. "Would you please escort Mr. Shavaughn, Cecil, and bring his wife back?"

Plug rose and started toward the kitchen, followed by Cecil. Dragging a bit, Plug allowed the gunman to get close behind him, then turned to him with a big smile. "Hey," he said, "that was pretty good." Cecil knew a friend when he saw one. He smiled. The gun drooped.

Plug was toying with the idea of slugging the guy, which he was quite confident he could do, especially if he could collect the big, round, solid glass paper weight from the desk as he passed. That, wrapped in the Shavaughn fist, should put a hippopotamus out. But it would still have left the other two armed clowns standing over Midge, Mabel, Gemma and Zeke. He abandoned a very inviting idea, but decided to keep his newfound friend. In a low voice, he advised the man, "You ought to ask for a raise!"

They passed through the kitchen, and the exchange of signers was made. Plug said to Midge, "It's okay. Just sign whatever he wants."

Midge disappeared into the house, tailed by Cecil, who was preoccupied. As they parted, he asked Plug, confidentially, "How much?"

Plugs eyes couldn't accommodate the darkness for a few moments, but he could make out shapes. "Everybody okay?" he asked, and got a chorus of affirmations. Zeke spoke,

"Like John D. Rottenfeller said, 'it's really very pleasant out here.'" Still, it wasn't a conversational kind of pleasant.

It seemed but a short passage of time and Midge was back, announcing, "He's got autographs to last him for years in Leavenworth. Actually, he's so rich he'll probably get Danbury."

Gilbert deVille suddenly loomed in the doorway, a shiny-topped silhouette. "Now, wasn't that easy?" he asked. "Beginning tomorrow morning you can sleep as late as you like and never worry about a thing again."

Plug couldn't stand it. "There is no way this 'deal' is ever going to get finished. A contract's got no weight in law until both sides have delivered. You've got all that lawyer paper, but I don't have the million dollars, and when you give me the check, I'm going to hold a little bonfire with it. You can forget this Robber Baron garbage, deVille!"

Gilbert deVille still stood in the kitchen door, making sure that his briefcase was securely locked. Now he stepped into the weaker light on the porch.

"Would you turn the car around, please?" he said to the chauffeur, who leapt to it. To Cecil and the Law Abiding bodyguard he said, "Now, Gentlemen, we may go and dine." He turned to Plug.

"No, Mr. Shavaughn. I am not that simplistic. You are now a millionaire and I am now the owner of this land. The fact is that you have had your million dollars since this afternoon. About 1:30, I think, if you'd care to make a note of precisely when you became wealthy. The money was deposited directly into your account at Hartford Mutual and has been yours for many hours. I understand that it is an axiom of your calling that farmers live poor but die rich. You have beaten the system, Mr. Shavaughn, and I congratulate you. So! We are all signed, sealed, and delivered. As for possession, I can be reasonably patient. There's no reason for you to vacate immediately. As a gesture of goodwill, I can leave you here, rent free, through the balance of the summer. Off we go, Gentlemen—Mr. Shavaughn, be rich, not dead!"

This was a far perkier Gilbert deVille than any of them had ever seen before and therefore more revolting. Everyone was of the opinion that he had pulled a fast one; that by putting the payment in Plug's account, he had carried out his part of the deal, and the signed contracts might even be binding. They all, of course, were witnesses to the fact that the sale was forced. But they also knew that the simplest truth, e.g., a disputed bill complete with proof of payment, wasn't

proof against extensive and expensive litigation. In simple terms, the question was "Would it pay Gilbert deVille to tough it out in court. It seemed to be his opinion that it would, and he was precisely the kind of chiseling bastard who would know!

Somebody said, "I don't see how he can get away with it. Now you've got a million dollars, you can fight him in court practically forever."

Plug said, "If I spend a dime of that money, on law cases or on an ice cream cone, it would mean acceptance of the money and of the sale."

Somebody said, "Oh!"

XXVII

"Simultaneity" is the *mot juste* we seek, although several others might do nearly as well. We refer, of course, to the condition extant on that evening of August twenty-second when Gilbert deVille, his assorted spear bearers, and what he fondly presumed to be the airtight contract-of-sale for Quandary Farm, were rolling luxuriously westward down the dark farm road toward the distant highway.

"Simultaneity" is selected because, at that very same moment and also westbound—but on that segment of the farm road leading from the Old State Route—an automobile, a motorcycle and a pickup truck were wending toward the farm. Very acute ears might have detected a sloshing sound emanating from the back of the pickup, although that fact has nothing whatever to do with the simultaneity of the situation.

Had they all been going to the same place, the arsonists could have been said to be behind—several miles behind—the extortionists, but as we have seen, the extortionists were leaving while the arsonists were arriving. To everybody at the farm all this damned traffic could have been irritating, but Plug, Midge, Able Mabel, Zeke and Gemma were already pretty irritated.

Plug was also on the phone—before deVille had gone a hundred yards down the road, Plug was on the phone. He tried Chief Fine at the police station, but that's not where rural police chiefs are at ten o'clock at night. He conned the desk man into giving him the chief's home number and called the man there. He explained the circumstances, including deVille's claim that *he* hadn't written any postcards, and he got a response from Chief Fine. "Sounds screwy to me," the chief responded. But he said he'd stop deVille and have a chat with him. He told

Plug to get off the line, which Plug did. Fine instantly made some calls of his own.

Which is why town cruiser #4 became part of the simultaneity thing. Bearing its one occupant, Officer Pansky, it headed for the farm road, turned in, and following Chief Fine's instructions, parked on the little arched bridge. Nothing wider than a roller skate could pass over the bridge while #4 was on it. Officer Pansky reported his position and waited for the promised reinforcements. Far ahead, he could see headlights bouncing toward him through the darkness.

His nearest support had a ways to go to join him, so he was surprised when, suddenly, he also saw headlights behind him—close behind him. In fact, David

W. Dimble ran right up to the police car's tail pipe before he got his foot firmly on the brake, and was really quite taken aback to find himself so closely associated with the police. Intrinsically, he had nothing against police. He was, after all, a wholly law-abiding swindler. He just hadn't penciled in "police" on his program for the evening.

Officer Pansky now discovered what was wrong with his position on the bridge. He couldn't open his door to get out and talk to the newcomer. He pulled ahead a few feet, giving himself door space but still making passage over the bridge quite impossible for any other vehicle. Since he didn't really know what the hell was going on (the Chief hadn't sounded worried, but!) he drew his gun as he stepped from the car, and he darted behind the arch abutment, squatting there to shout at David W. Dimble to turn off his headlights.

That made DWD jumpy. The day had already provided as much excitement as one day should be allowed to provide. But he dimmed his lights and leaned out his window to ask, diffidently, what was the matter?

Officer Pansky was an honest cop, so he told the little man—he could now just begin to see the figure in the reflection from his own his own bright lights— that he didn't know, exactly, but he wanted to keep the bridge entrance clear for a few minutes. And he asked DWD who he was and what he was doing there.

David W. Dimble started to try to explain that he wanted to buy Quandary Farm, but even to him this sounded a little weak at ten o'clock at night in the country darkness. Officer Pansky asked him to get out of his car and put his hands on top of it. DWD did.

Pansky reached into his cruiser, turned on his rooftop lights, and pulled out his radio mike. It was while he was trying to raise the station, which took only a couple of seconds that the deVille limousine flashed around the bend behind him and screeched to a stop. Officer Pansky found himself in a sudden blaze of lights, his own and deVille's. This illumination was immediately augmented by the awaited cruiser, wheeling off the highway and slamming to a stop just behind the Dimble Cadillac.

A police cruiser flashing brightly in the dark night had thoroughly flummoxed deVille's chauffeur—who strongly suspected that something he didn't understand was going on—something highly illegal. Worse, he had fibbed just a little bit himself—to get the job. Unlike the Law Abiding Bodyguard, he *had been inside and was wholly prohibited from bearing arms under any circumstance. The second cruiser scrambled him completely. He backed the huge limo in a tight reverse, ran forward, backed again, and taking a goodly amount of greenery with him went racing back up the road he had just come down.*

By now, deVille was screaming at him. "What do you think you're doing? Stop. Stop right now!"

It wasn't deVille's directives that did it. The limo was back around the bend and just out of sight of the cruisers. The man hit the brake, and before the car had even responded he was out the door and bounding through the bush. As he went, he got out his gun and threw it as far as he could, which in the pitch dark of the wood was about a foot and a half, where it hit a tree and fell to earth. It is a measure of God's good intentions that in just one more bound the bounder did the same; he smashed, brow first, into the limb of a hefty little ash and fell to earth. When he came to, there was still a hell of a lot of noise on the road just a few feet away, but nobody came near him. He was a man of minor intellect, but major instinct. He lay very still until morning, and then disappeared from our ken forever!

Without him, his large limousine had coasted into the roadside brush, and it was on this whirl of the spheres that Cecil blossomed as a bodyguard. He vaulted from his jump seat in the back, leapt into the vacated chauffeur's seat and roared off up the road. This action, in no way concerted with the desires of Gilbert deVille, was accompanied by reassurance to deVille, loudly and almost joyously delivered.

"Don't worry, Boss," Cecil bellowed. "They ain't gonna getcha. Hang on!"

Officer Pansky had rather a short interval to try to guess what to do. He still had no idea what in the world was going on, but the huge car that had so suddenly come and gone must be the one he was supposed to stop for the Chief. He would pursue!

But he did want a little succor. That had just pulled up on the other side of the bridge. He screamed at DWD to, "... get that car the hell out of the way!" It was a rational request; there was no way in the world that the second cruiser could get across the bridge with the Dimble yacht anchored in the passage. Two cops slid out of the newly arrived car and one screamed at Pansky, "What the hell's goin' on?"

Just as loudly, Pansky screamed back, "Goddamned if I know, but I gotta get that limo for Fine. Follow me." The screaming wasn't really necessary; the policemen were only a few yards apart over a now peaceful little brook, but somehow it seemed appropriate.

The new arrival screamed, "Where's the driver?" He was looking into the darkened Cadillac, which was as empty as a fully appointed vehicle of that mark can be. David W. Dimble had disappeared. He was, in fact, scrunched down behind some dense bushes, but readily visible to the second cop from the new car. This willing, if confused, youth dragged David W., rather roughly, out into the bright headlights, where his waiting partner screamed at poor David, "This is your car?" David nodded. "MOVE IT," the cop bellowed. Then he backed his own so that Dimble could.

Instantly the Cadillac was out of their path, the two new arrivals were over the bridge in pursuit of Pansky who had bravely, if reluctantly, blasted off alone in pursuit of the deVille limo, now a good quarter mile up the farm road.

In it, Cecil was having the time of his life. He'd never before driven anything nearly so big or so powerful, and he'd never before been a real bodyguard with a real body to guard. He was feeling fulfilled. The limo was almost flying over the rough road, bottoming out at ten second intervals. Gilbert deVille was hanging on to the rear seat strap and screaming at Cecil to "Stop, you damned idiot. Stop right now!"

The accepted method for the well-bred limousine owner to employ in conveying this kind of order to his chauffeur is, of course, to pick up the tasteful handset, which will be found conveniently nested in the armrest at his side. This causes a small red light to glow before the chauffeur's very eyes, and a piercing shriek of a buzzer to go off directly over his head and this, in turn, will usually arouse the attention of even the most languid chauffeur who will, thereupon, push a little button on his steering wheel and say, "Yes, Sir." At that point, the well-bred owner may proceed to scream down the horn, "STOP THE CAR THIS INSTANT, YOU GODDAM BLOODY BABOON!", or whatever comes to mind.

But Gilbert was much too shaken for this procedure, and Cecil was much too much into his delicious new role to pay any attention even if Mr. deVille had been capable of the full, formal format. The limo was now hitting nearly fifty miles an hour in an area where twenty-five was deemed good going in a jeep. DeVille, and it must be said, the Law-Abiding Bodyguard, were both being thrown about in the back seat like a pair of rag dolls, screaming, enraged rag dolls, for the Law-Abiding Bodyguard had now taken up the cry and was also trying to beat upon the glass panel that separated him from Cecil. Cecil, too, was being thrown about a bit, but he at least had a steering wheel to cling to, as well as a whole new purpose in life, his first! His accelerator foot became yet heavier.

They were just cresting the farmhouse hill when Officer Pansky's siren started. This caused a variety of reactions in several places. For beginners, it seemed to sober Cecil a little; he slowed the limo down to missile speed, as if he had heard a traffic cop distantly hailing some other miscreant. The limo scooted past the farmhouse where five late diners had just come to attention at the first whoop of the siren. Plug rushed to the window and was quickly buried by four other close observers.

It was difficult to identify anything in the outdoor darkness, especially peering at it from the indoor brightness, but Zeke was intuitive in automotive matters. With total confidence he stated, "That's Poohbah's limo!" And then its headlight vanished.

Moments later the source of the siren roared into view, its urban discord sounding even more out of place than it was. It flashed by. Then another, not so noisy but with the same garish rooftop lighting. As suddenly, they were both out of sight.

They were all totally imbued with the evening's goings on; certainly, no other subject of conversation had arisen. So nobody was surprised when Gemma said, quietly, "If that man is running away from the police like that, he can't be quite as sure of himself as we think he is!"

They returned to the table, hearing the siren distancing itself and at the same time rising and falling with the topography of the rolling road. They were almost settled from the window excitement when they heard—and then felt—the blast!

Again, they all rushed to the window, then piled out onto the porch. Away to the east, where the three speeding cars had just gone, the entire landscape was awash in brilliant white light while a rising fireball quickly burned itself out, and then the night went black again. The three women stared in silent amazement. So much in unison that it sounded like one voice, Plug and Zeke almost whispered, "Jesus Christ!"

XXVIII

When Officer Pansky's siren first slew the stillness of that pleasant summer's evening, our co-actors on the stage of simultaneity were already positioned on the old farm road, having recently turned their automobile, motorcycle and pickup truck off the Old State Route and pointed them and selves toward the incendiary climax of their visit to Historic New England. In fact, by the time the deVille Missile—under the guidance of Cecil-the-Consummate and hotly pursued by three perplexed policemen—hurtled past the farmhouse, the Signori Tamy, Tommy, and Tony from Toledo, Tacoma, and Tucson, had already brought their little convoy to a halt and were preparing in their businesslike way to burn down Quandary Farm.

They had laid their plans with the skill and thoroughness of experience. Their vehicles were now parked, unobtrusively, so as to facilitate quick departure if required; perhaps haste would be unnecessary or even undesirable, but one never knows.

They had unloaded many heavy cans of gasoline onto the edge of the deserted road and were getting ready to make a series of unseen forays to and from a selection of barns and outbuildings and one farmhouse, all clearly in sight. They had allowed a full four hours for preparation, and anticipated a restful pause at about

2:30 or 3:00 a.m. to watch, from a prudent distance, what should be one helluva pyrotechnic display in the darkness of early morn!

The only unpleasant part of the entire project, in fact, was the part now due; they had to carry a lot of heavy gasoline over a lot of space. Still, they were young and healthy, and the paychecks—now in escrow—were positively bountiful! And it was a beautiful night. Starting to cool off! Dark, and shadowy, with lots of tall corn and stuff growing everywhere to simplify getting around unseen! A little workout never hurt a guy. And tomorrow, five deep in broads!

The dog meat was ready—the shoulder straps were in place—the siren was ... the SIREN WAS BLOWING?

Detection had not been one of their serious worries, so what the hell were police sirens doing screaming around the place?? They could suddenly see, still at a pretty good distance, to be sure, bouncing lights—apparently headlights, and headed in their direction. The siren rose and fell in intensity, but it was definitely coming toward them.

Tamy said, "Ciao," and trotted off toward the motorcycle.

Tony said, "Buon' notte," and trotted off toward the automobile.

Tommy said, "Eh, guardie! Che cosa, carabiniere? Sei Piu cornudo di San Giuseppe!" It was pretty much all the Italian he knew, but it made him feel better. He trotted toward the pickup. All three seated themselves on their vehicles, ready to go if necessary, but well hidden.

Their supply of combustibles wasn't nearly so well hidden as they. It stood on the side of the road, some of the cans in high grass, others right out on the narrow dirt carriageway, but all packed and stacked together.

From their own vehicles they really couldn't see the oncoming car—nor did they know that it was an oncoming convoy—and even when Cecil's headlights started flapping over nearer-and-nearer crests, the three "T"s had no view of the action.

But they could certainly hear it. First the siren, then the motor roar, then the screech of cornering tires, the screech, the screech, and then the crash as Cecil stabbed the long limousine over the final crest and cascaded it onto the small army of cans. He never braked!

There was the crash sound, then a "crump" as the many cans of gasoline ignited almost as a unit, the deafening "whoosh" as all the oxygen in the region was sucked into the inferno, and then a general tumult as the two police cars managed—by inches—to avoid the already raging pyre.

And suddenly the night was white. For many moments, neither the three "T"s nor the policemen could see anything in the intensity of the fireball. Then it was gone and darkness returned, cut only by the ongoing fire that ate deVille's limousine and deVille and Cecil and the Law-Abiding Bodyguard.

The policemen pulled their own cars further away from the intense heat of the blaze, then got out to watch in awe. No one even considered trying to approach the white-hot limousine, which proved fortunate. Officer Pansky turned back to his car to call the station. As he moved, his back to the immolation, there was a second horrifying "crump" and another sucking "whoosh" as the limo's own large fuel tank went up.

This time the police officers were in the explosion area and one was knocked over by the concussion, while another took a violent blow to an arm from a piece of white-hot debris. Pansky was blasted face-first into his car, but was unhurt and got his call through. By now, the entire limousine looked like one huge white-hot welding flame.

Slowly, the intensity of the fire diminished. In a surprisingly short time the first of the volunteer firemen arrived and moments later, their pumper truck. Within twenty minutes, there must have been a hundred people and dozens of vehicles collected in a space that hadn't seen that many passers-by in a month.

Plug and company were among the first arrivals, all in Gemma's car, which happened to be the easiest to break loose from the farm's erratic parking arrangements. Zeke drove the few hundred yards. Headlights, spotlights, police and fire flashers, even traffic warning tapers stuck in the road, provided an ever-growing floor of light, so that even the final damping of the limousine blaze left the area looking like a ballpark setting up for a night game.

Tamy, Tommy, and Tony had joined the onlookers one at a time and carefully ignoring each other at first, their various vehicles now mixed in among the rubbernecking traffic. After a while, they managed a quick and quiet conference, then drifted off one at a time. They would be back. Wooden buildings will burn even without gasoline, and their contracts called for burning buildings, not specified technique. And all that money was waiting in escrow.

Slowly, headlights began to crawl away. Little by little, the crowd thinned, the lights dimmed, and at last, the event of the year was over. The final act was three strong-stomached volunteer firemen, working with hydraulic equipment, getting the last of the crisp remains out of the limo and into the waiting ambulance, and its slowly revolving blue light moving off toward the Old State Route.

Zeke had driven the women back to the farmhouse, but Plug stayed on to give reprise after reprise of the evening's events. Chief Fine had arrived not long after the crash, and a State Trooper had been pulled off his highway beat by the two blasts and the on-going fire and crowd.

Finally, night claimed its countryside again and the burned out limo was left black beside the road with one miffed cop set to guard it. Officer Pansky would have substantial explaining to do when the official forensic investigation came up. The State Cop went off eastbound, passing but giving little thought to a slow-moving pickup truck whose driver seemed sober enough.

Chief Fine drove back to town westbound and dropped Plug at the house, promising to have Fuss and Fury in the act first thing in the morning. He *almost* accepted Plug's belief that the threatening cards had been sent by someone other than the late Gilbert deVille.

Plug walked up the drive and went into the darkened house through the kitchen, as if there were no other way. Everybody was in bed—it was just on one o'clock—but Midge was sitting up. "How about doubles tomorrow night?" she suggested, "I'm beat." Plug nodded and climbed out of his clothes. "I don't think I'd do you a lot of good right now, anyway." Even so, there was some very friendly smooching before they both dropped off to deep sleep. Plug's last perception, barely remembered later, was of a car going quietly up the road. Any other night that would have been unusual at that hour, but tonight nothing was unusual. He slept.

And then it was 2:30 a.m., and he was wide awake again and the night outside had turned to white again. Through the open window he could see that the cow barn was ablaze and in its light he saw a black figure trotting toward the tractor barn. He found himself shouting loudly, "The goddamned barn's on fire— there's some sonofabitch out there setting fires."

Midge was pouring out of the far side of the bed as he slid into a pair of jeans and some loafers. He heard Zeke and Able Mable screaming as he leapt down the stairs and dashed for the phone. He roused the fire people, thinking, "Twice in one night is tough."

Zeke, Midge, and Able Mabel shot past him toward the yard as he nursed the phone, then he saw Gemma pausing in the next room long enough to pull a T-shirt over one of the truly spectacular sets of mammary glands ever released on the East Coast. He just didn't have time for art appreciation.

Racing into the yard, he realized that the invader was really invaders. Two shadowy figures were throwing blazing sticks at the base of the tractor barn. Zeke raced into that building while Plug kicked the firebrands away from the stone planking. He judged that the fire would not take and dashed into the barn where two fire extinguishers hung. As he entered, he was almost run down by Zeke, driving out on a large and valuable tractor. He got the extinguishers, dashed off toward the cow barn and noted Gemma coming into the tractor barn as he left. She, too, climbed up onto one of the big green monsters and started it. As he approached at a dead run he could see that the cow barn was not going to be saved, but he could still get equipment out. Happily, the big stupids were all far afield. For minutes he was frenzied, back and forth into the sterile room, getting out expensive gear, making instantaneous economic judgments. As he came out dragging a segment of a separator, he saw Gemma again, this time wheeling out of the other barn and down the drive on the second tractor, looking terrified. He had lost the two guys who were throwing fire around, but they suddenly reappeared way up behind the silo on a motorcycle.

Now, he located Zeke, once again rushing out of the tractor barn, this time with the third tractor and a combine dragging behind.

And he saw Gemma. She had pulled her tractor far down the drive, well away from potential fire, and was starting to climb down. She saw the motorcycle at the same time he did, and climbed back. The motorcycle, with two men aboard, was picking up speed as it got to the drive and was almost wide open when Gemma jerked her tractor forward and took the bike broadside, climbing right up over the fallen two wheeler and its driver. The postillion man was thrown off, violently, and lay still for a moment. Then he started to stir.

From his viewpoint, this might have seemed an astute move. He had, after all, a vested interest in continuing to leave the scene. But from Able Mabel's viewpoint it was a major blunder, and the spot where he slithered to stillness was exactly where her viewpoint was focused. As the man groped to his knees, she took two short steps forward and clobbered poor Tocama Tommy smack in the middle of his skull with the eighteen-inch birch log she had just pulled off the firewood pile for that precise purpose. He instantly became insensate, inarticulate, and inanimate.

Able Mabel now moved forward toward the fallen, pinned driver—it was Tamy from Toledo—and raised her log again. She had found the prior shot immensely satisfying, but it was overwhelmingly obvious that Tamy needed no further sedation. He was awkwardly bent over his half-crushed motorcycle and neatly straddled by the two front wheels of a two-ton tractor. She subconsciously classified his likelihood of departure as minimal and, rather sadly, lowered her *ad hoc shillelagh*.

The cow barn fire raged hotter and Plug was in and out like a piston, carrying anything portable and trying to make economic value judgments on what to save next. Zeke had joined him. Able Mabel went into the kitchen for some twine. Midge now ran toward the blazing barn to help, but spotted a third skulking figure as she ran. And screamed!

Gemma had seconded Able Mabel's analysis of the 'cycle driver's' immediate mobility potential and was also running toward the blazing barn. Her eyes followed Midge's pointing finger and saw Tucson Tony (without a decent introduction, she had no idea that that's who it was, but we, by simple deduction, can make this determination), obviously trying to stay out of sight and failing. She took up the screaming and Tony decided that his best bet was a dash for the road where his car was, even though this meant dashing past the screaming women.

He dashed!

Midge is small, but tough. Gemma is magnificent, but not what your normal defensive line coach would call "big." And Tucson Tony is husky and in pretty good shape. Working from the form sheet, one would have expected him to be able to break through, but form sheets are not written about seriously angry women. As noted, he dashed. And he was tackled by the two screaming women, who had been heard! Tony and the girls went down in a thrashing of arms and legs. He clawed his way to his feet, with both ladies hanging on. And then he made that kind of unimaginable blunder which, *in extremis*, even balanced, intelligent persons can make. But it is well known that guys in Tony's line of work tend to run to, well ... perhaps not actually stupid, but certainly not balanced and intelligent.

What he did might have been merely foolish in other circumstances, but as things stood then, it was monumental among twentieth century errors. He took a swing at Gemma.

As advertised, the girls had been screaming and had been heard. Plug and Zeke were just arriving, having abandoned the hardware in favor of salvaging the more precious software. When poor, stupid, suicidal, unknowing Tucson Tony took a swing at Gemma, he could not have understood that her husband of only a few weeks was bearing down on him from behind at approximately Mach III, but in an instant he learned.

Zeke hit him full in the small of his back, lifting him about a yard, then proceeded to beat him to a jelly over a period of several minutes. While he was able, Tony kept trying to surrender, but he wasn't able for long and he was probably unconscious the last eight or ten times Zeke belted him. When Gemma finally dragged her mad dog off, Tony was in a state of inertness unmatched by either of his colleagues, and they had been far, far out of it for several minutes.

Plug had come to help, but it was quickly apparent that any such effort was superfluous, if not positively wasteful. He headed back to the milk room, Midge at his side, while Zeke got on with the disassembly of poor, stupid, suicidal, unknowing and unconscious Tucson Tony. Then he picked up the remains and carried them a few yards, dumping them unceremoniously on top of Tacoma Tommy, who didn't care.

Able Mabel rolled back from the kitchen at this moment with her twine. She started tying—"stitching" may be a better word—Tommy, Tamy, and Tony to the fence. Thereafter, for about an hour, everyone who saw them instantly perceived that they required no attention except medical. That wasn't immediately available, so they could bloody well wait. When the time came to set them loose and patch them up, it took the State Trooper—yes, the same fellow; he, too, was having a helluva night—nearly twenty minutes to cut them loose.

The crowd for this early morning event wasn't as big as it had been for the 10 o'clock show, but there were still a lot of people around for a small, apopulous farm at 4 a.m. The cow barn was structurally a dead loss, but a gratifying amount of equipment had been got out. A nice hot summer had left that well-baked board building tinder dry, even after a couple of good soakings, and, lit, it had burned without hesitation. The suddenness of the uproar had probably saved the rest of the establishment. The tractor barn was essentially untouched and nothing else had even been attacked.

August dawns come early and that particular New England breed of anonymous hero, the volunteer fireman, leaves late, if that scheduling is dictated by the situation. Plug was shaking hands with a couple of the guys and seeing them off to a few hours sleep, happy in the thought that at least nobody was hurt. One of the last, who had been rolling hose after soaking down the black space where the cow barn had stood, passed by to say "good luck," and added, "You gotta give up this goddamn nightlife, Shavaughn, it's killing me!"

Plug waved at the guy and said, "Go sleep. An' thanks!" And he thought to himself, "Now all I've got to do is empty the big stupids—without benefit of gadgetry. And think of a way to say 'thanks' to all these guys."

In the cool breaking dawn—it looked to be a nice day—he noticed that the kid had showed up early, and then he realized that there were six or seven people wandering around the meadows, gathering the cows into a crowd and cornering them in a neck of fencing down by the brook. And he saw that every one of them had a bucket and he knew perfectly well that every one of 'em would remember how to turn the faucets by hand.

He put an arm around a passing Midge and guided her up steps into the kitchen, where Able Mabel was making coffee for the third regiment. And he said to his wife, "What the hell are we going to do for an encore?"

XXIX

Coming around on Friday was a slow business, done in shifts. Able Mabel napped on the living room couch after feeding multitudes, still with neither fishes nor loaves. Gemma was allowed to sleep until nature nudged her. Plug and Midge and Zeke managed a couple of hours each, but at ten o'clock Fuss and Fury showed up—without Fine.

The FBI seemed a little cool about being called out, but very interested in the events under report. They had been briefed by Fine and had started the necessary balls rolling. It developed that the three "T"s were being held—on charges that amounted to vandalism.

"None of 'em," Fuss stated, "has a record. The guy named Tony—he's from over in Woonsocket—is all beat up."

A connection between the crash that killed deVille and Co. and the farm fire was still suppositional, although it had been established that the car had crashed into a dozen or more gas cans, good old Army surplus five-gallon models. "The culprits claimed no knowledge of gas cans. A car and pickup truck had been found nearby and were being studied.

"We think it may be time for the reward," Fuss told Plug.

"The reward?"

"Yes. Normally, in cases like this, we try to run down the possibilities. Just like we've done on this one. Then, if we don't bag at least a name—that is, someone specific to look for, we'll usually offer a reward. Let it be known in the right places that there's a reward for information on such-and-such.

That usually gets some action. Sometimes, dozens of accusations. We've had mothers name their sons. 'Course, it's not always very dependable. We had this one out west, this woman said her son killed his wife and claimed the reward. The son had been in the slammer in Idaho or some place for three years, but the mother didn't know that. She just hated him and thought it would be nice to have the five."

"Five grand?" Plug asked.

"That was the reward we offered on that one. 'Course, it can go pretty high, sometimes. But you never know how reliable the claimants will be."

"Yeah, I see," Plug said. He wondered why they didn't just offer the reward in the first place. Then he pursued it a little further.

"You figure if you offer a reward *now*, you might find out who sent the cards threatening to burn down the farm?"

"Yes," Fuss told him. "You never know when somebody'll come forward with the facts you want."

"We *caught* these guys trying to burn the place down. They *did* burn down my cow barn, and they tried to burn down my tractor barn. *They* ought to be able to tell us quite a bit about *why* they were doing it! And who sent the cards. But I wouldn't want to give them any reward!"

Mr. Fuss was very patient. He explained, "Well, you've got to remember it'll be tough to prove anything in court. If they get a good lawyer, he'll have the jury believing they were just roasting marshmallows and the barn was hit by lightning."

Plug had the sense that he had just walked into Judge Groton's court again. He was beginning to twitch when the word "lawyer" was spoken. Or, 'iterated,' as a lawyer would say.

He let the rest of the conversation take its course. The combination of G-Men, fatigue, and the word "lawyer" left him in the mental equivalent of bankruptcy, and as soon as he got Fuss and Fury into their car and down the drive, he went indoors and collapsed. He wanted to call the lumberyard and talk with somebody about materials for rebuilding a cow barn, but he fell asleep on that one.

Weekend was better, and by Monday Quandary Farm had progressed all the way back from chaos to mere pandemonium. Somebody had rustled up a couple of local lads who knew how to empty cows and still had a week to go before school started again, so the hand milking only took about an hour longer than the old pocketa-pocketa. In the afternoon, a guy came around from the lumberyard to assay the damage and ended up selling Plug on a cinderblock barn and a metal silo. The hay barn was intact but the silo was gone and with it a fair amount of silage, although most of the corn hadn't been cut. Tuesday morning, the first truckload of cinderblocks arrived—and then stood in a large pile through the week, the fire had been intense but brief, so the concrete foundation had suffered no buckling or cracking. After a close examination, Plug reported this fact to the Lavender Hour Mob, with the observation that it was the first thing God had got right in four months. In that determination, he was being a little hard on the opus of the Dei.

Because, as we will recall, Senator Hadley Ware, who had fomented so much of the summer's hash, was still running around loose out there, just waiting for justice to triumph. God was working on that!

We will recall, further, that the senator had, in the early evening of August twenty-second, entertained the three "T"s to dinner at Honiss's. And, as we have long known, the senator was—while financially rich in that degree often called 'stinking' (strange, that no one ever seems to turn his nose up!)—pretty close to destitute between the ears.

It was this intra-auricular indigence that had led him to wine and dine his tame incendiaries publicly, in the strange belief that being seen with the sinners would, should the need arise, demonstrate his dissociation from them. Who in his right mind, Ware cogitated and would argue, could believe that he would knowingly socialize with arsonists just hours before they arsoned?? Such (one may say, 'alas') is the Ware level of subtlety, but there you have it.

In the event, Ware alone connected Ware with Tamy, Tommy and Tony. That didn't help our Hadley much (though it may show that the rich are luckier than the poor) because he was developing a twitch, which in concert with his wobble, could leave even the wealthiest of persons aspenesque!

The police had more or less convinced him that somebody really did hoist him on a Pearl Street petard. Then, there was that crazy ride when Gilbert deVille's chauffeur didn't seem to know what he was doing. And the complete stranger who tried to shoot deVille and ended up blown up! And now deVille had been incinerated on the very road that ran beside the farm that they were both trying so hard to buy. Suddenly, the deVille/Ware axis appeared dangerous.

Worse, the senator had in his possession the piece of paper that correctly identified William Thackeray Shavaughn as legatee of the strip of land, which constituted the middle of that same farm.

Reading a rundown of the events in the Sunday paper, he thought that what he really wanted was *out*. It occurred to him that Gilbert deVille was no longer in a position to interfere. Hadley was on an intellectual roll! He went right ahead and had one more throw! He would unload the codicil. On Whiffletree!

Why he didn't just burn it is one of those questions that must be put directly to the senator, but he didn't. Instead, he personally delivered it to the office of Thos. S. Whiffletree, where there was nobody home but Gemma.

Most men, seeing her, tend to become idiotic. Some drool. Others spring in the air and click their heels together. At least one has been known to drop his hotdog. And a good many simply stare, leer, or make moronic remarks which they instantly regret because the remark terminates communication. Senator Ware just handed her an envelope and told her to, "Give this to Whiffletree when you see him." Given the unacceptable behavior of others, this would seem the paradigm, but virtue is frequently just the absence of perception.

Gemma recognized him. Gemma waited until he went. Gemma opened the envelope. Gemma recognized the codicil. Gemma put the codicil in her handbag. Gemma never mentioned the incident to Attorney Whiffletree. Gemma is beautiful, honest, trustworthy, loyal, helpful, friendly, courteous, kind, obedient, cheerful, thrifty, brave, clean and only moderately irreverent. But Gemma is not stupid!

That very day, Plug begged off for a couple of hours and ran into Hartford to confer with the bank. To his surprise, he was almost immediately put in the hands of a banker who could read and write and do simple sums.

The man even answered some questions, pending clarification. *Pro tem*, according to the records, Plug was a millionaire. He immediately had the money transferred to the savings bank next door, which was paying five percent. He had no idea who owned the money! But Plug is not stupid, either.

Senator Hadley Ware, after leaving Whiffletree's office, found himself without further employment. It was his custom, when brought face to face with the horror of ennui, to head for the Shaker Club. He headed.

Even within the membership of the Shaker Club, hereditary wealth like Ware's was unusual. Most of the members had to spend at least a little time each day in an office, albeit a very comfy one, leaning on someone else to get some work done. And yet, at any given hour of the club day there was apt to be in attendance somebody with whom the extremely rich might mix without fear of pollution.

The Senator disengaged himself from his taxi and made his way through the muggy midday heat into the enveloping cool of the air-conditioned Club. The basic A.C. of the Shaker Club was, in those distant days, a trifle primitive, having been among the first building-wide systems installed in the region. Once in, its purpose—one-upmanship—had been served, and because a large percentage of the members hated it, modernization was annually procrastinated. The Ways and

Means Committee, no member of which would consider driving last year's Continental while his corporation was still providing cars, would find neither a way nor a means to up-date the air conditioning. It was, therefore, noisy and localized. While half the reading room froze, the other half checked in at eighty-eight degrees Fahrenheit. It was one of those hair shirts, which only the monied can afford.

Senator Ware sat in the cold part, cooled, moved to the hot part, warmed, moved again to the cold, subsequently tried hot one more time, and finally chucked it for the Gold Room. There, two provincial executives sat eulogizing the President of General Motors, but they couldn't agree upon whether his genius was best exemplified in his social philosophy or in his command of language. Executive "A" opted for the man's unflinching insistence that unemployment was good for the country, while Executive "B" felt that the brilliance of his aphorisms, e.g., "Basic research is what you're doing when you don't know what you're doing," was pre-eminent.

Here in the bar the room's extra dimension provided four temperature zones, two too hot and two too cold. Senator Ware waved at the Wilson fan club and then joined them, confident that anyone as stinking rich as he would be welcomed by anyone as predatory as they. This was an accurate judgment, especially since each of them had a little favor to ask of the Connecticut State Senate. Ware didn't hesitate to let Executive "B" buy the Glenfiddich.

Either way the reader may interpret Dr. Johnson's word, the threesome in the Gold Room were all "clubbable," so the afternoon passed in good fellowship and bonhomie—at least as interpreted at the Shaker Club. Neither cabbages nor kings were mentioned, but the conversation did give passing recognition to the amazing circumstances under which Gilbert deVille had been sprung from the mortal coil. It was a subject thrashing about in the cranial cavity of Senator Ware, but not one he wanted to talk about.

His knowledge of the methods of his pyrotechnologists was limited, but he knew he had handed over money—cash—for the gas cans and the excessive amount of gasoline to fill them. He hadn't been able to bring himself to even think about how Gilbert had managed to blow up the whole works, including himself, and incidentally to screw up the entire program.

There was quick and rather *pro forma agreement that the Club must do something in recognition of the passing of an old and honored member. A Memorial. Plaque or something. Committee. Junior members, of course. Get on with it. There was other light chat. Bonds. Interims. Chat.*

Then there was a minor interruption, possibly Dei opusing or maybe just another cock-up over at the celestial TV studio behind Alpha Centaurus. A messenger came in, found nobody at the front desk, and stuck his head into the bar to page, "Mr. Gilbert deVille? Ya got a Mr. Gilbert deVille in here? Any a you people Mr. Gilbert deVille?"

The name had caused Ware to jerk around in such a way as to suggest to the bearer of tidings that he, Ware, was him, deVille. The man strode over to the table and handed Senator Ware a large manila envelope, said, "Here y'are, Mr. deVille," and strode off without even requesting a receipt signature. Nobody demurred. Ware set the envelope on the table, face down, so fast that only he had time to see the word "Buckeye" in the corporate return address. He said, "I can drop it off with his wife when I go home." And then, so that his listeners would understand that this was the most normal thing in the world, he added, "He's right next door."

His interest in sitting around the club was suddenly diminished. He was deeply curious about the envelope from Ohio. That's where deVille had been negotiating with somebody about the Fallout Shelter idea. He was forestalled by the offer of a refill from one of the pleaders-to-the-Senate, which militated against his desired hasty departure. He was not preeminent among the world's seriously wealthy in the matter of being cheap, but he was a contender. Mere millionaires are often not vastly different from human beings in the matter of avariciousness versus generosity, and many of them are very well presented indeed on the virtuous side. But the seriously rich, billionaires and up, seem to be uniformly crippled in the matter of pocket-reaching and positively insatiable in the matter of receipt. Ware went for the refill. And drank it. Then he went home!

He hardly had his legs crossed in the back seat before he was carefully slitting open the envelope. Insofar as anything can fill him with anything, anticipation filled him with something. The contents were simple; several brochures describing the products of "Buckeye Hi, Inc." And a letter to Gilbert deVille.

Dear Gil,

Nice to talk with you on the phone just now. Here's some background on the stuff we do—and you can be sure nobody does it better!

What you'll really like, though, are the prices I can give you, as follows: That's all FOB, but as you can see on the back of the blue and grey brochure, we've got plants everywhere. If we move fast and really ram this thing, we can saturate the market before anyone else really moves. So far, it's been just one-off stuff, here and there, with no concerted effort like you suggest.

Shelter, as described	A	$700
In my prior letter	B	$890
	C	$1150

Jack F. Reynolds

I'm sure you'll understand that I've left a little cushion in these prices, so there'll be a decent reward for everyone. A couple of my guys, incidentally, have already talked with a couple of municipal fireballs, west and south. They saw the light instantly. Presented your way, with heavy P.R. and a little flag waving (have you thought of trying to get the Legion and the VFW in the act?) it should be the biggest things since God's Mother's Apple Pie! And heaven help the poor dumb 'commie' bastard who comes out against it!

As you'll see, I'm sending this SPEEDI-PARSELL, just so there'll be no nonsense about 'through the mails.'

In answer to your question about print-promo, my agency guy tells me that he can originate whatever we want, either right here or in New York, and have it printed almost simultaneously nationwide. Says he could do 5,000,000 in under a week.

Sales and Distribution: we've got sales offices in twenty cities. If my local managers hire in some freelance sales forces we can blitz this thing into every town council/State Assembly, etc., in America within a month. I can taste it now—a "Buckeye Hi" fallout shelter in every park, vacant lot, village green, well-off back spill over into Canada. (The Mex's can't afford an outhouse, so I guess that's not market!). On distribution, we'd work out of our local plants, and the patriots can just stand and wait while the work gets done. A little overtime should keep the union hoods happy.

Finally, I've got to hand it to you on your sales slogan! If we can't inundate the continent with fallout shelters on the wings of "Fall in Against Fallout," we're in the wrong business!

I'll expect to hear from you soon. Best regards to you and your good wife.

Sincerely, Wall

Senator Ware read the letter twice, glanced over the brochures, and then read the letter again. He was a little envious, but disappointed. It looked as if the project was ready to go, and he hadn't been brought into it at all. And, at this late date, how could he get himself into deVille's place. This Ohio cement mixer could just go ahead and take over the whole brilliant idea when he found out that deVille was dead. Usually given to no emotion stronger than a little hunger two or three times a day, Ware wasn't really able to get excited. Just vaguely disappointed. If it had meant *easy* money, the kind he was accustomed to from birth, it would have been alright. But now the situation seemed to call for action. Whereas his real talent was talking to people. Not all of whom always listened. It was Gilbert who normally did all this running around and simply told him whom to talk to. Funny, but he had never thought of that before. For the first time he felt a small but genuine twinge of sorrow at the passing of his late colleague. And another for that wonderful fallout shelter idea; he'd had such high hopes for that. He was cast down.

Thoughtfully, slowly—it wasn't easy—Senator Hadley Ware put the brochures and the letter back in the manila envelope and sat back to await, rather dolefully, arrival at his own hearth. There, he instructed his driver to wait, went inside and found the Scotch Tape, taped the envelope closed, went back outside and instructed the driver to take it along to Mrs. Gilbert deVille, just next door about a thousand yards. He had no desire to see Gilbert's widow himself. She had cried all over him at the funeral, and he didn't like her much anyway. Reminded him of his own wife. Whom he now went indoors to face. He had to.

One sometimes sees this kind of unfulfilled *tristesse* in the lives of even nature's richest bongleheads. It's just God, moving in a mysterious way.

XXX

"At Munktown Prison today, scene of the recent killing of prisoner Gordon Gil-bey, himself being held on suspicion of attempted murder of Rejuvenation Assurance President Gilbert deVille, officials confirmed that three men being held in connection with the Friday night vandalism at a regional dairy farm are also being questioned about the death of Mr. deVille and two unidentified men in a flaming inferno on a road adjacent to that same farm. No further charges have been made against the men, but hints of organized crime connections have come from FBI agents, on the scene of both incidents from the beginning.

"The three accused vandals are all from out of state and have not yet provided satisfactory explanations of their presence at Quandary Farm, where a spectacular crash of Mr. deVille's limousine into an apparent gasoline storage dump occurred.

"Police today confirmed that forensic investigations are going forward and that FBI facilities nationwide have been brought into the case, partly in response to pressure from the Connecticut Congressional delegation seeking a quick solution to the untimely demise of one of the State's and the nation's most prominent insurance executives. Further FBI involvement is thought …"

Plug turned down the volume and moved away from the radio to get on with the even more pressing matter of drinks for the thirsty. For his eager attendants he declaimed, "We got three dead ones right out here, including deVille; they *blew up* the guy who tried to shoot him before; this D.P. Gee guy who tried to screw me out of ten grand is shot in the head in New York; this whole damned thing has to be a huge conspiracy by the Undertakers Association."

"I keep asking myself," Midge cut in, "what that wet noodle Ware has to do with all this? I know from personal experience that the guy's got the intellect of a backward Aberdeen Angus! So, can anybody tell me how a clod like that fits into even the State Senate, to start with, much less our lives or this whole stupid scene. He was in Whiffletree's office, and right away somebody came mighty close to blowing him up. Then we see him hanging around with deVille all the time and somebody *does* blow *him* up. And then Ware walks into Whiffletree's shop and hands Gemma the codicil we've all been beating our brains out about. Just hands it to her! How the hell did he come to have it? He's got to fit into this landscape somewhere, if only because he's practically the only one left!"

A voice came from the vicinity of the refrigerator, Able Mabel's voice.

"Call 'im up and ask 'im!"

Midge looked at Plug. From Plug, a shrug. "Why not?"

Midge looked at Zeke and Gemma. Tenor and alto, a duet, "Call him up and ask him!"

These things are never as simple as they start off to be, but they do tend to be possible. Midge went to the phone, opened the directory, and discovered that Ware's number was unlisted.

"Well," she said, "that kind of fries that bright idea. Any more?"

Able Mabel was doing nothing but finishing dinner and putting an occasional row on a pair of argyles, which by her was pretty much the same as being comatose. She took the phone from Midge, got the information operator to give her the number of Republican State Headquarters, and rang them. She bald-facedly told then that she was Woman's Editor of the Suburban Weekly and absolutely had to talk with Mrs. Ware about tomorrow's luncheon. They were just suspicious enough to ask for her phone number—they'd call right back. She told them she was in a phone booth and gave them the Shavaughn number. And hung up. They called right back and gave her Senator Ware's unlisted number. Her moral code is rigid but not inflexible.

Midge took the number and dialed the Ware manse.

"Senator Ware? This is Midge Shavaughn at Quandary Farm in ... yes, that's the one. Senator ... yes, I know the legislature isn't in session right now. Yes, yes Senator. Senator! SENATOR, this is my dime. Let me ask the questions. That's right. Now. I have a little quorum of citizens-good-and-true sitting here trying to take the agony out of the day, and we want to know what you have to do with all the crime, bloodshed, and general mismanagement that's been going on in our neighborhood lately? I ... wait, wait a second! The death of Gilbert deVille. The death of the guy who tried to kill him. The death of D.P. Gee. The arsonists who burned down our ...! D.P. Gee, Senator. A New York business type. Ran a thing called the Intergalactic Macro-Conduits. Yes! Somebody shot him right through his little head—oh, several days ago. You never heard of him! Okay. How about the rest? We know you knew deVille. We know somebody blew up *your* car with you in it. We know somebody tried to burn down our farm, with *us* in it! We never actually caught you playing with matches, but we would like to know how you fit into all this! We'd like you to tell us ..." The Senator broke in and Midge listened. Then, "Hold it, hold it. I think that's probably a good idea. Let me ask my quorum." She turned to her crew. "He wants to come out here and talk with us. Tonight, like *now*! Okay? Senator? Okay, c'mon out. I'll put a candle in the window. Make it about an hour, okay, so we can get fed." She hung up and looked at everybody. "What do you know about that? He's coming here, right now. Should we have some cops on hand?"

"Can't hurt to call Fine or Pansky or one of those guys. Maybe tell 'em to park their car in the barn and sort of stand behind the door in here."

That was Plug, already moving to the stove to help Able Mabel get out a quick dinner service.

Midge called the police station and asked for Chief Fine. Gone home. She tried officer Pansky. Day off. She pulled names up from her mental file and arrived at Sergeant Klizwicz.

"Yes, maam. The Sergeant's here. Just a moment."

Midge told Klizwicz that she needed a reliable cop-cum witness, double quick. Could he come out himself? She told him she wanted a State Senator observed— and it was just possible that there would be people with him.

Klizwicz took it in and agreed to drive over and listen in. Quandary Farm was currently viewed as the town's private crime wave. "You think a State Senator's got something to do with this stuff? Geez. I met one once at an unveilin' I had to do duty on. I think he was Mensa defective. Okay, I'll come up now. Okay, out of sight in the barn. I'll just drive right in. Geez. Weird!"

Dinner was of the usual gustatory excellence expected of Able Mabel, but the diners got through it more rapidly than usual. They were polishing off some plain old ice cream and chocolate sauce—Mabel had planned on zabaglione, but even with her 8000 r.p.m. wrist that seemed a little time consuming in the circumstances—when a car came whirring up the drive and went right on into the tractor barn.

Klizwicz had made good time, especially since he had done all the things a good cop should do, notably recording his errand with the desk man and phoning Chief Fine at home. Fine wanted to know anything related to the crime wave at Quandary.

Klizwicz appeared at the kitchen door and pushed through the screen. "Ya want some ice cream, Sergeant? These gluttons haven't got it all yet."

"No thanks, Mabel. I gotta watch my weight." He turned to Midge, "What's with the State Senator of yours? Ya think he's involved with the barn fire?"

"Maybe that," she answered, "and maybe the more dramatic death of Gilbert deVille, also right here on the spot."

Klizwicz wouldn't buy that. "I don't think anybody exackly arranged that one. The officer who was pursuin' says that was accident all the way. They sure weren't trying to commit suicide, or anything, especially that way. But he says he doesn't know why they were evadin.' But I don't think there's any way anybody could have set 'em up for that. An' the way I got it, the guys they're holding on the vandalism rap—that's your barn—they're supposed to be mafia types. Ya think your Senator's tied up with the mob?" He paused, remembering. "Hey, you took those guys yourselves, didn't ya? Good goin'! Only I don't think ya oughta tackle punks like that yourselves anymore. That's what they pay us for, and those creeps can be very nasty!"

"They were," Zeke told him. But we had 'em outnumbered and we were armoured. My wife, here—this is Gemma—she took out two of 'em with a tractor, and she can hardly drive the thing." He didn't mention his assault and battering of Tony from Tucson.

As a local policeman, Klizwicz didn't know any more than the farm crowd about things like the blowing up of Gordon Gilbey or the earlier attempt on Senator Ware. But the mention of Ware raised the question. He asked, "He's the one somebody did an 'attempted' on in Hartford, right? Is *he* the one we're stalkin' here tonight? An' ya say he buddied around with this insurance president that got flamed? Weird!"

"Here comes a big car!"

Able Mabel was speaking loudly from the front of the house; everybody else was in the kitchen, where everybody else usually was. Plug took Klizwicz' uniform hat and slipped it onto a high pantry shelf, well out of sight. Midge took Klizwicz into the front hall and slipped him behind an open door, well out of sight.

Zeke took himself onto the back porch and waved at the wobble-headed Senator, just dismounted from his very large transport and apparently aimed for the front door. Communicating with Ware is not easy and Zeke was making no breakthroughs in that direction.

Even *he* couldn't sprint around the house fast enough to keep Ware away from the front door, so he stepped back into the kitchen and yelled, "Midge—the Senator's coming in the front."

She heard him and started to try to emend Klizwicz's hiding place, which was well out of sight of every point in the house except the front door. Klizwicz heard, too, and tried to slip from hall to living room before the guest of honor could see him. He partially failed, but with Senator Ware, it didn't matter. Fast perception is not his métier. Klizwicz uniform shirt and trousers, together with holstered pistol, handcuffs, and all the paraphernalia of his trade were in full view for a fraction of a moment, but it is arguable that Ware wouldn't have registered them in a fraction of an eon.

Midge caught the Senator at the door and allowed Klizwicz to scramble for the kitchen. There, Able Mabel ushered him into the back shed. This proved to be an inadequate place from which to play observer to Ware's quarry, because the quarry having entered as he did instead of as he was expected, everyone ended up sitting in the living room. When they were all settled and looked to stay settled, Able Mabel gently closed the kitchen door, retrieved a slightly rattled Sergeant Klizwicz from his bolt hole, led him up the back stairs, as quietly as possible to the front of the house, then down the front stair and back to his hiding place behind the door, right where he had been in the first place. It's really quite remarkable how difficult it can be to achieve the simplest damn thing.

Midge had been expecting that she'd pick up the interrogation pretty much where she'd left it when she and the Senator were on the phone. Instead, he started the ball rolling by telling the assembly that he really didn't want to say anything until his attorney arrived. "I'm an attorney myself, of course," he explained, his voice starting strong but fading. "Still, I think I should have counsel. In the profession," and here he managed a deprecating little—smile—"in the profession we say that 'he who is his own lawyer has a fool for a client'" There was a quiet pause. "That's a kind of lawyer's joke," he explained. Somehow, nobody could manage a laugh.

"Well, while we're waiting," Midge said, "maybe you could just tell us how you relate to the late Dorset P. Gee of New York!"

"It's like I told you on the phone, Mrs. Shavaughn. I don't think I've ever heard of anyone by that name." he spoke with apparent sincerity and Midge accepted the possibility.

"How about whatever you know about the guys who burned down our cow barn last Thursday night?"

"Ah. That," Ware mumbled. His eyes rather flitted around, then settled on a geometric pattern in the tired old inherited oriental rug.

"Yeah, that!" Plug picked him up … "That barn was a fairly expensive bit of country bonfire, and I'm not sure my insurance is going to cover the replacement, even with us doing all the lifting and toting." He had never really associated Ware with the fire or the threats. But it was a thought!

To himself, Plug thought, "why does the man say 'ah, that'? He may have been a pal of deVille's, but he can't have anything to do with our three little arsonists. In which case, why doesn't he just say so?" He decided that he did like Abel Mabel's direct approach. He'd 'jes'ask'.

"Senator, do you have any association with these punks who were out here playing Mrs. O'Leary with my cows??? Do you know these bipedal turds?"

Ware looked really confused. "Mrs. O'Leary? Mr. Shavaughn. I don't … I really can't answer any questions until my attorney gets here. If you don't mind waiting a few minutes."

Plug accepted the answer as the answer. "You *do* know these no-good mothers" he thought. Then he became audible. "What the hell is my brainless Senator doing involved in burning down my farm? Did you send those goddamned threats?"

In a matter of moments, Plug had gone from seeing Ware as a clod to seeing Ware as a hood. The metamorphosis confused him a little, but it made him angry a whole lot! He came to his feet, intending he knew not what. But whatever it was he was absolved from it by the telephone, which started to ring.

Plug being up, Plug went to the kitchen to answer the thing. It was Chief Fine, just checking in. Fine didn't know anything about the G-Men's reward scheme, but he knew that the FBI lads had turned up nothing from the threatening notes. Every conceivable test had apparently been run, and there was nothing to tie the cards to anybody. As stationery, the plain white cards with the plain white envelopes could be bought in any plain white stationers, office supply house, drug store, or news stand in America, and probably a few thousand other places. It would be possible to identify the typewriter that wrote them, but first you've got to identify a candidate typewriter. For that, you need suspects and warrants. "I'll get a warrant on Ware's offices and his home, but …" Chief Fine asked if his officer was there and got a "yes" from Plug. Finally, the Chief said, "Okay, Mr. Shavaughn. If you don't mind, I'll check in again a little later. I gather that you don't anticipate any trouble?"

"Not unless I decide to punch out a middle-aged Senator," Plug told him. "Call when you want. We're here all the time, but I hope I'll be asleep by ten o'clock. I'm about a season behind on sleep."

He hung up and started back toward the living room. From the kitchen, he had heard the car drive up and the burble of voices as another party arrived, presumably Ware's lawyer.

Midge had seen the car approach and ducked into the hall to get Klizwicz out of the way again. This involved being a little impolite and closing the hall door behind herself, pushing the Sergeant to the stairs, and taking up a sort of sentry position on the porch outside the open front door.

It had been an eventful summer, at least by Quandary Farm standards. Many strange events had occurred, but none of these had prepared her for the surprise of the week. Out of the car and jauntily up the walk came Attorney Thos. S. Whiffletree, showing signs of ecstasy.

Inside, the basic group attitude was astonishment, excepting Senator Hadley Ware. He knew who his appointed counsel was, but nobody else had anticipated Whiffletree. And that gentleman had not anticipated seeing his own secretary or Plug or the spouses thereof. The little lawyer's observations pretty well covered everyone's attitude. He babbled. "Oh, dear. Mrs. Giordano—er, excuse me, Mrs. Smith! I didn't expect to find you here. And Mr. Shavaughn, dear me Senator Ware didn't tell me you'd be here. Ah there you are, Senator. I hope I haven't kept you waiting. It was a bit of a rush—difficult to find, you know. As i understand it, you just want me to ... well, I don't understand, really. I mean, what I can do to assist. But of course, I'm completely at your service."

Plug strolled in from the kitchen as the arrival was at its most chaotic, looked at Whiffletree, looked at Midge, and said, "What the goddamnhell is *he* doing here?"

Midge told him, "I don't even know what *I'm* doing here!"

It took a little settling down, maybe ten minutes worth, but everyone was so eager to get on with the proceedings, whatever they may be, that they soon agreed on joint silence. Senator Hadley Ware, definitely the ranking focusee, finally spoke, although nobody could claim that it was his usual confidence, élan, and/or megalomania.

"Uh," he said. Then he started again. "Uh, I think. Uh." He turned to address Whiffletree directly. "Uh, Attorney Whiffletree ..."

Whiffletree leapt right in. This was not the Senator Ware he knew, but ... "Yes, Senator, yes, I am wholly at your service. I think it would be alright for you to go right ahead and say what you were, er, going to say. Until I find it desirable, as your counsel, of course, to stop you. To ask you to stop, you understand. I'm sure."

That left it back in Ware's court. Or lap.

"Well," he almost whispered, "the thing is—actually, Mr. Shavaughn just alluded to it a little while ago. I guess these people all know, but I don't know about you, Whif., but there were some men who burned down Mr. Shavaughn's barn, one of his barns, last week. At least, they are so charged and they are in prison. Well, the thing is, I had these gentlemen, well, just men, really, I had them to dinner. As my guests, sort of, at Honiss's. the night of the fire. You see what I mean?"

"You mean you took these goddamned hoods to dinner at Honiss's the night they burned my barn down?" Plug interpreted.

"Yes. Precisely, exactly, Mr. Shavaughn."

"Why the hell would you do a non-stop stupid thing like that?" Plug continued.

"Yes. Well. That's the part to explain. It's hard to explain. I think. I … you see, these gentlemen came to my office that afternoon and asked for … for various kinds of information. About this area. Where I'm State Senator. You see what I mean? They wanted, well, for instance maps. Mainly."

"They couldn't get a map from a gas station?" Plug asked incredulously. They've gotta go to a State Senator for a map?"

"An official map, Mr. Shavaughn. Very good maps. Free, of course."

"So instead of giving them a map, you just naturally took them out to dinner? Free!"

"Oh, no. Well, yes. I mean, I gave them the maps, free one for each of them. But you know how it is. We got to talking. They were from out of State—different places. And I naturally felt it was my civic duty, well, not dinner, of course, but to, well, boost Connecticut as it were. And they …"

"Excuse me, Senator." It was Whiffletree, doing his counsel thing. "I think it would be well to pause here. You simply want Mr. Shavaughn and his colleagues to know that you had an acquaintance, an accidental acquaintance, really, and that you dined with these men on the evening preceding the unfortunate fire here at this farm. Is that right?"

"Yes, yes, exactly right, Attorney Whiffletree." It may have been the first time in his life that an accent of gratitude had slipped into his speech. He went on.

"Of course, of course it was at Honiss's. Very popular place. And a lot of people must have seen me there. And of course I am very well known. And with these men. Of course, I had no idea they would do anything so dastardly as they are charged with doing. I just wanted Mr. Shavaughn and these nice people to know, the, the whys and wherefores. As it were. You see what I mean?"

"Yes, indeed. Yes, I'm sure we all see," Whiffletree picked it up. "And I should say that you had accomplished that most effectively. Quite obviously, there is no other connection between you and these alleged, or putative, vandals."

He turned to Plug. "You understand, Mr. Shavaughn, that I take no position whatever on the guilt of these men, although I understand that they were caught red-handed. But in law they are innocent until proven guilty.

Do you wish to question my client any further, Mr. Shavaughn?" He glanced quickly around. "Anyone?"

Before anyone could muster a question, Whiffletree had turned back to Ware.

"If I may say so, Senator, only a little while ago when I walked in here, I was dubious about the, uh, desirability, from your viewpoint, of raising these points of information. But I'm sure this company will join me in expressing admiration for your candor, although I'm sure no one in the world would seriously think that you would have any intercourse with the persons of the type I have seen described in the newspapers." He turned back to Plug.

"Mr. Shavaughn?"

Plug was totally bemused by the whole business. The idea of the three punks just walking into Ware's office looking for a map—it was so damned idiotic that it could even be true. He raised a shrug at Whiffletree and said, "I've got no argument. We were just probing for clues. So, I guess I should say 'thank you' for coming out, Senator, and you, too, Mr. Whiffletree. We'll just have to look elsewhere for rational explanations."

Whiffletree, who was riding a high that made his day with the two New York District Attorney lads look like a tropical depression, bolted for the door, propelling his client before him, and out that door the two strange LL.D.s went merrily.

Plug's normal elbow rest was the kitchen table, but now he collapsed into the armchair and spoke, weakly.

"Mabel," he said to the round lady who was fluffing cushions all around the room, "I know you just can't find anything to do to amuse yourself, so would you please bring me one helluva big bourbon with two negligible ice cubes. Not suicide big, but the next largest size."

Midge dropped into the huge chair, between his legs. "Mabel, if you don't mind—for me, the baby-bear size."

Zeke and Gemma stood mid-room and Midge addressed them jointly. "You guys like a drink?"

Zeke answered for both. "Nope. Bed."

"I understand," Plug said. "Beginners. Need practice."

So, while a stately car bearing a smug, neatly explained and off-the-hook Senator Hadley Ware and a less stately one bearing a euphoric Attorney Thos. S. Whiffletree rolled down the farm road and Plug and Midge sipped nightcaps, Zeke and Gemma made their way upstairs to bed. It would be hard to argue that they had anything but the best of it.

XXXI

Reviewing last night's events, one might think that God, being expected to lower the boom on Senator Hadley Ware, was goofing off. Or, under the kindest interpretation, putting off until tomorrow that which might better have been done last night. But, hold! It's in the mail.

Because our Hadley, however smug he may have felt driving his great big motor vehicle home from Quandary Farm last night, was already in the tureen. It is true that when Midge had phoned him his mood had been such that he more or less panicked. At least, he felt cornered in a degree, which even his excessive funding couldn't help much. And, he therefore blurted out the suggestion that he visit the occupants of Quandary Farm. He made that suggestion with the idea of putting into service his own personal Plan "A", i.e., putting aside their suspicions by giving them a candid explanation of his association with the arsonists. "Candid" his way, of course.

This was an intrinsically moronic idea!

So, this being the planet earth, it worked like a charm. His listeners, excepting possibly his own attorney, brought along solely as a kind of social crutch and witness, were sound, intelligent people. So, this being the planet earth, they bought it! Senator Ware was pleased, but not surprised. He had thought it a brilliant scheme, and its success justified his opinion of it and of himself.

But, this being the planet earth, he should have ducked. Other factors were afoot!

Eloise Cecchinni, as soon as she stepped from her bath one busy morning, was afoot. And putting it in the mail!

She had had posted, from a suburb of Boston, a masterfully anonymous invoice, so presented that an outsider might have thought it no more than a statistical analysis of Milwaukee's run-up to the World Series. But Eloise wasn't much interested in baseball, and her invoice would have been comprehensible to Senator Ware, if only because he was expecting it and knew what it would say. It would say "$25,000." He just didn't understand the potential permutations of statistical analysis.

But Eloise had been in the trade for some years, and she understood. She also knew that her three soldati were in the slammer and that she had to get them out. That constituted out-of-pocket expense. She had arranged lawyers for Tamy, Tommy, and Tony as soon as she heard of their misfortune, and she had done it in such a way that even the lawyers themselves thought they were hired by Tamy, Tommy, and Tony. They never heard of Eloise.

We have seen earlier that Eloise was a woman of significant orchestrational talent. She used this God-given talent to arrange things so that only Tamy spent any significant time in prison—sixteen months—while Tommy and Tony got off with stiffish fines. Tony, in particular, was softly treated because he was in bad health.

Such arrangements are not cheap, and it was essential to have decent remuneration for the Three "T"s and herself, as well as money to pay fines and lawyers and costs. Then there would be the eighty grand for Tamy (computed at $5000 per month inside) and appropriate contributions for local charities like Sam, Guido, Al and Al., Jr.

So, one month after the first invoice she sent Senator Ware a duplicate. A few days later, she happened to be in New York at the time, she phoned him and explained that on that same date each month—until ordered to stop, which wasn't likely—he should send the same amount, in cash. He would receive occasional notification of new addresses.

Hadley, as we know, is a little slow. It took him several seconds to get into full splutter, and he was still spluttering when she hung up. But he was not so slow as to miss a payment.

If one were of a tender disposition, one might incline to feel some degree of sympathy for Senator Ware, especially since he hadn't even originated the idea of threats to the farm, although it is certainly true that he put into practice that very naughty idea. One might even feel for him on the grounds that he is a congenital meathead. But a realist must ask himself, "why bother?" Our Hadley is a man who, through absolutely no fault of his own, can afford to offload three hundred grand a year plus postage—and never feel pain! Sometimes it's hard to know which side of the street God is working.

Perhaps more to the point, one might sympathize with poor Eloise who laid upon the barrelhead a cool $10,000 simply to have a small pellet placed in the brain of D.P. Gee. This was practically an act of philanthropy, and Eloise had to eat the entire cost herself because of the singular stupidity of Gilbert deVille, who not only removed himself from eligibility to pay her bill, but screwed up the entire program at Quandary Farm!

Well, in all honesty, she didn't actually take a bath on that one. DeVille understood these matters and had paid C.O.D. But she had allowed her associates to believe otherwise! Anyway, her commission was a lousy $2500, hardly enough to make a girl rich, although it would buy a lot of bath salts!

Other people came out of the summer's divertissement more fulfilled than Eloise. Gemma leaps to mind, and John-called-Zeke. He was even able to return to the dirt tracks for part of the autumn season, although Gemma had already started a subsequently successful campaign to get him into a less hazardous hobby.

And when Gemma went to work on the morning after the interesting evening with Senator Ware, her small employer was already there, looking and acting as fulfilled as Billy Graham holding an evangelical whizbang in Fort Knox. He—the Att., not the Rev.—was convinced that the eminent and extremely wealthy Senator Hadley Ware had decided to use his professional services whenever needed. Of course, Attorney Whiffletree started off every day afloat on this kind of optimistic Cloud Nine, and ended up pretty much every day inside the cloud.

David W. Dimble, on the other hand never knew when he was fulfilled. He had his high points and low points, certainly. Cheating the blind widow in Glastonbury had been a high by any standard, but he felt it wouldn't match the glorious triumph that had to come when he got that ghastly Farmer Shavaughn to let go of that rotten rock pile of his. There had been problems, but he, David W. Dimble, was not a quitter. Tenacity was the thing. Keeping everlastingly at it. Soldiering on. Never giving in. That was the secret!

It was already in his program to go back, despite all the unpleasantness that had transpired on the evening of this last attempted visit. Policemen; cars full of policemen! And maniacs. That maniac, deVille, killing himself right there on that valuable property!

That, David W. Dimble had read about in the papers the next day, although he had seen and heard the distant explosion while getting his very large car turned around on that very small road. He had then driven home to Suffield in some haste. But now, today, he would breach the line again. He'd have to go very carefully across that tiny little bridge! But surely Shavaughn, one of the toughest bargainers he'd ever come up against, couldn't refuse a sincere offer of, of (he could barely *think* it) *two* million dollars!

Jack F. Reynolds

While everybody's mind was individually on his or her own aspect of the goings-on of recent days, they tended to miss the fact that today was a perfectly glorious specimen of the genre. Late summer at its primal best, it was, with the savage humidity nearly blotted from the clear air and the warmth dry and pleasant while a light zephyr zephed across scented meadows. In truth, if you had to rebuild your cow barn this is just about the best possible circumstance in which to do it. Plug and Zeke were hard at it when David W. Dimble moored his twenty-one foot Cadillac under Mabel's kitchen window. His arrival was hidden from them by a brand-new cement block wall.

Nimbly, D.W.D. stepped out into the nearly mud-free yard. His highly polished wing-tip found the only wet spot within three yards. He pitched. He slewed. He flew. Implied in that last action was its corollary, his landing, which followed immediately and violently. Mr. Dimble may be persistent, tenacious, perseverant and deeply greedy. But he is also breakable.

Able Mabel witnessed the entire performance, and before the crash was fully completed she had an ambulance on the way. Then she went outside and did a masterful job of first-aid on the compound fracture of David W. D's left fibula and the disabling break in his mandible, or talking bone.

The staff at Hartford Hospital are a splendid lot. During a very expensive stay with them, our David was so comforted that he had time to ruminate. He chewed and reviewed the events associated with his deep interest in Quandary Farm. He thought of the fire. He thought of the murder. He thought again and again of two million dollars. In private, he cried. And, in pain, he withdrew from the market.

THE END